# THE BABY AUCTION

To: Maggie
with very best wishes
Peter

*The Baby Auction*
*Published by The Conrad Press in the United Kingdom 2016*

Tel: +44(0)1227 472 874
www.theconradpress.com
info@theconradpress.com

ISBN 978-1-911546-00-9



Book cover design and typesetting by:
Charlotte Mouncey, www.bookstyle.co.uk

The Conrad Press logo was designed by Maria Priestley.

Printed by Management Books 2000 Limited
36 Western Road
Oxford
OX1 4LG

# THE BABY AUCTION

PETER TAYLOR-GOOBY

The author will be donating profits from this book to Shelter.

For Sue

- and thanks to Diane Dane, David Ewens, James Essinger, Dawn Lyon, David Pick, Tim Armstrong and all the others who helped me with this book.

Matt was six years old and he was frightened. Mummy was holding his hand but everything was terribly wrong. They'd gone further down the track into the forest than he'd ever been before and it was getting dark. The trees were different here, taller, packed closer together. He felt they were crowding towards him. If they got right round him he'd never find his way out.

Mummy had stopped walking. He wished she wouldn't hold his hand so tightly. They stood there, staring down the track. You could just make it out in the evening light and then it turned at the crest of a rise and you couldn't see it any more.

The pine trees towered over him. He caught the smell, rich and harsh, but there was another odour he didn't recognise, with sweat and iron and something like lamp-oil in it.

He gripped Mummy's hand. She wouldn't look at him. She just stared down the track.

'When's Daddy coming? I'm hungry,'

She glanced down but she didn't smile. The sun was now touching the tops of the trees. It was night already between the trunks and the black shadows were reaching out across the track, towards them.

'Later, Matt.'

She squeezed his hand. Now she had a different look on her face, as if she was listening out for something far away.

The forest was silent; there was no wind among the trees, no bird-song. He wished she wouldn't grip his hand so hard. He felt so hungry he couldn't stand still. He wished Daddy was there and they could all go back to the village together.

He heard a rattle, like a harness being shaken hard, and the clatter of hooves on the track, then the special low whinny a horse makes when it recognises the smell of its own stable. That's when he thought it might all be all right. He shouted:

'That's Duke!'

Duke was his favourite, the best, the most powerful horse in the village. His father always used Duke for the ploughing. Daddy sometimes lifted him up onto Duke's back. He loved the soft warmth of the horse's body. He loved burying his face in the mane and stretching his arms round the sturdy neck and feeling the great muscles move under the skin.

He let go of Mummy's hand and started to run forward. Duke rounded the corner and plunged toward him. A man, his Daddy, sat astride his back, urging him on.

'Daddy!' he shouted, 'Daddy!'

Daddy drove the horse onward, towards him. All around the great trees crowded in, the shadows black as pitch between their trunks.

He saw one of the shadows move and he felt as if his heart was being squeezed in his breast. The shadow heaved forward, separated itself from the darkness under the trees and swept out of the forest onto the track. It reared up, forming itself into a shape like a man, but black as the night between the trees. The hair rose stiff on the back of his neck. He felt Mummy's arms round him, clasping him against her. She was trembling.

Others came, men like black shadows flowing out of the forest. They made no noise. All he could hear was the pounding of hooves and Mummy screaming:

'No!'

The first figure hurled itself upward at Duke, grabbing at the bridle. It lurched sideways and was dragged along, clinging to the flank of the horse. Duke's head was wrenched round. The black shapes swarmed round, reaching up and fastening themselves onto Daddy, dragging him down. He was on his feet, throwing his body from side to side to shake them off. Then something swept up over his head from behind and he was gone. Matt stood there watching it all happen. His whole body quivered in horror.

Then he woke up and it was dark and he was eighteen and Ed was there beside him and he loved her so much he could hardly breathe and he was telling her his dream.

# PART 1: MATT AND ED

# 1

He was standing there, right at the back of the main stand, almost against the rear wall of the City Stadium. Ed was beside him, and she had her arm tight round his waist and her head on his shoulder. Ed's name was really Eden, but she'd told him she only wanted to be called Ed. She was eighteen too, just over a fortnight younger than him. They'd met in Re-education. She had skin the colour of cinnamon, long brown wavy hair which she often tied back, brown eyes and a smile that made Matt feel he was worth something. There was a scar the width of his thumb under her right eye, healed so close to the colour of her skin that you scarcely noticed it. That warm August day she was wearing blue jeans and a crimson tee-shirt and she was the only person out of the thousands who packed the stands who mattered to Matt.

He couldn't understand why everyone was so intent on the giant screen that dominated the stadium, on the words that kept appearing on it, all about 'Citizens' and 'Exchange' and 'The One Law'. He was more interested in the family in front of him - a couple and a boy who must have been only about six years old. *The same age I was when they came for Dad,* Matt thought.

There were more people in the stadium than Matt had ever seen in one place before. He felt uneasy. He knew that the message on the screen and the speeches of the well-dressed people he could barely make out on the platform in front of it were part of Celebration Day and that was why they were all here. He just didn't believe any of it would make any difference. Celebration Day wouldn't help him find Mum or Dad.

The parents of the small boy in front of him stood rigidly at attention, chanting the words on the screen. Matt felt his heart go out to the child, who tugged impatiently at his father's hand. He guessed from their shabby blue work-clothes and the fact that they were here, at the back, in the cheapest area, that they came from the poorest class in the city, just like him and Ed. You never got paid very much. They'd sack you if they decided they didn't want you and that meant going hungry. They were on an outing together as a family. He thought maybe that didn't happen very often.

The child tugged harder, almost swinging on his father's arm. Matt watched, the familiar ache at his heart, thinking of his own father and of his mother, of what it was like when you were a child with no-one to look after you.

*All he needs is a smile,* he thought. *Don't ignore him. It's not right.*

All around them the crowd were shouting:

THE ONE LAW PROTECTS PROPERTY!
THE ONE LAW PROTECTS FREEDOM!
THE ONE LAW PROTECTS DIGNITY!

The noise battered at his ears. He saw the father swing round and glare down at the child. He felt the anger gathering in his chest. The father suddenly shoved the child away, so violently that he fell. Matt started forward.

The child picked himself up and stared at Matt with solemn, dark eyes. Matt couldn't help himself. He tapped the father on the shoulder:

'Careful with the kid,' he said. 'You'll hurt him.'

The father, thin, his narrow face prematurely lined, made to answer. Then he caught the expression in Matt's eyes, half pain, half anger, and turned abruptly away.

Matt felt a hand gripping his wrist. Ed slipped in front of him.

'The One Law protects everyone,' she said to the man. 'That includes kids.'

The man grabbed his son with one hand and the woman with the other and pushed his way into the crowd. The child dragged behind, staring back at Matt, unsmiling.

Ed released Matt's wrist.

'You OK?' she said.

'Yes, I'm OK.'

He relaxed his shoulders and forced his attention back onto the ceremony. No-one paid him any attention. They were all gazing up at the screen, shouting out the words: 'The One Law!' ignoring everything else going on around them. Ed was mouthing the words on the screen beside him. He opened his own mouth in time with hers, but could say nothing, his throat constricted.

Ed looked up at him:

'It's OK. Just pretend you're saying it.'

Matt never saw the point of the One Law. They taught you about it in Re-education but none of it made sense. The only good thing about Re-education was that that was where he met Ed.

Matt knew he was special to Ed. Happiness tickled inside him whenever he was with her. For the first time since they'd sent him to Re-education he felt he could make something of his life.

# 2

Matt remembered his first day in Re-education, the noise the gate made slamming behind you, the stone wall that shut out the rest of the world, the way the officer who took him there turned and marched back to the waiting transport without a glance at him as soon as she'd got the receipt signed by the guard at the gate.

He was fourteen then. He knew Re-education wasn't like the school he'd gone to in the village. He'd learned he wasn't much good at writing and things like that, but he loved the work experience. They sent him to a farm most days and that was where he first worked with horses. The men in the stables taught him about harnessing and feeding and mucking out and combing and saddling up. Most of all they said you had to respect the horse and then the horse would respect you. They said he was a natural and sometimes they'd let him take a horse out by himself. That had been when he was with his great-aunt, Naomi.

Mummy had held both his hands in hers.

'They've taken your father,' she said. 'I have to go to the city to find him. I'll bring him back. We'll be together again soon. I promise.'

When he asked her who they were, who'd taken Daddy, she looked at Naomi and said:

'Black shadows. It was the black shadows. Don't think about them.'

Naomi would look after him while Mummy was away.

They stood watching Mummy as she set off down the track through the forest. She turned round once and waved to him. He started forward, but Naomi held him with her thin strong hands. Then Mummy went on round the corner into the darkness among the trees.

Naomi was a cheerful older woman with a spare, lined face who had buried two husbands. 'Neither of them as much use as a cart-load of cabbages,' she always said.

A week passed. Mummy didn't come back. He stood there one morning staring up the track. Naomi came out and took his hand in hers.

'Sometimes people go away to the city,' she said, 'and it takes a long time for them to find their way back. You'll be all right with me for now. Just do your best.'

So he got on with things, but the dreams came, with Daddy and the black shadows and he couldn't tell the difference between dreams and memories. Sometimes he got angry, so angry he was frightened and he had to go away from everyone into the forest. Naomi would come and find him. She never asked him why he'd gone, she just took his hand and led him back to the village. If he tried to tell her about the dreams she just said:

'Black shadows. Doesn't do any good to talk about them. There's potatoes need peeling.'

Time passed and he went to the school, then the farm. Then one day people came in a strange sealed vehicle with tracks and said he had to go to Re-education. His great-aunt argued with them but they didn't listen.

Re-education was where they sent you for something you'd done. They said it was wrong. You couldn't undo it, you just had to go to the place on the edge of the city, three day's journey away, and stay there behind the grey stone walls until they let you out. You were with all the others they wanted to get out of the way, all of you waiting until you were eighteen. Then they threw you out. It felt like you were in a warehouse for people who made a nuisance of themselves. Perhaps it was something your parents had done, they never told you what it was.

He remembered Re-education as an emptiness. No-one had any time for anyone else. There were endless training sessions on the One Law, on Entrepreneurial Skills, on Jobs Mart Day, on Citizenship, on the Broken Lands. They kept giving you tests and when you failed they punished you. They called it 'experiential training'. They put you in a windowless cell with blank brick walls and a mattress on the floor. You got bean stew and bread to eat.

'This is what you're worth,' they said. 'If you want better, you've got to earn it.'

He didn't care. When he was in the cell he thought about what he'd do when they threw him out, how he'd walk for days down a track far into the forest and find a farm where there were horses. Then at night came the dreams and the anger. He hated them, the guards, the instructors, the people who'd brought him here, all of them.

He'd seen Ed at the front of one of the classes. She always seemed to be in a world of her own, disciplined, in control, distant from where Matt would ever be. She always came top in the tests.

One day, when Matt was sixteen, the instructor announced that they would be studying what she called 'the good society'.

'You, Torman!' she said. 'On your feet! You're from outside. Tell us what the main cash crops from the villages are.'

Matt stood up. He had no idea what to say. He saw the faces all round him, looking up, ready to laugh at him, like they were watching a show. He felt the anger inside him. He breathed carefully.

'We didn't sell food much,' he said. 'We grew it to eat, us and the rest of the village.'

'Undeveloped,' said the instructor, addressing the rest of the class. 'That's why we have the One Law. How do you make a profit, how do you make progress, if you don't sell things?'

Matt caught at the word.

'Apples,' he said. 'We sold a few apples in the autumn, but we mostly gave them away. We had so many.'

'Idiot!' barked the instructor. A ripple of laughter ran round the room. 'You're no better than someone from the Broken Lands. Criminals against the one law. If you give things away, why would anyone work? Then if you want something you just take it. Is that what they did in your village? Is that what your parents did? Is that why you're here?'

'But it wasn't like that.'

Matt realised he was shouting and lowered his voice. 'My parents worked for everything they had. We were in the village, we just wanted to help each other, it's what we did.'

He felt they were all against him, the instructor, all the grinning faces, then he saw Ed looking up at him. Her face no longer wore the usual detached expression. She seemed sad. Then she gave him a quick smile, like they were in a conspiracy together.

The instructor held up a hand for silence and continued:

'Fortunately the farmers near the city have a better grasp of civilised behaviour. Market prices, profits, investment. That's how you get high yields. The main exports from the rural sector are wheat thirty-six per cent, beans thirty-two per cent, livestock twenty-four per cent and fruit eight per cent.'

Then they were doing the test and he could think of nothing but how Ed had smiled at him.

He failed the test and spent the next two days in the training cell. The dreams came but he didn't get angry.

He was walking slowly back along the corridor when he saw her. She was leaning against the wall. Something made him talk to her.

'What are you doing here?'

She didn't answer.

'Ed,' he said. 'What is it?' Then: 'I'm sorry.'

He couldn't think of anything more to say.

At last she looked up at him. Tears glittered in her eyes. He wanted to hold her.

'They keep talking about primitive areas and the Broken Lands and how much better we are in Market World,' she said. 'What do they know about the Broken Lands?'

She looked away. He put a hand against the wall, his arm shielding her face.

'Are you OK? Can I help?'

'That's where I come from,' she said. 'My people were civilised in their own way. They wanted to help each other. It was the soldiers.'

Then she shook her head, turned and walked rapidly away.

He hung around in that corridor a bit after that and one day she was there again. You were taking a risk, but it was one of the few places people didn't go very much. He told her about his father and the black shadows and about how Mum went to the city and didn't come back, and about working with horses. He didn't tell here about the anger until later.

They started meeting after that, always it seemed by accident, always away from the others. He felt for the first time since going to Re-education that he mattered to someone.

It was much later that she told him about the Broken Lands. They were standing in the corridor again. She said she was a refugee from one of the wars.

'Soldiers came one night across the fields. They burnt everything, the crops, the houses, the church, everything. There was smoke, rolling towards us and you could see red flames in it and hear people crying out, screaming.'

She looked away and wiped her eyes with her hand.

'We walked for days and we came to the sea. I'd never seen anything like it. It was beautiful, like wrinkled silver paper. Mum and dad got us on a boat. Everyone was frightened. They thought the soldiers would come after us. The journey took days and we were hungry all the time.'

Somewhere in the building a door slammed. Ed went on:

'We didn't know much about Market World. We thought everyone was rich here. We'd be able to work, perhaps people'd be kind us.'

She paused.

'They didn't treat us badly, they just ignored us. We didn't have any money. We were living on the street, we were hungry. They just walked past us.'

She stopped again. The remote look came back into her face.

After a moment Matt said, as gently as he could:

'Tell me what happened.'

'My dad did what made sense to him. He asked someone for some money, just a loan to buy food. The woman muttered 'Don't pay, don't get' and pushed past, so he stopped the next person and asked him. This man started shouting about parasites and the One Law. Then the Enforcers came.'

'Why?' Matt asked. 'Who are the Enforcers?'

'They are the One Law. They hate anyone who asks for anything and they hate gifters. They enforce the One Law. I hate them.'

She glanced up the corridor.

'The Enforcers beat Dad with the butts of their whips, like he was an animal. They seized him, and Mum too. Mum screamed at me to run for it so I did.'

She touched the scar under her eye.

'I found out how to live in the city. That's how I got this. Then they caught me and sent me here.'

She paused again.

'I know what happened to Mum and Dad, Matt. They sent them to a colony, a long way away.' Her voice hardened. 'That's why I hate them, all of them, the bosses, the Enforcers, all of them. Anyone who loves you, anyone tries to help you, they take them away. You don't pay, you don't get.'

She looked up. Her eyes were heavy with tears. He felt clumsy with his tenderness for her.

'I think I'll never see them again,' she said, 'but I have to find out the truth. Don't tell anyone.'

# 3

It was the morning of July the twelfth. Matt was eighteen. He stood at the gate watching the gate-keeper fumble at the lock. Re-education was over. Ed had fifteen days to go.

'I'll wait for you,' he said. 'By the gate.'

'See you,' she said. She moved closer, her face turned up to his. 'Maybe.'

She kissed him and he held her close, closer than he'd ever held anyone.

Then she turned and walked swiftly down the corridor, without looking back. He stood there for a long time.

The gate-keeper fixed his eyes on Matt.

'One thing to remember: never owe anyone more than you can pay. And don't come back.'

He swung open the gate and gestured Matt through.

There was a road in front of him and a grey residence block, half-derelict with the windows boarded up, opposite. He looked both ways. No-one in sight.

He crossed over and found a shelter from the wind in the doorway of the block. He stood there for half an hour staring at the high stone wall that surrounded Re-education.

He pulled his jacket round him and glanced up the street. One way led to the city, where they took his dad, where Mum had gone, long ago. He could see high towers at the centre, glinting in the bright sunlight. Nearer were the ranks of grey residence blocks, like a barrier.

The other way led to open country, farmland first, then rougher pastures and in the distance the forest. He knew his village was somewhere there, three, perhaps four day's journey away. He shouldered his backpack, turned and set off down the road, away from the city. He thought of Ed. Fifteen days.

The sun was low in the sky when he reached the trees and almost instantly he was in semi-darkness. He took three paces away from the track and stood with his hand on the rough bark. He smelled the scent of the pine trees. They'd taken Dad away on the track through the forest. He couldn't make out anything in the darkness between the trunks. There were none of the strange odours, sweat and iron and oil he'd smelled that day.

He felt somehow comforted. The forest was silent. He stood there looking out over the pasture-land and the fields, over the jumble of buildings, to the towers in the distance. A searchlight stabbed out from the tallest tower and swept an arc halfway round towards him. Just as abruptly it was extinguished. Matt edged further behind the tree. *Maybe that's where Mum and Dad are,* he thought.

He moved deeper in among the trunks and found somewhere among the bracken where he could rest without anyone being able to see him. The night was warm and he pulled his coat round him. He could hear movement in the forest, small feet ruffling the twigs on the forest-floor. Once something touched his hand. He felt a tiny snout, then a tongue licking at his fingers. He moved his wrist and it was gone. Towards morning he slept.

Matt spent most of the fifteen days in the forest. He ate some fruit and roots. On the third day he found a stream that meandered down between deep pools. He remembered what his father had taught him about catching trout, luring them in over a motionless hand by dabbing at the surface with a blade of grass, then suddenly snatching upwards and flipping them onto the bank. He watched their eyes film over, the scales on their sides grow dull.

When he had a dozen, he washed carefully in the stream and made his way back to the track. After a while he reached a village.

He'd watched Dad trade and he knew how to bargain. He told the villagers that he was from Fernhill. Some of them had heard of it, but no-one had ever been there. He let the first three fish go cheap, he was a stranger after all, then raised the price. Soon he had everything he needed: a blanket, some bread, dried meat, cheese, berries, a sliver of soap, and a welcome to come back next time he had some fish to sell.

He was back outside the gate half-hidden in the angle of the wall just after the sun came up. He stood there for three hours. There was no-one else waiting. Finally the bolt snapped back and there she was, a hesitancy in her stance he'd never seen before as she looked both ways up and down the street. He wished he could stop time at that moment, Ed seeking for him and him watching out for her, and all the future before them.

'Ed! Over here!'

He ran forward and swept his arms round her. Then he was kissing her.

'I was in the wood, I caught fish and sold them in the village. We can go there, I'm sure we can …'

She smiled at him:

'Slow down,' she said. 'We can't hide in the villages for ever.'

She turned towards the city, then glanced up at him.

'Besides,' she said, 'there's Mum and Dad. And your parents. We have to find out. There's nowhere else to go.'

They set off up the road, Ed walking slightly in front of him.

Soon they were among the residence blocks. The buildings cast deep shadows across the streets and there were people on all sides, too many of them to keep track of. He felt he was somewhere where he didn't know the rules. Ed grasped his hand firmly and led the way, through a maze of dingy streets, across a square and into a doorway below a flickering neon sign. She said something Matt didn't catch to a fat man who sat on wooden chair at the entrance. He grunted.

They were in a dingy room at the top of an uncarpeted stairway. She turned and she was kissing him hard on the lips, her arms around him, tight as promises. She reached up and her rich brown hair suddenly flooded out, framing her face. They were together on the bed, her slight body powerful against his. She was kissing him endlessly, her face against his. He forgot everything. There was just this moment, just him and Ed together at last.

'I love you,' he said. 'I love you so much.'

*Never owe more than you can pay.*

He owed Ed more than he would ever be able to pay, however long he was with her. It was beyond him, as distant as the moon on a winter's night.

She ran her hand tenderly down his back.

'We'll be together now, won't we?'

It was more a statement than a question.

Matt was fascinated by Ed's competence, the way she could deal with people, bargaining endlessly, never losing her temper. The rest of that day, the first day he'd ever been in the city, passed in a rush, walking past crowds of people with his head down, keeping against the buildings, passing through alleyways strewn with litter and knocking at doors and asking about rooms. Once they ate something that smelled of beans in a noisy back-room crowded with people.

Later, they were by themselves in the room she found for them, sub-let from a flat on the edge of the city, up five flights of grimy concrete stairs. It had a cracked washbasin and a cupboard in the corner and most of the rest of the floor-space was taken up by the bed.

'It's cheap,' she said, 'and we'll soon fix it up OK.'

They stuck some pictures from magazines on the walls. Matt liked the one he got from a calendar at the market best even though it had a slogan about cow-fodder across the bottom. The picture showed a peaceful valley with a herd of cows gathered at the trough and the farmer and his family looking on. The family looked so content in the evening light. The farmer had one arm round his wife, the other round his son. Matt knew it was just an advertising picture. You'd never really be able to support a herd of that size on that much pasture.

They spent a few days wandering round the back streets, looking for work. Matt still felt nervous in the city. He knew the anger was still there somewhere within him. He loathed the endless offers of things for sale, the way no-one ever paid you any attention as they pushed by, the endless babble of noise, everywhere the glare of light reflected from concrete walls, from the roadway, from the huge glass windows on the shops, beating down on him from above. Most of all it was the smells that overwhelmed him, the jumble of different scents and odours, none of them he could recognise, everything tangled, nothing like the village, where you could pick out each animal, each plant, each neighbour.

He tried to explain it all to Ed. She said:

'No one in Market World'd give you the dirt off their shoes. They're all frightened of the One Law.'

Matt found he could get labouring work, cash in hand, unloading the sacks of vegetables from the wagons in the wholesale market on the edge of the city where the farmers brought in their produce. They were from the country, like him.

'Recognise that accent anywhere. You're not from round here are you?' they'd say to him. They liked to see someone they felt they could trust. The maze of streets frightened them. Matt understood they were like himself, unused to the traffic, to the crowds of people and the uproar, to the jumbled smells of everything in your nostrils all at once. They sometimes gave him produce, cheese, the best of the fruit, kept in a compartment under the seat: 'just so you don't forget where you came from – but if anyone asks, we bargained and you paid me a fair price for it.'

He'd share some of it with them, sitting on sacks out of the way, at the side of the market hall, but he always took most of it back to Ed. Once he traded some of the fruit for flowers. He found they had enough to keep going with what he earned and the money Ed brought back from a casual job in a supermarket owned by someone called Franklin.

Then he asked the farmer he worked for most about finding his parents. They'd unloaded the wagon and were sharing a loaf of bread. The man looked at him and felt in his pocket. He counted out the two credits he owed and put the money in Matt's hand without speaking. Then he gave him a five credit note extra. He shook his head, turned and walked away. Matt couldn't find anyone else who wanted him to work for them that day.

When Ed got back, he put the money on the table and told her what had happened.

'You've got to be careful,' she said. 'Some things people won't talk about. You don't make friends in Market World.'

'But how can we find out what happened to Mum and Dad?'

She took his hand and warmed it between hers.

'The answer is here, in the city,' she said. 'I know it.'

'But we have to do something.'

She looked up at him.

'It's Celebration Day soon. We'll go to the arena. You'll see what Market World's really like.'

# 4

Dain felt a cold pride as he stared out over the city. He was seated at his desk, opposite the window in the room on the tenth floor with 'Captain of the City Guard' on the door. He knew pride was incorrect. He served where he was best fitted to serve, that was all.

He fingered the three stars at his collar that denoted his rank.

His parents had always wanted him to become a priest like his father.

He imagined what the scene in the Great Hall two weeks ago would have been like, if they had lived. He knew they'd have stood right at the front, smiling proudly, accepting the congratulations of their friends, of the Council, perhaps of President Wells herself. They would tell him how smart he looked in his new dress uniform, with the two rows of medals and the Star of the City on its silver ribbon, promoted to Captain of the City Guard at the age of twenty-six. How proud they would have been, if only everything had been different and they had been there.

But perhaps his father, the priest without a parish, would have taken him on one side earlier that morning and reminded him in his careful insistent voice:

'Dain, we are both so very proud of you. You have accomplished so much. But to serve God first and then to serve your fellow man: that is the highest duty. You would not be the first to discover that duty even now …'

No God ruled in Market World, only the One Law. It was the One Law that made Market World possible, and the higher duty was to enforce it. The Captain of the City Guard serves the people, no god and no one man. And the One Law means that noone has to fail, as you did, my father, in the Broken Lands. He nurtured the obduracy of his heart. My duty. There must be one man steadfast in the law, so that citizens are safe to lead free lives in Market World.

Dain stared out over the city spread out in front of him: *my parish. I will serve you, all of you.* The great towers dominated everything, dwarfing the frail half-finished spires of the cathedral. Beyond the towers he could see the ranks of identical grey residence blocks, the streets dark canyons between them. He could just make out, yet further off, the land rising up to the darker green of the forest on the crest of the hills that encircled the city. Deep in the forest there were still villages where the writ of One Law did not at present run, where Enforcers only went on authorised pursuit.

Dain glanced at the clock, then at the silver-braided uniform cap lying on the desk in front of him. The crest of the city was picked out in gold above the glossy peak, the scales of justice with the motto in tiny letters: 'Property, Equality, Dignity, Trade'

He rose to his feet, picked up the cap in both hands and placed it firmly on his head. The reflection of the Star shimmered in the opaque glass panel of the door. August the fifteenth. Twenty-first anniversary of the foundation of Market World.

No-one would question his right to march at the head of the Enforcers on Celebration Day.

# 5

Dain loved the way the crowd fell silent and cleared a path in front of him as he led the Enforcers through the packed streets. The entire city force marched behind him, more than three hundred men and women chosen for their stature and their air of stern authority. The crowd watched awestruck as they marched down Exchange Avenue and entered the arena.

The faces at the front of the crowd were prosperous, admiring, above all respectful. Behind them, in the cheaper stands, Dain could see the ranks of less prosperous citizens, their clothes drab, their faces leaner, their expressions blank, accepting. No-one spoke. Dain ignored them, his eyes on the crimson banners of Market World on either side of the main stand. He would enforce the law equally, without fear or favour, for all of them.

He directed the Enforcers to the centre of the open space in front of the podium, brought them to attention and raised his right fist in salute. Their black uniforms stood out against the yellow of the sand and the crimson banners draped across the front of the stands. They wore black leather gloves and boots. Their whips were coiled neatly at their belts and their helmets were stowed in the vehicles.

Dain was aware that at five foot eleven inches, he was the sole male Enforcer below six foot in height. He alone had the three silver stars of rank at his throat and the silver edging to his cap denoting his rank, Captain of the City Guard.

The others had always treated him with respect. That had been true at the College. Now he was twenty-six he understood that this respect was paid not only to his rapid promotion or his rank or the Star of the City on his chest. There was something about the direct gaze of his grey eyes and his decisiveness that he knew carried an air of calm authority. That, and his reputation for putting the Law before patronage, personal advantage or even friendship. That was his faith.

The City dignitaries saluted in turn. Franklin, Master of the Guild of Entrepreneurs, the only figure not in uniform, gave a casual half-wave. Dain glanced swiftly at the red-haired businessman in the dark suit that fitted perfectly, with his handkerchief dangling from his top pocket as if he'd just used it to clean his glasses. *You too,* he thought. *The Law is also for you and I will enforce it.*

President Rebecca Wells, Co-ordinator of the Council, looked directly at Dain and saluted him smartly, raising her right hand, fist lightly closed, to her right shoulder. Her black linen trouser suit was tailored to remind the audience of the Enforcers' uniform, the jacket buttoned to the neck. The silver motif on the jacket pocket caught the sunlight and flashed like a row of decorations. She had intense brown eyes and shoulder-length ash-blond hair. It was known that she was fifty-one years old, but she looked ten years younger.

Dain stared straight ahead. Bright sunlight lit up the stadium. Noon, the time without shadows. The banks of loudspeakers, on either side of the podium, were flanked by the gigantic vertical crimson banners, each as high as a residence block. The banners carried the City's crest, the scales of justice, under them now visible the words:

PROPERTY, EQUALITY, DIGNITY, TRADE

and above them, in capitals as high as a man, the order of the day:

CELEBRATE THE ONE LAW

Dain stood at the centre of the stadium, the podium directly in front of him, his Enforcers drawn up in the open space behind him. All around him he could hear the hubbub of the crowd, thousands of people, everyone in the city who was able to get there, gossiping, shuffling, pointing things out and trading, always trading. His Enforcers contributed nothing to the noise, each standing rigidly still, unmoving and alert, as if rooted. Adam Steele, his deputy, whom Dain trusted completely, stood to his side, older and fitter than any of them, the scar from the incident that had earned him his reputation running diagonally from the corner of his right eye across his mouth to his chin. Dain squared his shoulders.

The din of the crowd hushed as the image of President Wells appeared in close-up, perhaps fifty times life-size, on the giant screen behind the podium.

Dain's mind went back to the promotion ceremony two weeks ago, when he'd first met President Wells face-to-face, the day after he'd led the raid that had smashed the price-ring in the Old Market. A few of the senior traders had controlled the entire food supply of the city. He'd stopped that and now the food shortages which meant that the poor were always hungry were at an end.

He thought with satisfaction of how he'd undertaken the operation on his own initiative with a few officers he trusted in support. Adam was the only one he'd taken into his full confidence. They'd caught the ring-leaders red-handed handing over the briefcase with the bribes in it to one of the highest-ranking Enforcers, the Chief Inspector of Markets. Dain smiled briefly. The senior officers who'd been happy to accept their pay-offs so long as they turned a blind eye were now paying their debt to the city: forced labour in the North Colony.

That ceremony was the proudest day of Dain's life. President Wells had leaned forward to place the ribbon of the Star about his neck, her hands on his shoulders. He smelt the sharp tang of her perfume. She had straightened, looked him in the eyes and announced:

'Enforcer Dain Lucas, congratulations! We award you the Star of the City for meritorious and exceptional service. You have more to offer us. I hereby appoint you Captain of the City Guard. You have shown that you have the integrity, the courage, the honour to lead our Enforcers.'

The applause of the City Council behind her rang in his ears. *If only my parents had understood about Market World,* he thought, *if only they hadn't thought they had a better way, they would be here, part of all this.*

# 

Nothing, Dain thought, could equal the intensity of President Wells' brown eyes now, on Celebration Day, as she stared straight into the camera, straight into the face of everyone in the arena. Her voice rang out, echoing back from the sheer walls of the residence blocks around the stadium.

'Citizens! Today is Celebration Day. We celebrate our city. We celebrate the One Law. We celebrate our Enforcers, guardians of the Law. And we celebrate that we alone do not endure the lawless life of the Broken Lands.'

She paused. There was complete silence. The only sound Dain could hear was the rustle of the banners.

'Perhaps I can remind you of that time, not so distant, when humanity emerged from the shadows. Men and women discovered machinery, they mined, they invented, they made, they grew crops and they bought and sold.'

Images flashed onto the screen: a family, mother, father, two children, smiling as they surveyed a field of golden corn, men and women hammering at a metal blade on a bed of glowing coals, a craftsman fitting the ploughshare, a woman driving a team of horses, people trading among the gaily-coloured stalls of a village market, all in bright sunlight.

'That was our Golden Age.'

Dain noticed a sudden movement at the front of the premium stand, not twenty yards to his right.

A woman, her black hair neatly cut to frame her face, was standing up in the front row, her face rapt. She had deep brown eyes and her skin was strikingly pale. Her white suit stood out against the dark business clothing of those surrounding her, like a lily in a coal-yard. He guessed she was in her early twenties. She was standing in the front section of the stand reserved for the leading traders and those who had made their mark, the 'Heroes of Enterprise'.

'The world changed,' the president went on, her voice sombre. 'The gulf between rich and poor grew wider, unimaginably wide. Life for most people was no better than slavery, a life of endless poverty, without dignity, without respect.'

The images darkened. A factory appeared, a huge dim hall filled with endless rows of machines. Women, men and children bowed over the machines, ragged, dirty, moving with the exhaustion of the half-starved. Then a mob in rags fought for places around a great cauldron, their arms reaching out, their faces desperate, their feet slipping in the mud. A soberly-dressed man smiling piously, a guard on either side of him, handed down a bowl of soup.

'After many years, men and women could no longer tolerate the burden of their lives. The poor rose up and fought the rich and their police in bloody revolutions spreading throughout the lands. The outcome was endless disorder, and finally the Great Hunger swept across the world.'

Chaotic images rushed across the screen, almost too fast to register: slaves chained to a great wagon, hauling it over a rutted road; an armoured car, its machine-gun blazing at a crowd outside a football stadium; the golden meadow seen earlier in flames, great clouds of black smoke rolling out over the village; horsemen with whips beating people away from the market-stalls, throwing them to the ground, trampling on them, the stalls smashed, a child, its face distorted with terror, screaming soundlessly, falling forward onto the camera as the horsemen swept through the crowd.

Dain glanced across at the woman. To his amazement, she was staring back at him with an expression he couldn't fathom. There seemed to be admiration in it, and respect. He found himself wondering if she'd watched him on the newscasts.

President Wells looked intently out at her audience.

'We drove out the rulers and we drove out the gifters. Those who would exploit us and those who would shame us. We outlawed corruption and we outlawed welfare. We burned out the cancer. Their chains and their hand-outs we gave to the furnace.'

The giant screen was filled with fire, great tongues of flame blazing up. The stadium echoed with the roar of the furnace.

'Slavers, warlords, the charitable, the gifters, all oppressors we sent to the Broken Lands. Here in Market World we found a better way.'

The familiar map Dain remembered from the school-room appeared, a bright blue sea, with the tongue of the Great Continent reaching into it, the camera dropping down to discover far out in the ocean, beyond the tongue, the speck of an island growing rapidly larger. He'd learnt how distant from all other lands Market World was, how remote, so that no-one came to interfere with their special way of life.

Dain glanced back at the black-haired woman. Her eyes were still on him.

She stood out against the business people around her, bulky men and women, sleek as seals in their dark suits, their faces accustomed to power. He decided at that moment to make it his business to get to know her.

A sudden blare of music brought his attention back to the giant screen. The camera dived down. The image of the island expanded to reveal Market World at the centre, around it the forest: the city on its fertile plain, divided north to south by the river, the towers at its heart, the river-side park, the stadium, the market halls and then the residence blocks neatly arranged around them.

'In Market World,' President Wells proclaimed, 'we came to understand that only in a society that had fair exchange at its very heart can citizens truly be individuals, truly have dignity, truly be free. No citizen a sharer, no citizen a gifter, no citizen dependent on charity, no citizen a slave to another, as in the Broken Lands. But in Market World all are equal, all are respected equally.'

She paused, and Dain, looking up at the giant screen, saw how her dark eyes seemed to gaze into the faces of every member of her audience.

'Only through payment, only through trade, only through the bargain struck freely between willing buyer and willing seller is there equality, respect and dignity. All else is charity, dependence and …'

She paused again, her gaze embracing all of them. She spoke the final word with a new gentleness.

'Tyranny.'

Her voice rang out across the stadium.

'I give you: Another Twenty-One Years of Property, Equality, Dignity, Trade - and Peace. I give you the One Law.'

Dain saw in crimson letters on the great screen the words:

THE ONE LAW

Dain glanced back at the contingent and signalled with his left hand. They shouted out as one:

THE ONE LAW!
THE ONE LAW!
THE ONE LAW!

The crowd were on their feet shouting:

THE ONE LAW!

swelling the chant as it rose up, above the arena, out over the city and beyond, perhaps, Dain thought, as far as the dark forest on the surrounding hills.

# 7

The loudspeakers went on booming. Matt looked round and remembered where he was, with Ed, right at the back of the stadium. He felt the anger stirring within him. There were too many people here, he thought, people who ignored you, people who brushed you aside, people who took your Mum and Dad, who put you in Re-education.

He stared up at the giant screen. A man who Matt thought must have been somewhere in his mid-forties, a man in a business suit with untidy ginger hair, stared confidently out at the crowd, his face stamped with the habit of command.

'That's Franklin,' Ed whispered to him, 'Big boss, he owns the market hall, the shop I work in, he owns everything. Look at how his suit fits, they're the only people who can afford that kind of stuff.'

Matt watched as Franklin grinned at his audience and raised both hands to quiet them.

'Citizens! Fellow-citizens! Fellow-traders!'

The new speaker's gaze swept across the stadium. He spoke in a coarse, grating voice. Matt recognised the accent of the residence blocks, the run-down inner-city streets where the poor lived.

'You know me, I'm Franklin. I'm an Entrepreneur, but that's just a fancy word for a trader. I come from the blocks, same as you do. I started with nothing. I'm not proud. Anyone can do it.'

He stared out at them, his head thrust forward, both hands grasping the sides of the lectern. Matt glanced at Ed. She was looking up at the screen, an expression of contempt on her face. She shook her head and whispered to Matt:

'Yeah, Franklin. We believe you. It was an easy as that. That's why you're rich and we ain't. It's all our fault.'

Franklin was still talking:

'I'm someone who buys and sells, who gives people work, who builds the blocks you live in. I make the things you buy in the shops, everything according to the One Law. I just want to make things work, for all of us.'

Matt saw him gesture to the banners with a broad, confident smile. Franklin continued, almost shouting his words.

'Everyone equal, no-one a slave, no-one a gifter, no-one a taker. Everyone with the chance to get rich and earn respect. That's how we made Market World – and it works, for all of us.'

He lowered his voice.

'I'm not a historian, I don't have the gift of words, not like President Wells.'

He smiled at the president. She ignored him.

'I say we did right when we drove out the gifters! Here in Market World everyone pays their way, no-one gets something for nothing. We don't live like they do in the Broken Lands, where the powerful enslave the weak, and starve them if they don't work hard enough.'

Franklin looked out over the audience, and nodded, as if agreeing with himself:

'Best of all, there's no discrimination here in Market World. In the Broken Lands people pick on each other just because they're different, black and white, gay and straight, men and women.'

'Here we have equality and respect. I'm equal to any of you and any of you are equal to me.'

He paused again. Matt saw his gaze travel across the audience to the gleaming glass and steel cliff of the New Market building next to the stadium. Franklin's grin broadened. He licked his lips and jabbed a finger at the audience.

'I don't care if you're black or white, young or old, gay or straight, a man or a woman. All I care is: can you pay me?'

Someone close by Matt started a chant:

FRANKLIN!
FRANKLIN!

The crowd took it up. Matt glanced at Ed. He was shocked at the hatred in her face.

'Ed,' he said softly into her ear, and took her hand. She looked blankly at him for a second, then seemed to come to herself and pulled him close.

'I don't forget, Matt. How can I? What they did to my parents.'

On the screen Franklin smiled as if momentarily embarrassed at the applause, despite his brashness. He pulled the handkerchief from his top pocket and polished vigorously at a pair of glasses. Matt watched as he slipped on the glasses and raised both his hands to acknowledge the cheers.

The first section of the One Law appeared on the screen. Franklin led the crowd in reading it out, squinting slightly at the words. Matt could hear the coarse voice, common as mud, echoing across the stadium, booming out over the harsh, raucous response of the audience.

ALL CITIZENS ARE EQUAL
NO CITIZEN TAKES FROM ANOTHER
NO CITIZEN GIVES TO ANOTHER
NO CITIZEN IS A SLAVE.

The words seemed to lose all meaning, the sound battering at his ears, the letters just shapes on the screen. Matt pushed the hair back from his forehead and leaned close to Ed's ear, so she could hear him above the clamour:

'I don't like these crowds, everyone shouting. I've had enough. Let's get out of here.'

Ed nodded and started to push her way to the side where the crowd was thinnest. The chanting kept on, waves of sound reflected from the wall of the stadium, pounding at them. The anger was there within him, growing stronger. He couldn't make it go away.

Matt saw that Ed had found a way through, right at the back of the stand, behind the last row of people, hard against the boundary wall. He felt trapped by the amplified voices echoing from the walls of the stadium, repeating the words that stood in letters a metre high on the screen above them.

They reached the edge of the arena. Matt leaned against the side wall. The only way out was to follow it, down towards the front.

'Keep your head down,' whispered Ed.

Matt followed her and glanced up, between the figures in the stand, at the next section of the law:

THE ONE LAW STANDS BETWEEN THE CITIZEN
AND SLAVERY,
AND THEFT,
AND ROBBERY,
AND RAPE

He put his hands over his ears, striving to block out the words bellowing out from the throats of fifty thousand citizens.

THIS IS THE LAW OF MARKET WORLD

The voices rose together into a great shout, led by the Enforcers:

THIS IS THE LAW

Matt and Ed froze as the arena suddenly fell silent. They were now close enough to the front for Matt to see the group on the platform clearly. President Wells rose to her feet. Franklin ignored her. He raised his hands to the crowd again, acknowledging the cheers, ran a hand through his hair and stepped back.

Matt watched as she saluted the citizens, her smart uniformed figure contrasting with Franklin's bulk.

'Citizens! Now our Enforcers will renew their pledge to the city. Step forward, Captain Dain Lucas of the City Guard.'

Matt stared, not moving, his body suddenly tense, as a small figure marched smartly to the podium, mounted the steps and turned to face the crowd. The screen showed his face in close up, smooth-skinned, calm grey eyes staring out authoritatively over the people.

'Citizens! All are equal before the one law. All must be buyers and sellers and nothing else.'

The screen filled with images of Enforcers marching, saluting, in riot gear, advancing in ordered ranks on a mob with banners, spilling out of tracked vehicles, always in black, always helmeted, faces covered. Matt's chest tightened, he couldn't breathe. The black shadows flashed into his mind, the figures at the edge of the forest. Men in black uniforms. Anger was flooding through him, like a torrent.

He shuddered.

'It's them! They took my father.'

He forced his way forward, angling down the side of the stand towards the arena. Ed squeezed through after him.

Matt heard the Enforcer's voice, booming out above them:

'Only one stands outside the market. Only one does not buy or sell. The Enforcer.'

Captain Lucas glanced down at the contingent of Enforcers standing rigidly to attention in front of him, then out across the citizens in the arena. Matt felt the grey eyes staring straight at him. He crouched as low as he could and kept on forward, past a low barrier.

Ed caught hold of him. She'd never seen such pain in his face.

'Black shadows,' he muttered, 'they're the black shadows.'

The anger drove everything out of his mind. He pushed forward towards the steps leading down into the arena.

Dain stood motionless on the podium, staring out over the heads of the crowd, past the prestige seats at the front to the cheap stands at the back, past the towers of the Entrepreneurs, past the half-built cathedral, out over the city, to the grey residence blocks where the ordinary people lived.

He smiled grimly. His parish, and the black-haired woman gazing up at him from the stand. He descended from the podium, signalled with his left hand and turned to lead the Enforcers from the arena. They wheeled and marched towards Exchange Avenue, leading back into the City. He prepared for the last ritual, the salute to the One Law.

He glanced at the twelve-foot black basalt column on which the law was engraved. It stood on its own plinth at the entrance to the Avenue directly in front of the Premium Stand. The black-haired woman was right at the front, among the Heroes of Enterprise, her jacket white against the dark suits of the wealthy businesspeople.

Behind the stand he could see the facade of the New Market Hall, Franklin's latest investment, the largest and the most prestigious trading hall in the city.

Dain realised that the woman had positioned herself just to the side of the column, her hand raised almost in a salute. He lifted his left hand again and gave the order:

'Parade, eyes right! Salute!'

Three hundred faces snapped to the right. Three hundred fists were raised. Dain's eyes remained on the woman. Others in the stand were gazing at the big screen, the Enforcers or at Franklin himself. She stared only at him, Dain, giving to him alone her full attention. He became aware again of the innocence of her face, the purity of her skin, the sombre expression in her eyes. He held his back straight as a sword-blade.

He realised that Adam at the end of the rank had started to cough. They were well past the column now. His voice rapped out, without his seeming to give a conscious order:

'Eyes front!'

As the Enforcers swept on past the stand, Dain caught side of two hunched figures bent down against the side wall. The larger of the two straightened and threw himself forward, directly at Dain, waving. He was shouting:

'What did you do with them? Where's my father? My mother?'

Dain had an impression of fervent blue eyes, black hair and a deep resonant voice.

The man was nearly on him now, still shouting nonsense:

'It was you! The black shadows.'

Dain realised as the Enforcers swept forward that his attacker towered over him. The second figure, smaller, wavy-haired, darker-skinned, a woman he was suddenly aware, had caught up with the first. She was reaching up to grab at him, yelling:

'Matt! What are you doing?'

Dain hesitated for half a second and a ripple ran back through the ranks behind him. Adam's voice rang out from the end of the first rank:

'March on!'

- and the ranks of Enforcers swept forward, like automatons, forcing the man to throw himself aside. He heard a sudden grunt as one of the Enforcers in the first row stuck the man a sharp blow to the stomach.

The attacker doubled up and another Enforcer tripped him neatly.

Out of the corner of his eye Dain saw the wavy-haired woman leap back. The man went down, boots kicking at his sides, at his belly, one slamming down just in front of his face. He rolled sideways. Adam, at the end of the rank, stepped carefully over him.

Dain heard Adam's growl:

'Compensate the citizen.'

The Enforcers reached into their pockets and flung the coins down hard at the figure on the ground. Dain heard nothing beyond the crunch of boots on gravel. He ached to turn his head, to see whether the dark-haired woman in the stand was still staring at him. He led his company on towards the exit.

# 9

Matt managed to get his hands over his face as the coins pelted down around him. He crawled forward and collapsed gasping at the side of the Avenue, against the front of the stand. The taste of blood filled his mouth, salt and iron. His side felt on fire, the pain forcing everything from his mind. The anger was still blazing through him. He tried to get up and fell back. The crunch of boots diminished into the distance.

He found himself staring up into the face of a black-haired woman, her eyes wide, her mouth open. She was reaching down towards him. She had pale skin, a delicate small-boned hand and startlingly red finger-nails. He gazed up into the dark eyes. He could hardly make out the division between the pupil and the iris.

He felt Ed tugging at his arm.

He realised the woman's eyes were filling with tears. Ed's voice was insistent:

'Come on, we have to go.'

The woman in the stand was speaking, saying something to him but he couldn't make out the words. The sunlight shone bright all around her, glinting on her short black hair. The light dazzled his eyes. Ed was still tugging at his arm.

He pulled himself slowly to his feet, gasping at the jolt of pain in his side. Ed had her arm round him, she was holding him on his feet, urging him forward. He stared up, unable to take his eyes away from the woman in the stand, just a few feet above him. He could hear Ed speaking, insistent in his ear:

'Hold onto me. We've got to get out of here.

The image of the face of the woman leaning over the edge of the stand, staring after him, the sun behind her, glinting from her black hair, her skin pale, her eyes wide, drove everything out of his mind.

'Come on.'

Ed tugged at his arm. He was astonished at the strength in her slender body.

# 10

Anna Pascal had been delighted, proud and thrilled when she was elected a 'Hero of Enterprise' with the chance to bid for a seat in the premium stand. Quality Catering was one of the big success stories of the city. She'd started it from virtually nothing, and now it ran everything from street-stalls to high class restaurants. The deal she'd made after the Old Market scandal secured supplies and she'd just recapitalised for further expansion. The award meant the Entrepreneurs took her seriously. *I'm only twenty-three,* she thought. *Some of it's luck, but not all of it.*

Her heart swelled when Dain marched in at the head of the Enforcers. She knew him by reputation, she'd followed the newscasts avidly. *He's a risk-taker, just like me.*

She was immediately struck by the graceful, precise way he moved as he entered the arena. She gazed up at his face on the giant screen. She couldn't understand why everyone looked back at Franklin and the President as soon as he finished speaking.

That was when the idea of standing right at the front, just next to the column, occurred to her. She found herself directly in front of Dain, no more than twenty feet away, when his head turned in the salute and the grey eyes met hers. She could find no expression in his face to answer her own, but his eyes remained fixed on her until he turned away to march forward.

It was then that the man dashed out, right at Dain, shouting something about black shadows. A woman with coffee-coloured skin and wavy brown hair was trying to hold him back. Anna gripped the rail. The ranks of Enforcers continued forward with Dain at their head.

She saw the man twist round, off balance. Dain was unscathed, but the man was on the ground, rolling over towards her, clutching his side, in a litter of small change. He tried to rise and fell back. He was directly beneath her now, staring upwards, straight at her.

She glanced towards Dain, but the Enforcers were marching away from her towards the gate, and he was at their head, eyes to the front.

She looked down. The face below her twisted in pain, then relaxed. She saw startlingly blue eyes, opened wide, a broad, red-lipped mouth and square chin. She was sure he was trying to say something, to speak to her. He gasped, his face contracted with pain. She felt a rush of feeling for him.

Instinctively, she reached down towards him. As his friend helped him to his feet and supported him, she realised he was a big man, muscular, and young, perhaps twenty. His eyes were still fixed on hers. There was a passionate intensity in his gaze.

The woman he was with was urging him along. Anna leant over the rail and stared after them. They limped painfully to the corner of the stand. He was looking back at her the whole way. She could see the blood streaked red across his forehead, soaking into the thick tangle of black hair. The woman pulled at him. They disappeared round the corner.

Anna sat down abruptly. She could hear the crunch of the Enforcers' boots on the gravel at the end of the Avenue. Dain wasn't hurt, she was certain of that.

The image of Dain's face, of his gaze, calm, confident and direct, again filled her mind. She couldn't understand why her eyes felt heavy with tears.

A voice spoke, it seemed in her ear:

'Are you OK?'

A pale-skinned young woman with light, almost straw-coloured hair cropped close to her scalp, dressed in jeans and a white tee-shirt was bending over her.

'It's nothing,' Anna replied.

She felt something soft in her palm. She looked up. The woman was pressing a handkerchief into her hand. Anna felt automatically for some coins but when she turned to pay the fair-haired woman was nowhere to be seen. She stared up Exchange Avenue. Dain and the Enforcers were gone. She could see no sign of the black-haired man and the woman who had helped him, just the coins glinting on the sand.

# 11

Matt felt the gentle pressure of Ed's arm across his back as she helped him along the road away from the stadium. The pain jerked in his side. He let her decide where they went. The anger was somewhere deep within him.

He was aware that she was leading him through a maze of brightly coloured stalls. On all sides people were shouting their wares. Celebration Day was good for trade. Cakes, drinks, shoes, cosmetics, T-shirts, coffee, electronics, hats, dresses, jeans, dental care, drugs, pawn-broking, you could get anything here. The noises were too loud, the colours too vivid, he felt it all as a weight bearing down on him.

Ed steered him through the mob of people, the clamour of everyone shouting, trading, bargaining, the jangling colours of the stalls. Images of the black uniforms and of his father jostled in his head. The pain retreated. He felt safer now. Ed had got him away from the stadium and they were among the crowds on the street.

After a few minutes, they turned into a side street. He couldn't see any stalls. The racket from the main road ebbed away after they'd gone a few yards and he could hear his own footsteps dragging on the pavement. Ed pushed him onto a chair outside a nondescript café.

Residence blocks rose on both sides, eight stories of grey unfinished concrete with small shuttered windows. Matt noticed there were cracks running zigzag down the building opposite him. Someone had tried to fill them with a lighter grey mixture that crumbled and fell out in uneven lumps.

Rubbish littered the street. He could see more rubbish, cardboard boxes, bottles, rusty cans, torn plastic, spilling out of the dark alleys between the blocks. Further along he noticed some children playing. He looked at them and realised it wasn't a game, they were picking through the rubbish, searching for anything of value. Otherwise the street was empty of people.

He felt Ed's hand on his shoulder.

'What the hell were you doing?' she said. 'You'll get yourself killed. You scare me.'

Matt looked up at Ed, at the fear and concern in her eyes. He felt a glow of warmth.

'Thanks. You saved my life.'

He straightened his back and grunted. The pain in his ribs had faded to a dull ache.

'No problem.' She smoothed the hair back from the cut on his forehead. 'But don't ever do that again.'

'I won't.'

He stared past her, down the street, trying to clear his head.

'The black shadows in the forest. I hate them.'

'They're Enforcers, guardians of the One Law. If you want to live in the city, you're going to have to get used to them. You need looking after.'

Images of life back on the farm flooded back into Matt's mind: the meals, his mother serving the food out to the men, great steaming platefuls; the cold of the attic room on a winter night, frost patterns growing across the window as you breathed on it; his great-aunt next to him, telling him one of her old stories about the village and about dragons and heroes and goblins.

Somewhere in his memory there was a big, fair-haired man, smelling of horses, on a bright sunlit day like today, with a barrow and a cart and a vast pile of apples, laughing, sorting through them, choosing the ripest and bending down to offer it to him. He could still smell the sharp sweet tang of ripe fruit.

'I have to find Mum and Dad. I have to find out what happened.'

He glanced down. His hand was shaking. Ed spoke carefully:

'Best to forget about it.'

'But it's there, in my mind, I have to know. I have to.'

Ed met his eyes. There was a silence. Then she spoke in a hesitant voice.

'Something I've never told you.'

She paused, staring at the residence block opposite them.

'When they took Mum and Dad people were laughing at them, calling them free-loaders. "Pigs at a trough" they called them.'

She fixed her eyes on his.

'The Enforcers liked that, the officer said, "That's right, pigs." He pulled out his whip and started flicking it at my father. They didn't treat us like people. They treated us like animals. They had cattle-prods.'

Her face was close to his, her eyes glowing with tears. She was speaking so softly he had to lean forward to catch the words:

'I don't forget Mum and Dad. I hate the Enforcers. That's why I'll help you find your mother and your father.'

Her arms were tight round him and her face was no more than two inches from his. He pulled her head down onto his shoulder and held it there for half a minute, then lifted her gently back.

'Thanks,' he said.

There was a silence. Ed's eyes never left his. She leaned forward and kissed him tenderly on the lips. They kissed for some time, then he gently broke the kiss. She looked down. When she spoke it was in her usual voice.

'You'd do the same for me, remember that. But it's going to make trouble, for both of us.'

# 12

Matt clasped Ed to him. A few moments passed and he looked up. He saw a lean, middle-aged woman striding towards them, glaring at them. Her face was careworn, her hair greying and tied back. She was wearing a creased apron with white and blue stripes.

'If you want to sit there, you've got to pay.'

Ed held up both her hands, palms open.

'The Enforcers got him, they gave him a kicking.'

The woman glanced up and down the street.

'Bloody Enforcers, they won't leave anyone alone.' She sniffed. 'They'll say I'm a gifter, you owe me a note for those seats. You been watching my TV.'

Ed shrugged and helped Matt to his feet. He felt her arm round him as he limped down the street. The café-owner came some way after them and stood there, shouting something about credits. There was a burst of noise from the end of the street. Ed swung round, looking back.

'There's some kind of protest happening back there. We've got to get off the street.'

Matt put a hand on the wall to steady himself and looked back. He saw a confused knot of people at the end of the street. Someone was waving a banner with a slogan on it, he couldn't make out the words.

The chanting became louder:

FRANKLIN! FRANKLIN! SHOW YOU CARE!
FRANKLIN! FRANKLIN! PAY US FAIR!

'It's a strike. Franklin's cut the wages.' Ed said. 'They were talking about it at the supermarket. Going on strike's against the law of course, damages trade.'

She glanced back up the street and tugged urgently at his arm. 'The Enforcers will be here any minute. Keep moving.'

He stumbled on. The children had disappeared. He realised that the chanting had stopped. He could just hear a faint echo from his footsteps in the silence. Then there was a scream from the end of the street, cut off abruptly.

Ed kept looking over her shoulder. She stared.

'Those poor people!!' she said softly.

Matt swung himself round. No sign of the banner. Black figures in helmets, visors down, had surrounded the demonstrators. He saw their arms swinging up and down rhythmically, in unison. They were using the whip handles as clubs, battering at whatever was on the ground in front of them. He felt the anger uncoiling, his body thick with blood.

Ed shoved him forward. The street was completely empty apart from the rubbish along the edge of the pavement. He caught the sound of running feet and the blast of a whistle behind them.

'Look out!'

He staggered back as two blond young men, handkerchiefs over their mouths, dashed by and cut across in front of them into an alley.

Ed pushed him: 'Get in there, quick.'

Matt stumbled forward into the alley, nearly tripping over a pile of boxes. The youths were ahead of them, their feet clattering on the paving stones.

Someone shouted:

'Christ! A bloody dead end.'

The grey concrete walls stretched up on both sides. Matt could see that the gate at the end had a steel padlock on it. The nearest youth was staring at them, wide-eyed. They could all hear the whistles on the street.

'Get down,' hissed Ed, pushing the youth in the chest. 'Hide - not you, Matt.'

Matt leaned on the wall watching her as Ed pulled at the rubbish stacked at the entrance. She threw the boxes further up the alley to cover the youths, huddled down against the gate. He felt the roughness of the concrete under his hand and forced his shoulders to relax. The harsh sound of people running in heavy boots was nearly on them.

Matt turned to the sharp bar of daylight at the end of the alley. A helmeted face appeared, visor down, then the rest of the figure, bulky in the black uniform, cutting off the light, the whip gripped in one hand.

Matt felt his heart racing. Everything seemed to go silent. Ed pushed herself past him.

The Enforcer pushed up the visor to reveal neatly cropped fair hair, bright red lipstick and the eyes of a hunting dog. She had a single silver star on her collar.

'Get yourselves out of there, you two. What's going on?'

Ed slipped sideways out of the alleyway, one hand shielding her face from the sun, the other holding Matt's hand in a gentle grip. He leant back, against the wall.

He noticed Ed was standing in a way he'd never seen before, one knee bent, her hips thrust forward, her spine arched backwards, her small breasts prominent, her head tilted to one side; not four-square with her weight evenly on both feet as she usually stood.

Ed smiled warmly at the Enforcer and glanced down.

'Nothing, officer, we were just hanging out, you know, personal trading, just him and me.'

The Enforcer looked past her, back up the street at two other black uniformed figures twenty metres away. Matt saw one of them was shining a flashlight into an alley, the other was stamping down on a pile of rubbish, kicking the shards of broken bottles across the pavement.

'No sign of them,' the one with the torch shouted, 'they're in the alleyways. I'm not going down there without back-up.'

The Enforcer turned to Ed:

'So where were you when there was all the trouble outside the supermarket?'

Matt could see a small scar across her lower lip, behind the lipstick.

'In the café,' said Ed. 'Ask her.'

She pointed across the street to where the careworn woman from the café with the striped blue apron was standing, arms folded, watching them. The woman nodded.

The other Enforcers joined them, their visors still down. Matt knew he had to hide his anger somewhere deep within him. He felt sick. One of them jerked his whip towards him.

'What about him? He looks like a trouble-maker.'

Ed giggled.

'Oh I don't think so. Look at him. He's a big guy, but he's not up to much just now. Not worth much of a bid.'

She put a hand over her mouth, and took it away.

'Bit of a disappointment.'

Matt grunted and pulled himself upright. He winced and fell back against the wall. The concrete grated against his arm. The one-star Enforcer was standing back, watching him. One of the other Enforcers poked the butt of the whip hard into Matt's side. It was if someone had stabbed him in the ribs with a red-hot blade. He doubled up and fell forward onto the pavement.

The dark shadow of the Enforcer looming over him as he lay there, his cheek against the pavement. He curled up and lay motionless, his eyes filled with tears.

The one-star Enforcer glared at Matt and Ed and pulled down her visor.

'You two can get off the street. I know your faces. If I see you again, you're in trouble.'

She threw some coins onto the pavement and added: 'That's for your time, citizens.'

She turned to her subordinates: 'Come on, back to the squad.'

Matt felt their shadows move off him. His side was throbbing with pain. He couldn't think clearly. He watched the Enforcers as they went back up the street, one of them idly kicking the piles of rubbish across the pavement as he passed by.

The cafe-owner stared at them in silence as Ed knelt down and helped Matt roll over and get into a sitting position. He put a hand on the wall and pulled himself to his feet.

*I owe you Ed,* he thought. *More than I can pay. I'll get back at those Enforcers for you one day. I'll do that for you.*

He heard the cafe-owner sniff again. She said ruminatively, to no-one in particular:

'All this talk about how they're there to protect you. They just like kicking people.'

Ed kicked the coins into the gutter and shouted 'You can come out now.'

Matt heard noises in the alley. One of the youths sidled out, bits of plastic in his short fair hair, and an ugly green stain on his T-shirt. The other followed him. They pulled the handkerchiefs down from their mouths.

'All right?' said the first. He was slightly-built, no more than eighteen, with striking blue eyes, freckles and a complexion pale as water. He kept glancing round.

Ed looked up at him.

'Yeah. You'd better get moving.'

The youth grinned. He touched her lightly on the shoulder, then snatched back his hand:

'Thanks, that was brilliant, the way you sorted those Enforcers. Maybe do the same for you someday.'

Matt suddenly realised that the second youth was a girl, dressed just the same as the boy, with the same fair hair, cropped short. She looked sideways at Matt with concern in her eyes.

'Are you going to be OK?'

Matt glanced at Ed. She nodded.

'I'll look after him,' Ed said, then, with sudden vehemence, 'I hate those bastards.'

'Come on.' The other youth glanced nervously up the street. 'We've got to get going.'

Matt could see the girl following him towards the alleyways. She paused and turned back.

'I hate them too. See you again. Do you ever come to the park?'

# PART 2: ANNA AND DAIN

# 13

Anna showed her pass to the dark-haired young woman on the door of the Guild of Entrepreneurs. She smiled and slipped some credits into the woman's hand. The girl started forward, then curtseyed and mumbled:

'Thank you, madam.'

Anna knew she'd given her too much. The woman reminded her of the girls she'd once sold cheap cosmetics to, in the shop. They had the same hopeful expression; they believed their lives were going somehow to get better.

Anna was dressed in her best, a full-length white silk gown flecked with gold. She was delighted with the way the gold in the chain of the 'Hero of Enterprise' award about her neck brought out the highlights in the dress.

She would be meeting some of the most important people in the city perhaps Franklin himself. She wanted them to think of her as someone whom they should take seriously, who was fully their equal in business. She knew that it was at these meetings that the real deals were done. She dropped some change into the hand of the slim young man who took her cloak, took a deep breath and stepped across the threshold into the Trading Hall of the Guild.

This was the first time she'd been in the Guild's residency, next to Franklin's Tower at the hub of the city, and dwarfed by it. She'd glanced up at the Tower, the tallest building in Market World, raw concrete cased in steel and studded with small uniform windows, stretching up into the night sky. It always made her think of the citadel of a fortress, a place of secrets. She knew that the Guild Residency was one of the few buildings dating from much earlier, before the Great Hunger and the remaking of the city. It was a graceful building, built of grey stone, with a pillared portico, a broad sweep of steps leading to the entrance and tall uncurtained windows spilling light out onto the street.

Anna paused and looked across the crowded room. A band was playing dance music, a quickstep she thought, their instruments glittering in the lights. An odour of alcohol, cooked meat and sweat rose to meet her. The bright dresses of the women shone out against the dark business suits of the men, roughly equal numbers of women and men.

It was impossible to miss Franklin, presiding at the bar at the centre of a throng of Entrepreneurs, the elite of the city, elected members of the Guild. The others like herself, just ordinary traders, were on the fringe of the crowd. Perhaps that's where I should be standing, she thought, networking.

Franklin was talking earnestly to President Wells, who stood stiffly next to him. He made a chopping motion with his right hand, then ran his fingers back through his hair.

A giant screen played highlights from today's celebration, the news feed flickering across the bottom: '*Celebration Day take tops 6 million*' and '*Strike ringleaders sentenced*' she read, then '*Index leaps*'.

Anna gazed at President Rebecca Wells, who was still wearing the smart black suit she had worn earlier. She had ceased to pay attention to Franklin and was looking away from him, towards the band and the empty dance-floor. She turned her head abruptly and, Anna realised, was staring directly at her, with her intent unsettling gaze.

Anna descended the short flight of steps to join the guests, who were talking, drinking, trading on the floor of the room.

'Anna,' someone shouted above the din, 'Good to see you!'

A short, elderly man dressed in a suit too tight for him gripped her above the elbow. He spoke with a wheeze, out of breath from the effort of attracting her attention.

'Welcome to the centre of power, a star in the setting it deserves, if I may say so.'

He was standing too close to her, the tobacco-smell of his breath on her face. Anna suppressed the desire to recoil. Why did he always have one of those cheap cigars in his mouth?

'Why Robert!' she exclaimed. 'I didn't see you there. It's good to see you too. We must get together sometime and discuss the speciality confectionery contract.'

She smiled with forced warmth and, at the same time twisted her arm, forcing him to release her. She smiled again, turned her back and moved on before he could respond. Robert Collis of Collis and Sons. Maybe he was a member of the Guild, but they'd soon vote him out. His parents had been one of Market World's success stories and her father had always wanted to do business with them but she knew he was on the verge of bankruptcy. She had no intention of trading with his kind of enterprise, self-consciously old-fashioned grocers, high-priced, too smug to see that their clientele was ageing and they had no future.

She passed easily through the crowd. She felt the eyes of the Entrepreneurs on her, appraising. She smiled vaguely across the room. Someone else was waving a hand to attract her attention. *Carol,* she thought, *I can never remember her second name, the one who calls herself the Ketchup Queen.*

She turned smoothly to the right, where the crowd was thinnest, passed through a doorway and found herself not in another crowded room, as she'd expected, but alone on a small veranda. The Central Boulevard stretched away in front of her, packed with the throng of early evening shoppers, the shop-windows glowing with their displays. She could hear the clamour of people busily trading even at this distance.

She paused, struck by the bustle, the activity. She noted that the Quality Catering mobile stall in position at the first cross-roads was doing a good trade. Speciality street stalls with top class food had been one of the first innovations in her business plan. She'd been proved right; you got a much higher return from the top end of the market than by competing directly with everyone else.

'Good evening.'

She recognised the voice and turned, rather more rapidly than was graceful. Captain Dain Lucas stood in the doorway she'd just come through, his black uniform (the dress uniform she realised, with silver edging, the double row of medal ribbons on his breast, dominated by the Star of the City) marking him out from the business people behind him.

She watched as he removed his cap and for a moment inclined his head respectfully in her direction. He moved more delicately than she had expected. She smiled, hesitated, and gave a swift imitation of the Enforcer's salute, right fist lightly clenched, the arm raised from the elbow.

'Captain Lucas. I'm delighted to meet you.'

'I'm very pleased to meet you, too.' He gestured towards her gold chain. 'People respect you.'

She smiled: 'Some do.'

He'd come towards her and she realised that he was closer than people would normally stand, perhaps half a metre away, but she didn't mind. She noted how serious his face was, even when he smiled at her, those grey eyes as calm as they'd been when he'd addressed the people in the stadium. The skin on his cheeks was smooth, like that of a younger man, a teenager, but she guessed he was at least twenty-five, maybe older. She noticed a grey streak in his hair running back from his forehead. It struck her that everything about him was compact, efficient and direct, but not sophisticated. He was not someone who spent much time at receptions.

She wondered what it would feel like to run her hand along that streak.

She nodded to the city before them.

'It's such a wonderful view, isn't it?'

'It's Market World,' he said simply.

His eyes were unexpectedly warm. He continued, more softly:

'I hoped you'd come to this event. That's why I'm here.'

She laughed and flicked her black hair to frame her face.

'I'm pleased to meet you, too. But there are much more important people here. Shouldn't you be talking to President Wells?'

'Of course. But I'd much rather talk to you.'

'I bet you always say that. But you're a man of authority in the city, I'm just a trader.'

He hesitated and she felt a tiny prick of regret. He's not someone who's used to being teased, she thought. She said quickly:

'But I'm flattered.'

His face flushed with pleasure and she found herself smiling.

'That's a lovely dress.' He glanced away and back at her. 'I'm sorry, I'm not very good at this kind of conversation.'

She shook her head, allowing the chain to sparkle across her breast.

'You're doing very well. But let's go back. The others will miss us.'

He took her hand and led her back to the hall and bowed again:

'Ms Pascal, would you like to dance?'

He pulled a handful of credits from his pocket. *Far too much,* she thought.

She looked round. There was no-one on the dance floor, under the lights.

'I'd be delighted, but isn't that for later? People are only just arriving.'

He slipped his arm round her.

'I'd love to dance with you.'

She took the credits and slipped them into her purse:

'Someone has to be first.'

Dain held her firmly as he steered her through the crowd towards the dance floor. She was surprised at how strong he was for someone so slender. She was aware of a murmur running through the traders, of people glancing round at them, then falling back on either side.

He clasped her tight against his breast as they whirled round. She always loved dancing. She found she was relaxing joyfully into the rhythm, her head back, her eyes glistening against the lights. Somewhere in her mind was a memory, a birthday cake with white and pink icing, a circle of pink candles, and poised at the centre, a dancing princess in a glittering ball-gown, whirling, whirling round.

Her mother ran a small business making cakes. This one was for the daughter of one of the richer Entrepreneurs. They sent a uniformed driver in a black car to collect it, and settled the account six months late. She'd always hungered for a cake with a princess on top, and now she was the princess in the ball-gown, whirling, twirling, under the lights.

# 14

Anna became aware of movement at the edge of the dance-floor. People were turning to look at her and Dain. The band played on for a few bars and then halted abruptly. The sound of one person clapping broke the silence. She could hear others joining in.

She was surprised to see that it was Franklin standing at the edge of the dance-floor, applauding them. He nodded to Dain and reached out towards her, seizing her by the hand. His hands were smaller and neater than she'd expected.

'There is business to attend to, if the Captain will excuse you.' His coarse street-trader voice echoed in the hall. 'We'll enjoy ourselves later.'

She saw him glance at Dain, who stood to one side with a neutral expression on his face. It struck her that he was handsome, with regular features and wide, well-proportioned shoulders. You didn't notice it at first, perhaps because of that calm, detached gaze. She wondered how he felt, whether he was sad that their dance had ended so suddenly. Franklin looked sharply at President Wells then round at the assembled traders.

'We're all here, all of you, all of the big shots. That's what I call you. We're the people who make Market World work.'

He grinned at them, and thrust his head forward as if he was taking on a challenge. He released Anna's hand and clapped his own hands together, hard.

'Come on. Give yourself a round of applause. Louder! Louder!'

The applause broke out here and there among the crowd, then spread, swelling to a deafening barrage of sound. He held up both hands for silence. Anna wasn't sure if anyone noticed that she hadn't joined in. She could see that Franklin's pale blue eyes were fastened on Dain.

'I didn't see you join in, Captain Lucas,' Franklin continued, 'but I'm pleased you accepted our invitation this evening. You're not too popular with some people here.'

Anna was still watching Dain. She realised his eyes were on her, not Franklin. Franklin's grin broadened.

'Some of us've got friends from the Old Market who over-reached themselves a bit. We won't be seeing them for quite a while. All because of you.'

He suddenly smiled and shot both arms out towards Dain.

'But I say, those people who ran the racket in the Old Market deserved everything they got. We're all here to do a fair deal aren't we?'

Franklin paused and looked at the audience as if prompting them. Anna heard a nervous mumble of assent.

'I know I am. And we can only do fair deals if we have the Enforcers. No corruption, no rigging of the market, no - what do they call it? - cartels.'

Anna's eyes were still on Dain. His face remained calm as ever. He was still gazing at her, but she couldn't gauge what he was thinking.

President Wells stepped forward. She spoke in her gentle confident voice.

'Citizens. Traders. Members of the Guild. I salute you on behalf of the City. We owe much to you. You are the beating heart of Market World.'

Franklin's coarse voice cut in.

'Yes, yes, I just said all that. Isn't it time now for the Young Trader of the Year award?'

He rubbed his hands together and nodded towards Anna. *He can't bear anyone else being in the limelight.*

President Wells gave no sign that she heard him. She held out her hand to Anna.

'The winner of this year's award is: Ms Anna Pascal.'

Pleasure bubbled up in Anna. She realised she had her hand to her mouth, and dropped it. The princess whirling, whirling in the silver ball-gown, all eyes fastened on her. The President was beaming at her.

'Come forward.'

Franklin interrupted.

'Just a moment. Anna is also elected a Fellow of the Guild, my Guild.'

She felt his arms tight round her, his face against hers to kiss her. She let his lips just brush hers and stepped back.

'Mr Franklin, it's a great honour.'

All round them the Traders were cheering, clapping, stamping. Franklin released her and she pulled away from him. He was still smiling warmly.

'Her achievements: there's a long list here, but the thing is, she was the first to jump in after that unpleasantness at the Old Market. Well, you lot all missed out. She's a winner. Like me.'

He grinned round at them again as if daring someone to argue with him.

'Go on. President Rebecca's got a certificate or something for you. Then we'll all have dinner. I'm hungry.'

The tall double-doors to the dining-room were pushed open from inside. Anna stood there. *A Hero of Enterprise,* she thought, *and now Young Trader of the Year and a Member of the Guild.* She heard the hubbub of the traders gossiping, networking, bargaining all around her. If only Franklin hadn't tried to kiss her like that! Everyone started to move towards the food. She felt Franklin's grip on her elbow:

'Come on. Food's getting cold.'

She looked back towards Dain. He stood alone on the dance-floor, gazing towards her, his face impassive. She found herself wishing they were alone together at their own table. But that was silly. She was going to be an Entrepreneur.

# 15

The meal was glorious, just as Anna had known it would be: a soup she didn't recognise that tasted half of oranges and half of mint with the nutty texture of chestnuts under it; quail with salad and roasted lettuce, then veal with caramelised onions, the most delicate new potatoes she'd ever tasted, tender green beans, and everything delightful. She'd make sure they had that soup or something very like it on the mobile stalls next week.

She turned in her seat to look across the room, but she couldn't see where Dain was sitting. He would probably be at President Wells' table. She knew whom she'd rather be with, but she mustn't turn down the chance of a private conversation with Franklin. She hoped Dain understood.

Franklin gave her his full attention whenever he wasn't distracted by messages on his communicator or by an aide slipping behind his chair to whisper discreetly in his ear. He leaned towards her.

'There's something I want to talk to you about.'

He stared intently at her, as if calculating the effect of his words.

'Only twenty-three and you've done very well.'

He licked his lips. Anna remembered she ought to smile at him.

'Thank you, Mr Franklin, I'm delighted and, well, more honoured than I deserve.'

Franklin was leaning very close to her. She wondered if Dain could see them.

Franklin continued: 'I like you. In fact, I've a job to offer you. We have an unexpected vacancy running the Old Market operation. The previous director was called away,' he glanced down the hall to where Dain was sitting, 'permanently.'

He smiled, his lips lifting over his teeth.

'You'll get a seat on the board, share options. It's a great offer. I'll make you rich.'

Anna felt excitement flooding through her. He'd just offered her one of the best positions in the city. Franklin was far and away the most powerful of the Entrepreneurs, but she didn't want to be part of his empire.

'Mr Franklin, that's … unexpected. But I need some time to think. Do please remember that I'm in charge of a flourishing business, Quality Catering.'

'Yes, you've done well; maybe we can make you an offer for that, too.'

'Actually, I was hoping to talk to you about the catering at the Baby Auction.'

He waved a hand.

'Of course you do. I want you at the Auction too, but that's all detail. Think about my offer. You'd learn a lot with us, about how markets really work. And make up your mind soon. I don't wait forever,' he grinned, and his eyes swept down her body and back to her face, 'even for someone as talented and attractive as you.'

He took something from his wallet.

'Here's my personal card. That number goes straight through to me. I don't give it out to everyone. I'm sure I'll hear from you soon.'

He smiled and licked his lips, a hungry glint in his eyes.

'Mr Franklin,' she said. 'I'm flattered by your offer. But there is something I must say. My father didn't approve of your methods. You have a reputation as a very aggressive trader.'

She felt almost surprised at her own courage. She wondered again about Dain, what would he think of it all?

Franklin nodded.

'Your father trusted people. There's no room for trust in Market World. It's either the One Law or it's trust. Trust is cheap talk, worth nothing. That was your father's mistake. Don't make it yours.'

He squeezed her hand. She could see her face reflected in miniature in the pupils of his milky blue eyes.

An image from her childhood, before her father had died, flashed into Anna's mind. She was in the shop. She was supposed to be helping her mother with the cakes in the kitchen, but she loved the shop, the smells of everything from sweets to sausages, boot-polish to cheese, oranges to turpentine. The shop was at a street-corner among the residence blocks. Her father sold everything anyone in the neighbourhood might need. If she was lucky he let her read the comics.

She could see over the counter if she stood on tiptoe. She heard her father talking in the soft sympathetic voice he used for bedtime stories. He was near the door, bending towards a customer. He kept saying:

'It'll be OK, just don't tell anyone.'

Anna could see it was a woman, but not like the usual customers. *Her face needs a good scrub,* Anna thought, the dirt was so ingrained it looked like a stain. The woman was bundled up in ragged clothing and standing hunched forward. Suddenly Anna realised that among the tattered shawls across the woman's breast was a baby's face gazing incuriously out at them. She saw her father was pushing the handle of a bag into the woman's hand. Suddenly she took it and scurried out of the shop without looking back at him.

He caught sight of Anna watching him, her hand to her mouth, and came towards her, smiling. He bent down and whispered:

'It's a secret, you mustn't tell. She'll pay when she's got the money. You've got to trust people.'

He smiled again and patted her shoulder and gave her a jelly baby.

Anna felt overwhelmed by the sudden memory. It had leapt into her mind so vividly, it was as if the woman was there before her. She bowed her head.

'Anna.'

Franklin was looking closely at her.

'Here, don't get upset, girl, dry your eyes. I guess you're thinking about your father aren't you?'

He pulled the folded handkerchief from his top pocket and offered it to her. Automatically she passed him some coins. He waved them aside, grinning with his small eyes, and patted her hand again with his small, damp hand and left it resting on hers.

'Oh no, let's just call it a business advance shall we?'

His face was very close to hers. She could see tiny wrinkles around his eyes. She pulled her hand back.

'Mr Franklin, I like to pay my way. Please, don't demean me.'

'I'm sorry, I didn't intend ... There, you stopped me thinking about business for a minute! You'd go a long way, if you joined Franklin's. Maybe right to the top.'

She was standing at a cross-roads, forced to choose. She suddenly felt unable to eat any more.

'I'll think it over. Excuse me one moment.'

She picked up her handbag and pushed back her chair so sharply that the grating sound caused the others at their table to stare at her, and then at Franklin. She glanced down at him, the grin still on his face. She walked across the room, her stride confident, her breath coming fast. She couldn't see Dain anywhere.

She stood in the lobby trying to make up her mind whether to go back to Franklin's table. She imagined her father smiling proudly as she told him of her business success, just as he'd smiled and embraced her when she told him about the scholarship. What would he think if he knew she'd become one of Franklin's elite?

The dark-haired doorkeeper to whom she'd given the credits stood looking at her curiously, ready to direct her to the lady's room. The other attendant was standing at the side of the lobby, in the shadows. She could just see him, holding out her cloak in both hands. He came up behind her, unbidden, and fitted the cloak onto her shoulders.

'One moment,' she said, 'I'm not sure whether I'm leaving just yet.'

He spoke, very close to her ear.

'May I offer you a lift?'

'Dain!'

She turned, burst out laughing, and flung her arms round him. He pulled her close against him, held her for a second and stood back. She felt she was seeing him fully for the first time, the grey eyes, the streak in his hair, the alert stance, all his ardour now focused directly on her.

# 16

Anna strolled down the Central Boulevard of the city, her hand locked tightly in Dain's. She felt that the city was hers. It was only a week since they'd met and here they were, hand-in-hand on a bright summer's day, on their way to City Park.

She wore a yellow dress and carried a parasol shaped like a giant yellow dahlia, the petals reaching out a full metre wide. She loved the parasol and she was sure it was worth much more than she'd paid for it. Almost everyone they passed by looked twice at it.

Anne caught the reflection of Dain and herself in a shop-window. *We make a handsome couple,* she thought, *my pale skin against black hair and his black uniform, the silver stars gleaming at his throat and on his cap, the credits rolled tight in my handbag and fat in his wallet.* She saw how people pressed back out of their way as they realised an Enforcer was approaching them, the uniform standing out against the brightly-dressed summer crowd. Then they'd notice her and their eyes would widen, and stay fixed on her as she strolled past, paying them no attention at all.

She smiled at Dain, at his lean, young face with the fine eyes. He'd fallen into step with her she noticed. She squeezed his hand. He glanced at her and smiled swiftly, then turned to look ahead.

She thought of the residency reception one week ago, of how he'd driven her back to her flat in his official car. When they'd arrived he'd turned to her and said simply:

'I must return to my duty.'

She'd gripped his lapels and pulled his face close to hers and kissed him, then pushed him away. They'd met the next day, and after that whenever he had time free from his duties. She realised that he was drawn to her like steel to a magnet, the way he looked at her face, the way he'd touch her arm, take her hand, occasionally embrace her, but there was more. If she had to put it into words, she'd have said she felt he wanted her to respect him.

She loved that he was so unlike any of the other men she'd met. Business people often tried to impress you with their self-confidence. She felt that Dain was decisive and assured, more so than any of them, but she didn't find it unattractive in him. She thought about it. It was because he was always honest, she knew it wasn't an image he was trying to put forward to wring a better deal out of you, it was simply how he was.

She loved being with him. The first time he'd contacted her she'd walked straight out of a meeting with one of the biggest fruit wholesalers. She just told her buyer to make her own mind up about where they'd source the fruit for the new dessert range. She'd never done anything like that before, she knew she was taking a risk. That's what I am, she thought, a risk-taker. She found herself wishing there was a vulnerability somewhere in him. She couldn't understand why he needed her. She felt he was perfect, like an unblemished egg, and she couldn't find a way through the shell.

All around them the buildings of the city centre rose up in the bright sunlight, the stolid stone facades, the shop-fronts at street level displaying the most expensive goods, the scent of money everywhere, and ahead of them the towers of the entrepreneurs at the hub of Market World. Along the edge of the pavement were the stalls, wherever people could cram them in, mostly ramshackle affairs of plywood and canvas, some on wheels so they could be moved easily, some more permanent with steel frames, windows and shutters. All of them were decked out in bright colours, with any design that the owners could think of, anything to catch the eye.

The chocolates on the stall next to them were piled so high they were at risk of spilling onto the street. Anna could see the stall-holder trying to scoop them back, glancing nervously at the crowd. *He's checking if there are any children there, anything on the pavement is fair game.* She smiled at the flower seller, a fresh-faced young man in a straw boater, as he leant forward, a bunch of roses in his hand, trying to attract Dain's attention. Dain ignored him, but Anna felt she wanted to say something:

'What lovely flowers! Maybe when we come back.'

She loved the exuberance of it, the enterprise, the sense of everyone vying with each other, all of them pleading for her attention as she walked by, intent on one thing, to make a bargain, to give her something she wanted. This was Market World, and she was at the heart of it.

She loved the towers, too. Through them the leading Entrepreneurs showed the citizens the power, the exuberance, the splendour of their world. The towers were fashioned from steel, wooden beams, granite, plastic, translucent glass. She remembered the names that people had given them: the cascade, the exclamation mark, the pylon, the toadstool, the key, the swan, the temple, the sunflower, the gantry, the knife, the poplar tree. They gleamed brilliant in the sunshine, reflecting the light back and down onto the city from countless windows.

At the centre stood Franklin's Tower, the huge dull fortress with its myriad tiny windows, raw concrete faced with steel, over-topping everything else, the heart of the city. Surely, she felt, a civilisation which could achieve such glory, such flamboyance, such glamour must be accounted a success. She mused on how she might one day commission her own tower, more restrained, more tasteful and more commanding than any of the others.

She knew this area well. Quality Catering served prestige lunches at conferences, board meetings, partnership ceremonies, anywhere that business was being done. She'd often sat in the crowded back offices bargaining with hospitality managers, reassuring clients, dropping the names of the most influential customers, fighting the pressure to shave the price down further.

She always told her customers that what she paid her staff was not subject to negotiation:

'If you want the best quality food served courteously and without delay, you must pay for it,' she'd remind them, her eyes challenging them to deny it. 'That's what I provide. I rely on my staff and I pay them what they're worth. No-one, and that includes me, gets more than ten times the wage of the lowest paid worker in my business.'

Let it shock them. None of them could deny that Quality Catering was value for money. The company's reputation was assured. Being seen with Dain wouldn't harm it one bit. She glanced at him. She wondered who she'd ask to cater the celebration if they ever made a temporary contract.

She knew that Dain was completely unaware of the way people stood back for him. His eyes were ranging along the street, continually checking on everything round them. He looked intently across the roadway, squeezed her hand and halted:

'One moment, Anna. There's something I need to sort out.'

He let go of her hand, held up an arm to stop the traffic and marched across the road. She didn't immediately understand where he was heading. The plate-glass windows of Franklin's Executive Foods, the flagship of his upmarket chain, a place where she might go for ideas about the kind of food that would appeal to wealthy people but where she certainly wouldn't buy anything, were directly opposite.

She followed him into the road and found herself dodging between cars and buses before she managed to reach the other side. People were staring curiously at her. She smoothed the yellow dress and looked round. Dain had made for the dark entrance to an alley at the side of the building.

Anna slowed her pace and peered after him. At first she could make nothing out in the gloom. She realised there was movement further down the alley.

Dain's voice rang out:

'Everybody stay where they are. You, tell me what's going on.'

A burly man in a suit stepped forward. He had a fat face and a hairstyle that struck Anna as modelled on Franklin's. His hands swung loose at his sides.

'I'm Carl Snape. I run the store. I just caught this lot thieving from the bins. They're...'

'That's enough.'

Anna picked her way carefully over the rotting vegetables that had spilled out of the bins. She felt light-headed with the stink. She'd closed the parasol and she held her dress carefully away from the brickwork.

Dain was standing there, his back to her in the dim light.

He spoke again, always the calm, measured tones.

'Now, you two, don't you know taking things is against the law?'

She realised that there were two other figure in the alley, shorter, slightly-built, their faces downcast. They couldn't be more than eight or ten years old.

Snape started to speak again, more loudly:

'I tell you they're thieves, I caught them red-handed...'

Dain held up his hand.

'That's enough!'

His tone softened. 'I want to hear your side of it.'

Anna became aware that Dain had reached down and was holding the smaller child's hand. After a silence the child spoke in a curious snuffling voice. She knew he'd been crying soundlessly in the dark.

'We were hungry. It's only what they throw out, doesn't do nobody no harm. They don't want it.'

'Here,' Dain said. 'Wipe your eyes.'

He passed a handkerchief to the child.

Snape cut in: 'It's our food, they're stealing. I was going to teach them a lesson.'

Anna realised he was holding a metal chain of the kind used to close check-outs wrapped round his knuckles, the end bundled up in his hand, the last few links dangling. Dain stood there holding the child's hand, not moving, staring past Snape as if he was thinking about something far away. Then he shook himself, stepped forward and pushed Snape back against the side door of the building, seemingly without effort.

'Mr Snape, you are needed in your shop.'

'What? I want to see you enforce the law. That's what you're paid for isn't it?'

Dain jabbed a finger against Snape's chest, grasped the free end of the chain and, with a sudden jerk, whipped it out of the manager's hand. Snape gasped and stumbled backwards.

'You are needed in your store. Go there. Now!'

Dain dropped the chain neatly in the bin. Snape stood there for a second, staring at him, his injured hand cradled against his belly. He turned and lurched through the door, slamming it behind him.

Dain turned to the children.

'You go now. Don't come back until the shop's closed, OK?'

The children turned hesitantly and then the smaller one reached down and grabbed something, stuffing it into his mouth. They started running and Anna saw them disappear round a corner into the alleyways. Dain swung round and caught sight of her, silhouetted against the light from the street.

'Anna! You shouldn't have come down here.'

He reached out and took her hand.

'Those children, he was going to hurt them,' she said. 'But he's right isn't he? They're thieves, they broke the law.'

A shadow fell across his face. She couldn't make out his expression.

'My father always said you should be kind to children. Let's get out in the sunshine.'

Anna started to speak, then fell silent. What business had kindness to do with the One Law?

Dain halted abruptly and turned to her.

'Anna, do you know what it's like in the Broken Lands?'

She nodded.

'Yes, of course. At the Academy, at Celebration Day, they're always telling us how awful they are.'

Dain's grip on her hand was painfully tight.

'Yes, I know. I've been there. My parents took me when I was a child.'

'I never realised that,' she said, 'you seem... so much part of the city. In the Broken Lands, is it really like they say?'

She wanted to put her arms round him, to pull him closer to her. Suddenly the communicator on his collar buzzed. He spoke briefly into it, his grip on her hand slackening.

'I have to go, there's an incident in the park.'

He bent and kissed her briefly on the cheek. She watched him striding away from her, the crowd parting to let him through, people staring after him, his body vital, direct, powerful. He moved with a controlled intensity that was almost graceful. Her eyes shone with admiration for him. She thought of his duty and of the thick wad of credits in her handbag. She put her parasol up and followed him, more slowly.

# 17

A few minutes earlier Matt had followed Ed through the alleys that led out onto the promenade that flanked the river. It took his eyes a few seconds to adjust to the brightness of the light, then he saw the tall trees of the city park rising up against the skyline almost, it seemed, in front of him. Just like the forest, he thought, until you glimpsed the towers behind, over-topping any tree.

His ribs felt a lot better since Ed had wound the bandages carefully round his chest. He was lucky. There were no cracked ribs and the bruises had nearly healed. He drew in a deep breath. Just an ache in his side.

They joined the queue at the ticket-booth. He stared into the park through the railings, watching the families strolling in the afternoon sun between the gaily-coloured stalls that sold everything from food to art-works, toys to medicine. He wondered why the girl in the alleyway had talked about the park. It wasn't the kind of place she would go.

Ed had his hand tight in hers. She led the way, pushing through the crowd of poorly-dressed people outside the ticket-booth.

'What's going on? Why are there so many people?'

'That's normal. It's the only park in the city.'

He understood why as soon as they were through the gates. Ed found a route away from the throng on the main paths, the stalls and the trading, into a wooded area. The noise of the crowd was muffled by the leaves. For the first time in the city, Matt could distinguish the various scents, the odour of leaves and of cut grass and the earthy smell of the beds. She led him away from the path, across a lawn of close-mown grass, the sun warm on his back, and in among the tall trees. He reached out and laid his hand on the bark of a great elm. He sucked in a deep breath, then another.

'I haven't seen trees like this since I was in the village. It's wonderful. Smell that perfume, it's every scent of green at once, the air smells clean here. Just feel that tree-trunk, it's got life in it.'

She smiled up at him, the sunshine bright on her face.

'Ed, I want to find a way to say thank you to you. I mean it. You found somewhere to stay. In the arena, when I was crazy, and afterwards, when my ribs hurt, you dealt with those Enforcers and got me out of there.'

She shrugged.

'I did it for both of us.'

They were walking slowly now, drifting along between the tall trees. Ed was holding his hand, her fingers interlaced with his.

'We've got to do it, you know, what we talked about, when we were in Re-education,' he said. 'The small-holding. We could make it work, we'd get away from the city. There's places in the forest we could go, places where not even they would find us.'

She looked at him.

'Mum and Dad. Your Mum and Dad. We go back to the villages, we'll never know what happened to them.'

He caught a glimpse of a figure in a white T-shirt further in among the foliage. He could just make out a face, pale skin, closecropped fair hair, blue eyes staring at him. She beckoned. Then he heard the patter of children's feet running towards them on the path and someone shouted and she was gone.

'It's her, the girl in that alley,' he said. 'She's here.'

He forced his way into the shrubbery, the branches scratching at him, but there was no sign of her.

'She's gone,' said Ed. 'If she wants to, she'll find us.'

She slipped her arm round his waist.

They moved on down the path to where it came out on one of the main promenades, packed with people. The noise of the crowd surged round them, everyone chattering, pointing things out to each other and bargaining, always bargaining. In front of them he could see the boundary of the park and beyond that the river, dark and fast-flowing here, the deep green water sliding past. He looked round, but the girl was nowhere to be seen.

They leaned on the parapet, looking across the river at the entrepreneurs' towers on the far side. Matt watched a steamer midstream struggling to make headway against the current. He caught sight of a small half-decked boat, advertisements along its sides, holding its position nearer into the bank. It badly needed repainting but there were twin outboards at the back, churning up the water.

'What's that boat?' he asked Ed.

She glanced at him. 'That's a rescue boat. He's hoping someone'll fall in, maybe he can make some money pulling them out. Look at him sitting there by the tiller. He ain't there for charity,'

She spat into the river:

'It's Market World.'

Matt realised it was a good place for the rescue trade here. You'd be in trouble if you got carried out away from the bank. Even so there were families with their children paddling from a beach a little way up the river from them. He could hear the excited shouts. Too poor to afford the fee to get into a proper pool, he guessed. They'd found a way down near the residence blocks and sneaked along the river bank. He smiled. They seemed to be having fun anyway.

He watched Ed casting her eye over the knot of people. He guessed she was thinking about her own parents, when she was a child back in the village.

'Was there a stream in your village, where you were brought up?' he asked her.

'Yes, we used to play there, it was great, all the kids together.'

'Lucky you. Ours was too shallow, just muddy pools.'

Matt's mind drifted back into his childhood before the black shadows, bath night in the tub in the heat of the kitchen range, his towel draped on the fireguard to air. The sun shone warm on his face. He slipped his arm round Ed. They scanned the crowd for the fair-haired girl.

Someone, a woman, shouted out, her voice urgent:

'Emily, careful, keep back!'

Matt watched a small child in a pink flared dress with matching bonnet, no more than three years old, with a delighted smile on her face. She was balanced on the parapet of the embankment, reaching out towards the boat. *She's a bit younger than I was,* he thought, *when …* the child giggled, tilted forward, as if in slow-motion, threw up her hands and plunged head first, down into the water. A splash, then there was just the small body floating swiftly towards him, face down, her dress fanning out on the surface.

*They never taught me to swim,* he thought. *Who's going to get her out?*

He heard someone screaming:

'Help me! She can't swim. Save her!'

A woman, poorly-dressed, her face distraught, struggled to the front of the crowd. Matt could see other children following on behind her, clutching at her skirt.

'How much?' asked a pretty young woman in a broad-brimmed felt hat leaning on the parapet next to him. *How can you say that?* Matt thought. *Like you're buying bacon.*

'Twenty', shouted the woman. 'It's all I've got! Twenty credits! Here, anyone, take it, just get her out.'

She was fumbling with a handbag.

Matt heard a brusque male voice:

'Don't talk daft, she looks pretty healthy to me, she's worth at least a hundred.'

Matt stared in horror. The child was floating face down in the water just below him, turning slowly in the current. Matt could see the fingers of one hand opening, closing. The blood pounded in his ears. Ed tugged at his arm. She was pointing to someone in the crowd.

Another voice was shouting:

'Ten to one against she's rescued! I'll give ten to one.'

Without thinking. Matt hoisted himself onto the parapet, swivelled across it and fell clumsily towards the water. The pain jabbed sharp into his side. He felt the shock of the impact and had an instant's underwater view of the surface, green above him, the throb of the steamer's engine pounding suddenly loud in his ears. His head burst out above the water. He spat and gasped for breath.

He shook the water from his eyes and looked swiftly round. The child had already been carried past him. Kicking hard with his feet he caught her by the arm and turned her over. The blue eyes stared at him and closed tight shut in panic. The mouth stretched open to scream.

He shoved her head out of the water, his own body dipping under the surface, his mouth flooding. He kicked again and rose up spitting. There was something slimy in his mouth. He could hear the child screaming, high-pitched, and the shouting from the crowd.

His knuckle scraped against the roughness of the embankment. He sucked in another breath. The current was pushing him on. He fought to keep close to the bank.

There was the sound of an engine, loud as if it was inside his head. A wave washed over him, cold and choking. He forced himself up and out of the water and looked round. It was the rescue boat, swinging broadside to him. An older man with a wrinkled, sunburnt face, holding a boathook, was leaning towards him from the cockpit.

'What insurance you got? Credit card?'

Matt spat water from his mouth and kicked down hard.

'What? What are you talking about?'

'I said "what insurance?" No pay, no rescue, like it says on the boat. I ain't got all day.'

Matt gulped in water and spat again. The weight of the child was pulling painfully at his arm. He shook his head.

'No money. You've got to save us.'

The outboards roared into life sending the spray over his head. The eddy gripped him, whirling him round.

Above him he could see the faces of the onlookers packed along the balustrade, staring down at the free spectacle. Someone was shouting the odds, now five to one. *They think it's a bloody cattle-auction,* he thought.

Something smacked against his shoulder and he twisted himself round despite the pain in his side. The current had washed him against some wooden steps jutting out from the embankment. The river tugged fiercely at his clothing. He snatched at the handrail, his fingers closed on it and he felt his hand slipping on the slimy wood of an upright.

The child was kicking at him now, pounding on his arm, screaming even louder. His legs were swept sideways by the current. He kicked out as hard as he could but seemed to make no headway. He felt dizzy. He heard the roar of an engine revving hard. The rescue boat was back out in the river.

He felt a hand grasping his. He glanced up. It was Ed, heaving at him with all her strength, her other hand hooked round the handrail.

Matt managed to grip the upright with his free hand. Ed took the child, passed her back to someone behind him and then seized Matt. She pulled him up with all the force in her wiry body. Matt was half dragged over the bottom step.

'You rescued her. You're a hero.'

Ed's grin stretched right across her face.

Matt knelt on the steps, hunched forward, spitting out river-water, gasping.

'Is she OK?'

He coughed out more water and shook the lank, wet hair out of his eyes.

'They were watching her drown and arguing about money, it's crazy.'

He looked up and froze, catching sight of a figure in a yellow dress standing above him on the embankment. He recognised the black hair, the pale skin, above all the eyes, dark as the skin of an aubergine. She was moving towards him. He realised she was holding the child, cradling it against the dress, the skirt streaked where the water ran down it.

A figure in the black uniform pushed past her, then another, shoving her aside. Matt felt his heart contract. The black shadows - Enforcers! He tried to pull himself to his feet, his eyes still fixed on the woman in the yellow dress.

'Who are you?' he whispered.

She was speaking to him, but he couldn't make out the words. Then she said clearly:

'Are you all right? You saved her, if you hadn't dived in ...'

She took half a pace towards him. The Enforcer stepped in front of her and led her away. Matt felt a pang of rejection. She looked back at him, her face timid among the uniformed figures.

The nearest Enforcer moved to the top of the steps, blocking his view. They seemed to be everywhere, all around him. He could hardly breathe. Was this what happened to his father? He realised the Enforcer on the steps was saying something, not shouting, a voice used to giving orders:

'Get yourselves up here. You've got some explaining to do.'

A second Enforcer was carrying the child tucked awkwardly under his arm, like a bundle, Matt thought. He watched as he handed her to her mother, who clasped her tight on her breast. He could see the tears running down the woman's face.

‘Oh thank you, thank you,’ she gasped. ‘I don’t know how I’ll ever repay you.’

‘Silence,’ ordered the Enforcer at the top of the steps. ‘You’ll pay. Wait there.’

He turned to Matt:

‘I have reason to believe you have rendered a service to a citizen without charge.’

Matt flinched and glared at him. A double star glinted at his collar. The Enforcer pointed to Ed:

‘And you rescued this woman’s property from the river without charge.’

He turned back to the woman:

‘You demanded services without payment. You are all called to account. Take them.’

He stepped forward smartly and saluted to someone, and Matt at last was able to see past him. The woman in the yellow dress had gone.

# 18

A few minutes earlier, Anna had been walking slowly along the central avenue of the park, pausing frequently to survey the crowd by the food stalls on either side of her. She looked round at the array of sandwiches, pies, bean paste and fruit on offer, then at the customers. There were opportunities here for Quality Catering.

This was the only real park in the city and people were willing to pay a decent price to get in here. Anna guessed they'd also be willing to pay a bit more for a high quality product, attractively presented: fresh-baked rolls, speciality cheeses, quiche of course, perhaps smoked salmon and venison, mint beetroot soup, with reputable branding, her trademark sherry porridge, and, above all, the service: courteous staff and no queuing. She was confident that she understood her market.

Her thoughts returned to Dain. She realised that Enforcers were not as other men. At the centre of Dain's life lay his duty to the city, to the One Law. She thought of his calm, stern face, his compact, well-muscled body. She'd find him somewhere in the park when he'd dealt with the emergency. They'd resume their conversation. She wanted to know about his past, everything about him.

She lingered by the stalls, between two great elms. She felt herself different from the crowds about her, the parents teaching their children to recognise a good bargain, the young people exchanging glances, looking away and perhaps back again.

After a while she found herself on the embankment. She stared across the river. On the opposite bank, at the centre of city, stood Franklin's Tower, around it the lesser towers, at its foot the residence of the Guild of Entrepreneurs. There at the centre of the city, she thought, is where I will one day live.

Her thoughts were interrupted by shouting, just upstream. A young woman with short fair hair brushed past her. She heard the splash of something heavy plunging into the river, and the clatter of running feet. She leaned over the parapet. Below her she saw turmoil in the grey-green water. The rescue boat veered round, heading for the shore, a scud of white froth at its stern.

A few metres further along some steps led down to the water. People were pushing past her. She followed them. Someone was shouting the odds. Then she saw there was a man in the river, struggling towards the steps. She saw him pass a bundle dripping water to someone crouched down on the lowest step. It shrieked and a leg suddenly kicked out. She realised with a sudden shock that it was a child.

By now she was near the head of the steps. The person she'd seen crouching, a woman with wavy brown hair, was reaching up to her, offering her the bundle with both hands.

'Quick, take her,' she said, desperation in her voice, and turned back to the river.

Anna looked down at the tiny face. The bonnet was too big for the child, and carefully mended across the crown. A wisp of damp red hair had escaped and was matted onto the forehead. She stroked it carefully aside. The blue eyes gazed up at her as if she were the most important thing in the world.

Something flashed into her mind, the woman in her father's shop and the tiny face staring out from among the ragged clothing. She clasped the bundle to her breast, feeling the river-water soak into her clothing, wrapping her arms round the child, comforting her with the warmth of her body.

A black uniformed figure pushed past her, then another.

The man who'd saved the child from the river was now slumped forward on the steps. Anna could see that the brown-skinned woman with the delicate features had both her arms round him.

She heard him gasp. He looked up, shaking lank black hair out of his eyes.

She felt a shock of recognition shoot through her body. He was the black-haired man who'd rushed towards Dain in the arena at the Celebration, who'd fallen on the gravel below her, the blood streaked across his forehead. She felt a tightness in her chest. She forced herself to speak calmly:

'Are you all right? You saved her. If you hadn't dived in....'

Her voice tailed away. The only thing she could think about was his face. The wound across his forehead was starting to heal. He was saying something to her. She couldn't make out the words.

'Give me that,' said an authoritative voice. 'It's not yours. Free-gifting contravenes the One Law.'

An Enforcer stood between her and the river, his arm outstretched. Anna found her voice:

'You'll take care of her, won't you?' she said.

The Enforcer had his visor down. He seized hold of the child as if she were a parcel, pulled her out of Anna's arms and tucked her awkwardly under his arm. He grasped Anna's wrist with his other hand and started to turn her away from the steps.

'What are you doing? Careful with the child, she's only a baby.'

A woman ran up, her face white as paper.

'Give me my child,' she gasped.

'Yours is it? Here,' snapped the Enforcer and thrust the bundle at her. The woman embraced the child, feeling her body carefully, arms, legs, all of her.

'Oh thank you, thank you,' the woman gasped, 'I don't know how I'll ever repay you.' Her eyes were wide, tearful, her face lined, her clothes cheap and much-washed, Anna noticed. 'He got her out and...'

'Silence!' snapped the Enforcer. 'You'll pay. Wait there.'

He pointed to the ground a few paces away.

An Enforcer moved between them and took her arm turning her gently away from the river. She realised it was Dain.

'Anna! What are you doing here? You mustn't interfere. This is a matter for the Enforcers.'

He stood there, unsmiling, smart in his Captain's uniform with the silver trimming on his cap. She stared at him, then remembered how she'd planned to greet him, and raised her arm slowly in a salute. He frowned.

'I must attend to my duty.'

Her hand fell back. He must make sure they looked after the child, and the man who had rescued her. They were both soaking wet.

'They're arresting him. He just saved that child. The poor child! She's so cold.'

She reached out towards him, but did not quite touch the black uniform sleeve.

'He broke the law,' Dain said 'He must be called to account.'

'But…he just wanted to help her. He was like you in the alley.'

Dain's eyes met hers. A troubled expression passed swiftly over his face. Then he seemed to make a decision and drew himself up, straight as a gun-barrel.

'Sometimes the right course is not the one our hearts speak for. You must understand: the One Law is all we have. Justice must be seen. I will not betray Market World.'

His eyes were fixed firmly on hers with an intensity she could not interpret.

'I'm sorry. You must leave.'

He turned back to the Enforcers.

She stood looking towards the river, hoping to catch sight of the rescuer, but her view was blocked by the black-uniformed figures. The nearest raised his hand:

'Crime scene. Go.'

She turned and walked rapidly away, not looking back, her thoughts in turmoil.

Dain took a deep breath. He felt his hand shudder. He focused his attention on the squad of Enforcers forming up on the path in a neat square around the prisoners.

'Sergeant, take them to the holding cells. I want a report on my desk by eight-thirty tomorrow.'

The Enforcer saluted and turned to the squad.

Dain walked slowly back along the path under the trees.

# 19

Matt, Ed and the child's mother were marched along the embankment between two Enforcers. Matt was aware of other Enforcers marching in front and behind. The other children followed behind, crying, their mother glancing back at them.

Matt was chilled to the marrow. He could feel his clothes, still soaking wet, clinging to his body. Images raced through his mind. He remembered his father long ago, high on the cart in the sunshine; the black-clad figures coming out of the forest; the contingent of Enforcers marching straight at him, like automatons, in the arena; the black-haired woman reaching down to him by the river, her eyes filled with tears; the water dripping from the bundle against her breast, streaking the yellow dress.

He twisted his head round. She was nowhere.

'Eyes front!' bellowed the Enforcer to his right, fingering the whip in her belt.

He felt Ed touch his wrist.

'When they've got us in the Halls we've no chance,' Ed whispered, 'We've got to get away from them here. Just watch what I do.'

Matt could see a crowd gathered just outside the park gates, more of them than before. They were blocking the passage and shouting. He couldn't make out the words.

'Out of the way,' ordered the lead Enforcer. 'The free show's over.'

Matt watched as the other Enforcers started shoving people aside. One of them pulled the whip from his belt and cracked it in the air.

'Move it!'

'What's she done wrong?' shouted a small blond woman in a badly fitting blue dress right at the front.

'They're taking our children away from us,' someone yelled. 'Look!'

'And they've got the hero who rescued her. The big one with the long hair.'

Matt raised his arm.

'Stop that!' a voice snapped out from behind him and immediately he felt a sharp blow as one of the Enforcers struck the side of his head. Anger swept through him. He lunged forward.

He felt Ed's hand on his wrist.

'Not now!'

The crowd was now large enough to prevent anyone from getting out of the park. Those outside were pushing against the gates. One of the stalls went over, the awning crumpled in a ragged mass on the cobble-stones. Matt could see sausages rolling across the path by the gate, a child grabbing at a bun.

A man in a ragged sweater snatched up a ketchup bottle and threw it, hard. It hit the Enforcer with the whip in the face. A red stain of ketchup spurted across his cheek and down the front of his uniform.

The Enforcer growled: 'You'll pay for that!'

He ran forward, braced himself, flicked the whip up and brought it down hard. The tip cut across the small woman's face. She screamed. Matt saw a sudden streak of blood, bright red on her cheek. The crowd surged forward.

'Now!' yelled Ed, pushing hard at the uniformed back in front of her and ducking down. As the Enforcer swung round she kicked out at the back of his knee. The man doubled up and went down. Matt jabbed his elbow out sideways. He dodged past the Enforcer who'd hit him, and they were running back into the park where the crowd was thinnest. Ed led the way, towards the trees at the side of the promenade. He glimpsed the mother, her arms wrapped round the Enforcer with the whip, both of them toppling backwards.

People were shouting after them. Matt could hear the crunch of the Enforcers' boots on the gravel. His ribs were on fire and the breath grated in his throat. The wet clothes clung to him. He knew he couldn't run much further.

They burst through the belt of trees and doubled back. In front of them was the river. Matt turned. The pursuers were only about thirty metres away, running hard, their faces grimacing fiercely. He saw the one in front bring his whip up, ready to slash. He threw up his hands to protect his face.

Out of the corner of his eye he saw the fair-haired woman race out of the trees to the side, running lightly, like a deer. She was dragging a rope behind her, right in front of the Enforcers. She stopped, swung round and jerked the rope taut at knee height. The Enforcers crashed headlong to the ground. One of them started to rise on all fours, reaching out towards the handle of his whip.

Matt saw the woman leap forward and stamp down hard on the back of the Enforcer's hand. She stood back, then stamped again. Matt gasped as the Enforcer fell backwards, groaning. The woman beckoned to Matt and Ed:

'Come on,' she yelled, 'move!'

Ed was tugging at his arm, half-dragging him into the trees.

Outside the park, a woman in a yellow dress was standing a little away from the gate, a furled parasol under her arm. She stood to one side of the mass of people, staring out over their heads at the group of Enforcers, and behind them at the towers, rising up on the far side of the river, the evening sunshine still catching their windows. The Enforcers had got the gates shut and were facing the crowd through them, their whips ready.

Anna held a handkerchief gripped tight in her hand, but she wasn't weeping. She seemed lost in thought. She understood Dain's expression now. He had been pleading with her. He needed her to say she understood, that she believed he was doing right.

# 20

Matt strained to keep up with the woman who'd rescued them. She kept urging them to move faster. Behind them Matt could hear an Enforcer shouting something into his communicator. She got them into the trees and stopped abruptly so that he nearly ran into her, and knelt down. Matt leaned against the rough bark of a tree-trunk, gasping for breath. His clothes were heavy with river-water. He felt sick. He watched as she heaved open some kind of trapdoor and gestured them towards it.

'Quick, get down!

Matt watched Ed crouch and climb into the hole. She reached up and helped him manoeuvre his legs over the edge and get his feet onto some rungs. He realised that the trapdoor was an inspection cover and he was standing on a ladder reaching down into a vertical shaft. They descended a few metres. He peered round and could see only blackness below. He didn't know if he'd be able to make it all the way down.

He looked up at the circle of light diminishing above him. The woman was on the ladder, reaching up to pull the cover shut. There was a crescent of blue sky, then nothing, blackness, as if he were blindfolded. A bolt clicked into place. He clambered slowly down the ladder.

He felt the woman squeeze past him.

'OK, I'm Grisha,' she said. 'Follow me and keep your hand on the wall. No lights. No talking.'

'Thanks, that was wonderful, but how …?'

'Are you deaf? No talking or you go back up there. Follow.'

He heard her footsteps ahead of him, splashing through something. He forced himself to lumber after her. The bruise in his side throbbed. Liquid was washing over his feet, soaking into his wet clothing. He tried to ignore the stench all round him. They must be in the sewers under the city.

Grisha moved fast and kept having to wait for Ed and Matt. They came to a junction and turned into a side tunnel, then down some steps and into another. Matt grazed his head on an archway and crouched lower. Once there was the noise of rushing water to his left, then a waterfall crashing down, drowning out everything. Water poured over him, saturating him from head to foot. He reached back to guide Ed to the side. Then he started coughing again. Grisha hissed in his ear:

'I told you to shut up! They'll hear us. Sound echoes in the tunnels.'

They turned into a side tunnel and moved more slowly. Matt tried to stifle the coughing. He hit his head again, hard. Once he stepped on something that wriggled under his foot and squirmed away. He nearly fell.

He had no idea how much time passed before the tunnel sloped upwards.

'Steps, now, careful, they're slippery,' muttered Grisha ahead of him. He started to climb slowly. He heard a grating sound, as of a door being forced open. They passed through a narrow arch onto a level floor.

He judged by the echoes that he was in a space as big as several rooms. There was a gleam of light ahead. His head felt clearer. He blinked for his eyes to adjust.

He made out several figures, black outlines against the light. He shivered. The surface was dry underfoot. He reached cautiously down. He could feel rough brickwork, dry to the touch. Ed was beside him. He took her hand. The air was warmer here, the foul smell of the sewers not so stifling.

A voice spoke out of the darkness ahead, light-toned, quavering slightly.

'Better blindfold them to be on the safe side.'

Grisha replied:

'It's OK. I know who they are.'

She was standing in front of them talking to someone in the darkness in a soft guttural voice.

'I've been watching them since the Celebration. He's the one who made the demonstration against the Enforcers in the stadium, I saw it.'

'We'll take it on trust,' the voice in the darkness replied. 'Bring them forward.'

Grisha tugged at Matt's arm. They were made to sit on what felt like old sacking next to the light. He realised that whoever was there would be able to see his face, but he couldn't see them. He started to feel warm for the first time since he'd dived into the river.

The figure in front of them spoke again. Matt was sure she was an older woman.

'So who are they?'

'They're called Matt and Ed. She helped us get away from some Enforcers after the supermarket demonstration. They were having trouble with the Enforcers in the park, so I brought them down here.'

'You took a big risk. You've got to be careful.'

That was a new voice, a young man who spoke with the accent of the residence blocks.

'It's not your business what I do. I like to know what's going on.'

'It's a risk. You could have led the Enforcers to us.'

'One of those bastards won't be handling a whip for a while. What did you do for the Commonwealth today?'

'Leave it alone, always bickering,' said the older woman.

Matt heard a rustling sound. She was shifting forward towards them.

'Now it's time to hear from you two. Tell us your story. My name's Eve. This is Lars. You've met Grisha. We're waiting.'

Matt coughed and cleared his throat.

'Not you,' she said, her voice firmer. 'I want to hear from the other one, the girl.'

Ed answered her: 'I'm Ed, he's Matt. We were being chased by Enforcers. They were after us because Matt broke the One Law by saving a child from the river. We didn't ask for any money, we just saved her, that's the crime. I helped him. I hate Enforcers. Grisha,' Ed inclined her head, 'got us away from them. You should have seen it, there were three of them. She was brilliant.'

The older woman sighed.

'Yes, we know. But why break the law in front of Enforcers? Are you stupid? If you are, you won't be much use to us.'

'The child was drowning, someone had to help. And I helped Matt, we've always helped each other, we've never asked for payment, it's what we've always done, ever since we met. We're not like the others, we hate the One Law. We met in Re-education. We just finished, they sent us out.'

Matt squeezed Ed's hand. The woman was talking again:

'Yes, it's not so easy to get by these days. The bosses screw you down.'

She paused. Matt wondered if talking tired her.

'The One Law. It's supposed to be fair for everyone, but people act like sheep and they let the wolves be the shepherds.'

She gave a dry laugh, like gravel in a can.

'They call us Gifters or the Resistance, but we prefer to be known as the Commonwealth. That's what we're about, sharing things in common. We despise the One Law and what it does to people.'

Eve came forward into the lamplight. Matt stared. He saw an older woman, with a pale seamed face in a ragged fur coat. Something sparkled at her throat and ears amidst the tangled white hair and a huge rhinestone brooch glittering on the lapel. Her mouth was made up bright red. She supported herself on a heavy crooked walking stick.

Eve smiled and held out her right hand.

'There are more of us than you think. We're getting stronger every day. We're the rats gnawing at the foundations.'

Her eyes gleamed and her voice grew louder.

'That strike outside the supermarket. Have you noticed how many strikes there are these days? People have lived under the One Law for too long. They don't get enough to live on and they see Franklin getting fat. A good future's coming. You'll help us, won't you?'

The young man, Lars, laid his hand gently on her forearm.

'How do you know they're OK?'

He was standing close to Grisha: 'They smell like Enforcers to me.'

'I'll make the decisions,' said Eve.

'We ought to be careful. It's too easy, getting away from the Enforcers like that when you've been arrested.'

'You weren't there,' Grisha said sharply. 'It wasn't easy.'

'Sorry, I didn't mean it like that.' Lars touched her shoulder and his voice softened. 'You know I didn't.'

He turned to Matt and Ed.

'You can help us if you want, but I'm going to keep my eye on you two.'

He'd stepped into the soft circle of light. He immediately reminded Matt of Grisha, slight, lithe, his pale hair cut short, his eyes blue as the summer sky, his skin the colour of skimmed milk.

'Don't worry,' Eve said. 'I'll take you on trust. Let's eat.'

Matt spoke hesitatingly.

'There's something I have to ask. My parents. The Enforcers took my father twelve years ago. Then they took my mother.'

No-one responded. He tried to put the pain at his heart into his voice.

'I've got to find them. They took Ed's parents, but we think they're dead.'

After a few moments, Eve said 'So many people have disappeared. Maybe they were sent to the colonies and didn't come back. Your parents were probably villagers who tried to take food to the city and give it away during the Great Hunger. That was against the One Law, but people who wanted to help did it anyway. Franklin made sure it was illegal, he wanted his profits.'

She shook her head, swaying slightly.

'We can't help you. I'm sorry. Our task is to build the future. Now let's eat.'

Matt sat there, not moving, thinking about how Dad had taken the cart and how he'd only had Duke when he came back, thinking about Mum's face and how she'd set off a week later. After a while Ed took his hand and led him towards the food.

Matt got the chance to talk to Ed later, after they'd bedded down on some sacking at the side of the chamber. She reached out and gripped his hand in the dark.

'They hate the Enforcers,' she said. 'They're our kind of people.'

'Yeah, but I've got to find out about Mum and Dad – and your Mum and Dad too. Are they going to help us?'

'No-one else will.'

They talked a bit longer. In the end she fell asleep, still holding onto his hand.

He had no idea what time it was, or even if it was day or night. He stretched carefully. His side still ached from the blows to his ribs. Every muscle in his body felt sore. He could hear Ed's soft, regular breathing to his left, and the sound of someone else snoring further away.

He lay there in the dark. Confused images followed one another, tumbling through his mind. There was the time in the village in the golden light, alone and safe in the apple-loft. His father looked down on him from high up on the cart, his face serious. Then the black shadows, the Enforcers, came pouring out of the forest, tens then hundreds of them, swarming across the land like insects, marching rank on rank at him, towering over him on the yellow sand, boots slamming down all round him.

Finally, he slept.

# 21

Anna found she was seeing the bustle of the city with new eyes as she made her way back to her flat. She walked slowly, thinking of Dain, of how they'd parted, of the troubled expression that had passed across his face. She thought of how he always ended talking about his duty and how remote he seemed when he said it.

She'd always found the street life exhilarating, the endless trading, the stalls, the people all around her rummaging through the stock to find a bargain, sizing up the traders, the torrent of requests to remodel her hair-style, call her a taxi, manage her investments, clean her dress or sell her a ready-cooked supper. The city was alive and the life was centred on people, always people, people were what mattered, and Anna knew she was someone who mattered.

Now she noticed something else. Among the stalls there were others, people with just a cloth or a bit of cardboard on the pavement and a few vegetables, yellow sweetcorn, tomatoes or plums, or second-hand clothes or razor blades or cheap medicine, the pills doled out in twos or threes in plastic cups.

They'd always been there, she knew, she'd just never thought much about them. You didn't notice them unless you looked down at pavement level and back a bit behind the front row of stalls. When they saw she was looking at them, the people called out to her or gestured to their wares.

Anna wondered why she'd never noticed them before, not properly.

Some of them looked too weary to call out. They just sat staring at the crowd, as if watching an image on a screen. Some almost seemed to be begging, they had so little to offer that anyone would want. She saw a pile of worn-out work-boots lying in front of a ragged, unshaven man, the uppers cracked, the laces missing, one of them with the sole hanging half-off. His hands endlessly rearranged them as if that would make them more attractive.

Three or four used hair-brushes and a plastic coat-hanger were set out in front of another. The excitement of the city was still all round her, but she found herself thinking of the pavement traders as vulnerable, something she'd never thought before. Where, she wondered, did they go at night? Her parents always taught her to steer clear of the dark alleys, the mysterious spaces between the blocks, but now she could see there was a life in these openings as well, movement, people in there, among the piles of rubbish. Someone had chalked up something by the opening: *PAY US FAIR* with a crude image of a clenched fist beside it. She hurried on, suddenly chilled.

'Chair, miss?' said a rough voice.

A small dark-skinned man in a threadbare purple uniform, bent forward under the burden of a sedan chair, was at her shoulder. She waved him away as she always did. Anna had always felt that sedan chairs were for jumped-up failures, people who didn't have enough credits for a taxi and who thought it beneath their dignity to walk. She imagined Robert Collis having himself carried to the residency reception in one.

The carrier sighed, a slow, weary sigh, braced himself against the carrying poles, and continued past her at a shambling half-run. Anna saw how the poles cut into the shoulders of the other carrier at the back, despite the rough felt pads he'd made. His knees bent outwards at each step under the weight of the chair.

'Chair! Back here,' she shouted raising her hand.

The chair-men turned awkwardly in the crowd, bringing the chair lurching round. They were at her side in seconds. She gave her address, climbed aboard and perched herself on the dusty leatherette seat, holding onto the side rail.

It was less than half a mile to her flat. The chair swayed to the ground and the man was bowing her out, his cap under his arm.

'One note, miss,' he said, trying to stifle the wheeze in his voice. She took a five credit note from her purse, unfolded it carefully and handed it to him.

He looked up into her eyes.

'I've no change, miss.'

She interrupted him: 'No problem. Have a day off. I'm sure you deserve it.

She pushed through the double doors and didn't look back until she was standing by the lift. The sedan chair had gone.

# 22

Anna called a taxi to take her to the restaurant where Dain had suggested they meet. Three of the staff, their faces wreathed with professional smiles, greeted her one after another and ushered her through the main room of the restaurant. Their table was in its own booth, right in front of the picture window, with a magnificent view across the river to the lights of the city. She wondered if he realised how much it cost other people to get a booking here.

He was wearing his full-dress uniform with the silver edging to the jacket and the braided silver lanyard looped from the epaulette. She could see, above the Star of the City, a double row of medal ribbons on his chest. He rose, half-saluted, then reached out, as if to shake her hand. She gripped it and pulled him to her in a clumsy embrace. She felt a tremor in his body and curbed a sudden urge to stroke him. She kissed him on the lips. For the first time in their relationship she felt she was in control.

She picked up her menu and ordered, not the most expensive dish but the next one down.

As soon as the waiter had gone, Dain cleared his throat and started to speak:

'I'm so very glad to see you here, Anna. This afternoon in the park …'

'Let's not talk about that now,' she said. 'Earlier, when you dealt with that brute of a shop-manager, I was so proud of you.'

'I acted for the best.'

He spoke stiffly, but the hands on the table were more relaxed.

'You were telling me about your parents, about the Broken Lands.'

He didn't answer. She leaned forward and laid her hand on his wrist.

'It's OK, it doesn't matter. Tell me some other time.'

He spoke so quietly, scarcely above a whisper, that she strained to make out the words.

'I thought perhaps you wouldn't come tonight.'

She felt the blood pulsing at his wrist.

He continued: '... that child. In the river. I keep thinking about her.'

He took a deep breath and let it out slowly. Then he was sitting upright, his back ramrod straight as usual, his shoulders square, the grey eyes locked on her face. He picked up a knife, looked at it for a second and put it down again.

'An unpleasant incident. It was my duty.'

Just then the meal arrived. Dain ignored the food and went on talking.

'My parents were unusual people. You've got to understand, things were different then. It was the time of the Great Hunger. My father was a priest, but he'd had some disagreement with the church. My mother was a doctor.'

He paused and sighed.

'My mother ran a clinic. They helped people who'd broken the law. They ran a sort of training workshop, furniture-making, painting and decorating, that sort of thing. They knew Franklin's father.'

He glanced at his plate, then looked steadily back into her eyes:

'Franklin Enterprises were just starting to take off. They had this approach to trade which just pushed everyone else aside, but that was before the One Law. Then there was the Great Hunger.'

He paused.

'You know about the Great Hunger don't you? People starved. They fought over scraps of food, you'd see children in rags on the streets, abandoned by their parents. It was bad here, but it was worse elsewhere. The Broken Lands never recovered.'

She nodded.

'Yes, I know about it,' she said. 'My father once talked about it, said he hoped it never came back. He said the rich did well. It was the poor who suffered. Poor father! He was never much of a businessman.'

Dain thought for a moment and continued.

'The rich did well. Maybe. It was Franklin's time. He was young then, still in his teens, but he was the driving force. The market, only the market, that's what he said. Government must stand aside, it only interfered and made things worse.'

His gaze was remote. He spoke slowly, calmly, without expression:

'Anna, he was right. Slowly things got better here. The One Law is sometimes harsh, but it is the same for all. I've seen things, in the Broken Lands, how they treat children. Franklin has the smile of a wolf, but he was right.'

Dain clasped her hand on the tablecloth.

'Franklin's businesses did well. He gave people jobs, sold them food. Then he started building housing. Most of the residence blocks are Franklin's work, all to the same pattern, and the Halls of Law.'

His eyes were fixed on hers. She could feel the passion in them, the fear that she might not believe what he said.

'It's true, Market World, alone of all the known lands has found a way out of chaos. Your father was right, too. It was good for the rich and not so good for the poor. It wasn't good for my parents. But that's what I defend, the One Law, Franklin's Law. That is my duty. It's all we've got, all that stands between us and the Broken Lands.'

Anna stroked the back of his hand with her thumb.

'Tell me more about your parents.'

Dain sighed.

'Mother and father. They always wanted me to be a priest, like father. They were good people, but they didn't understand the times. The clinic and the workshop had to go. They were against the One Law. They gave people treatment for free, some of them they gave food and shelter, too. They said you should always look after people.'

He looked suddenly tired.

'I was young then, perhaps three or four, I don't know. I can remember helping with the meals, the smell of soup in a big bucket, the bread in the oven. It was a good time.'

He smiled.

'They used to sing songs, songs you don't hear now, about the harvest, about going away, about friendship and comrades, about trusting others. A lot of the people were from the countryside. They didn't understand Market World.'

He glanced down at his untouched plate.

'I'd better eat this.'

He pushed a forkful of the cold beef into his mouth, then another.

'Dain.'

She leant towards him. She could see deep in his eyes the tiny image of her face.

'Please, I want to know. Tell me what happened.'

There was a gentleness in Dain that she'd never seen before.

'One day some Enforcers came, all men, in black uniforms. The law wasn't so strict in those days. I can remember the brass padlock they put on the clinic door.'

He sighed again.

'My parents talked to each other. They didn't have much money, they'd been relying on other people to give the project food, on people helping the men and women they'd trained into jobs. All that was drying up. Everyone believed in the market. Who wouldn't? It changed our world, and my parents were left behind.'

He paused again. Anna became aware that his hand was trembling. She took it again and stroked it, calming it.

'That's when they got the idea. I think it was my mother, but she convinced my father. They'd get a boat and travel, go to the Broken Lands. They'd take anyone with them who wanted to come. They'd set up a little settlement there. They'd farm, they'd train people, help them, send them out. Maybe they'd just give people who needed it health care and food.

Little by little, they thought, the idea would spread. Perhaps it would just be a small thing, perhaps they'd build a better world than Market World. I don't know what they really thought, I was too young. I remember the journey though. There was a storm and rain came pelting down. I was chilled to the bone. I've never been so frightened.'

Dain's eyes were alive, almost glowing. Her heart went out to him.

'My mother sailed the boat. My father was sick. He hated it, hated the weakness of his body. I remember trying to get him to drink water but it kept spilling out of his mouth. There was lightning right across the sky, and darkness, darkness so close you could only see the waves, silver and black, the crests rearing out of the night and breaking all round us.

Eventually we came to a beach and got ashore and got the stores out of the boat. It was an empty country, moorland covered in thick prickly gorse with a scrub of small trees in the valleys. There was a warlord, a despot I suppose. I can remember him. He was a small lean man in a dirty uniform with calculating eyes, like a gambler. I remember the medals sparkling right across his chest, he'd even given himself the Star of the City.'

Dain smiled grimly and touched the shining star at his breast.

'His men didn't have uniforms, just a strip of red cloth tied round their right arm and another as a headband. They had boots and guns, all sorts of guns.

The warlord thought for a while. He was nervous, he couldn't understand my parents. Then he said they could stay. He took all the stores though, everything. No payment, no bargaining, he just said he would look after all the goods they'd brought, for the people, I remember how he said it because all his men cheered and they fired off their guns, all at the same time. I was terrified.'

Anna felt herself bound up in the story.

'My parents nearly starved. It was a terrible winter, we were hungry all the time. But they found a place on the edge of a small town. There were others with us, I don't know how many. They built huts. People must have given us some food. My mother had medical training and she treated the people, so they came to us, more and more of them.'

The waiter came up, an enquiring expression on his face. Anna waved him away. Dain continued as if he hadn't noticed the interruption.

'Life was hard there but, for a time, things went well. More people came to the settlement, more every day. We started farming, we had seeds, we were good at it. People started to hear about us, sick people came to us. That's when it happened.'

He fell silent, his eyes cast down. Anna felt a tremor in his hand.

'Dain,' she said. 'We're going.'

She dropped a heap of credits on the table and led him out of the room. She saw some of the other diners look up, their eyes on the Enforcer in full uniform following the successful young Entrepreneur, clad in evening dress.

*A handsome couple*, that's what they'd be saying to each other.

Anna ordered a taxi. Dain held the door for her and climbed in. He spoke in a low uneven voice, as if he had to force the words out of his mouth:

'One day soldiers came. They were from the warlord. They said they were recruiting, everyone had to go, everyone over the age of twelve. People hid in their houses, some ran away. My father stood in the middle of the street barring the way. He had his priest's robes on. He hadn't worn them for years. My mother and

I were with him. He made a speech, he said violence never solved anything, we had to help people.'

Anna could see his face pale in the dark interior of the vehicle. She put her arms round him and pulled him gently against her. He went on:

'They didn't say anything. They shot him, Anna, one of the soldiers spat on the ground and shot him. I heard him laugh: "No worries. He's too old anyway," that's what he said.

They started shooting everywhere, at the animals, at the houses, at children, everywhere. People were screaming, running, some of the soldiers had horses, they rode people down. There was a child, a little boy. He reminded me of that child in the alleyway. Some of the soldiers had bayonets . . .'

He made a gesture as if pushing something away.

'They were laughing, making jokes, like it was a carnival. My mother got me away, I don't know how she did it. My father was just lying there, in the white robe, in the mud. I wanted to go back but she wouldn't let me.'

He was silent for a while again. She reached out and took both of his hands in hers. They were so cold. She started to stroke them, gently, so gently.

'I remember there was a beach in the dark, no moon, just a line of surf and the edge of the sand and an old sailing boat drawn up. It was cold as a winter's dawn. She got me on it and she stood there.

They wouldn't take her. She'd paid them, but they just said they didn't have room, they'd come back for her later. They never did. She stood on the beach silhouetted against the sand as we sailed out, and soon I couldn't see her. She didn't wave to me, Anna. That's the last time I ever saw her.'

He looked up at her. She felt herself crammed full of love for him. He smiled.

'So that's my story, Anna. My parents had a dream and it failed them. That's why I'm an Enforcer. The One Law, it's all we've got, it's what stands between us and the Broken Lands. Franklin's fat as a pig but he's right. Whatever your heart says, Franklin's right. I look at him sometimes and I think of that warlord. But Franklin can't just take what he wants, he doesn't send soldiers, he has to pay a fair price according to the One Law. It's my job, the job of the Enforcers to make sure he does. My duty.'

The taxi stopped. He released her hands, stepped out and helped her onto the pavement. Then he took a deep breath and settled his uniform cap on his head. He stood there, straight-backed as a soldier on parade:

'Anna', he said, his voice calm as the grey eyes, 'that's enough about me. You were ...'

She put her fingers gently across his lips.

'Come inside,' she pushed open the door to the block. He followed her, reaching out to take her hand.

She hadn't told him her story. It didn't seem important, just an everyday tale of Market World. There were thousands like it. Her father wanted to make good, and he'd failed, not in a big way. She was certain she wasn't going to fail. She wouldn't be like Franklin. She looked after her people, she made sure they got wages they could live off, whatever happened in the market.

Later, back at her flat, he put the credits on the dressing table, covered them with his hand and looked up at her.

She smiled tenderly at him. Excitement throbbed in her chest.

'Can't we leave the money out of it? I love ...'

The word felt strange in her mouth.

'... it's you I want to be with,' she finished.

Dain's face was serious, almost solemn, she thought. His skin was smooth as milk and his cheeks pink, but the grey eyes and the grey streak in his hair made him look older than he was. She longed to fling her arms round him, to hold him tight against her.

His voice was calm:

'We must follow the law. The money shows you how much I value you. There's nothing else you can trust.'

She looked at him for a moment and slapped down her hand next to his. Then she withdrew it, revealing a pile of coins and credits. He took his hand away from the credits he'd put down.

She gave a delighted laugh:

'Dain! Both the same! That's wonderful! Exactly the same: a perfect match!'

He stared at the two piles.

'I didn't believe you could value me as much as I value you.'

He looked up at her. She clasped her hands together behind his neck and drew his head down to hers, kissing him tenderly on the cheeks. She felt his arms holding her tight, his body against hers.

The thoughts tumbled through her head.

'I love you,' she whispered, 'why do I love you?'

Afterwards she lay there with him, caressing him.

'It's so good to be here with you,' he said, 'here, outside that world.'

'Hush, don't talk of it.'

He was silent for a long minute. She lay back wondering what the words meant to him, how she was now part of it, how she'd only wanted to be a success in business, someone her father could be proud of.

Later they talked lazily of a temporary contract, equal rights, equal payment, equal options for renewal.

'We should take a trip,' he said. 'There are places in the mountains, you can ski all day and never meet anyone. The air's so pure up there.'

She said nothing about what had happened in the park or the restaurant, all she could think was that he was here, with her, now.

'Yes, that would be wonderful. Just the two of us.'

Later he slept. She became vaguely aware of the noises from the street below, the city celebrating the twenty-one years of peace out there and both of them together, alone, in her room. Her thoughts went back to the stadium, stark in the noonday sun, just a week ago, but it seemed such a long time. Dain Lucas, Captain of the City, was honoured before all of Market World and now he was here in her arms. She thought of Dain in the restaurant, his eyes troubled, locked on hers, of her hand on his. She thought of the tiny cross he wore on a silver chain lying against the skin of his chest.

Then another image flashed into her mind, the park and the other man, the one who'd rushed out in the stadium, the man with the tangled black hair and the scar on his forehead, the man who'd looked up at her, his hair soaking wet, on the river bank, with the child clasped in his arms, his lips moving, saying something he wanted desperately to say to her, something she couldn't quite hear.

Later, on the margins of sleep, another image drifted into her mind: the child's face under the torn bonnet, the wisp of red hair and the blue eyes staring up into hers, as if she mattered more than anyone else in the world.

# 23

Anna felt more alive than she'd ever felt before, everything seemed new to her. She sat at the back of the chamber looking about her with interest. Bright sunshine shone down through the tall plate-glass windows across the council table onto the pictures of past presidents, all of them men, all of them Entrepreneurs, on the opposite wall.

It was the first time she had been in the Council Chamber in the Halls of Law. The Halls were President Wells' domain, a ten-story building just across City Plaza from Franklin's Tower and the Residency of the Guild, the whole area dominated by the Tower and surrounded by the lesser towers of the other entrepreneurs. The Halls were separated from the Plaza by the narrow strip of grass she'd walked across earlier.

The design was simple and functional, in keeping with the role of the building. When she looked up at the façade, she thought it resembled nothing so much as a larger version of a residence block, a giant shoebox, but faced with white stucco and with the emblem of the city, the scales of justice and the words 'Property, Equality, Dignity, Trade' in gold on a crimson backing over the double entrance doors. Here were the offices of the council and the headquarters of the most important arm of government, the Enforcers.

Anna realised, with a throb of excitement, that Dain was probably seated in his office within a few yards of her, a couple of corridors and doorways distant. She wondered if he was thinking of her. She knew that the building joined onto the main hall of the courts, with its white dome and pillared public entrance, where those accused under the One Law were brought to account.

She was disappointed by the Council Chamber. It was a high-ceilinged oblong room, panelled in light oak with a rich grey carpet, much less splendid that any of the meeting rooms she'd seen in the towers. The only furnishings were the table, light oak to match the walls and long enough to seat a dozen people on each side, and the simple upright chairs, occupied by the council members. On a bright day like today, the eye was immediately drawn to the windows.

Anna stared at Franklin's tower, steel-faced concrete, with its endless rows of tiny windows reaching up, lesser towers grouped behind it. Between them she could make out the residence blocks and in the far distance, just visible, the green fringe of forest on the hills surrounding the city.

She'd never been outside the city. She wondered how people lived out there, what it felt like to stand hidden among the trees and look down. Was it a city of towers and light you saw, or could you also make out the grey expanse of residence blocks and the dark canyons of the streets between them? Did you shrink from the power of the people who could build such towers, or did you wonder who lived in the alleyways, dimly visible as cracks between the blocks?

Her attention was called back to the council chamber as the members of the Council filed in. The Council was made up half of representatives chosen by the Guild of Entrepreneurs, ranged along one side of the table, with Franklin, Master of the Guild, the handkerchief neatly folded in his top pocket, at their head. On the other side of the table sat an equal number of representatives elected by the people. President Wells, dressed in a severe blue business suit with no jewellery, her blond hair swept back, her handsome face showing little sign of make-up, entered and sat at one end. Anna couldn't see any marks of rank or insignia of office by the seats, just name cards in front of each person.

She was seated on an upright chair in the gallery at the end of the room furthest from President Wells. She was pleased to see how the president had dressed. She was confident that her own choice of the dove grey suit with the faint pin-stripe and broad lapels and the cream silk shirt was appropriate.

She was here as an observer. Transparency of information was a city-wide policy. Her status as an elected member of the Guild gave her the right to observe, although she noticed she was the only person present who was not a full member of the Council. She guessed the other Guild members had better uses for their time.

She didn't really know why she was here. She just felt she had to understand more about Market World, more about the city that Dain served.

She thought tenderly of him, of what he had told her in the restaurant last night, of his commitment to duty, of how different he'd been when they were together in her flat, of his tense and suddenly powerful body.

She'd been woken that morning by the smell of coffee.

'Breakfast. Buttered toast?'

She opened her eyes and levered her way up the bed. He was offering her the coffee in one of her flower-patterned mugs. He was already in uniform.

'Thanks.'

She didn't know what else to say.

He drained his mug.

'I have to go. I'll call you. My duty.'

He raised his fist in the salute, then dropped it and bowed forward in his formal manner. She caught him by the shoulders and pulled him towards her. Just before he overbalanced she kissed him on the lips. Then she set him back on his feet.

'No, let me call you.'

She took a bite of toast.

He looked at her for a second longer and turned to go.

'I want to be with you,' she said.

He half-turned in the doorway and smiled, his face suddenly like a child's.

Anna forced herself to pay attention to the meeting. She realised that President Wells was already speaking:

'Let's not waste time on formalities.'

The President's eyes were on Franklin, who was gazing out of the window at his tower, seemingly uninterested in the proceedings.

'The scandal at the Old Market struck at the very heart of Market World. The matter has been addressed. The guilty have been punished and the market has recovered.

However, there are ...'

She paused, her eyes sweeping round the room and resting briefly on Anna.

'... ramifications.'

She paused again. Franklin continued to ignore her. She spoke more loudly. Her voice had an edge to it:

'We all know that the price-fixing cartels extended far beyond those who were arrested three weeks ago in the successful Enforcement action.'

She laid a hand on the thick wad of papers before her. Anna thought of Dain gazing out across all of Market World on Celebration Day. The President continued:

'I instructed the Information Division to pursue the matter. I have here their final report.'

*But Dain arrested all those who were in the racket, didn't he? Surely it's finished?*

She realised the President was still speaking. President Wells looked at each member of the Council in turn, as if weighing them up:

'There is evidence that many other traders were involved, including some of the most senior figures in our trading community, perhaps even members of the Guild. The question before us is: what action we should take? My Enforcers wish to proceed further.'

Franklin ran both hands through his hair and sighed.

President Wells fixed her eyes on him:

'You wish to comment, Master of the Guild of Entrepreneurs?'

Franklin sat forward in his chair.

'Only to say that would be unwise.'

He stared directly at President Wells. After a second she looked away. He continued in his coarse residence block voice, glaring round at the council members:

'Do I really have to remind everyone here that this city depends on trade, healthy, vigorous trade? We're Market World aren't we? Well, aren't we?'

He hunched forward, glaring round the room, challenging them to deny it. His gaze returned to President Wells.

'You politicians don't know what our world is like. Making a deal, it's winning, it's better than sex. What have you got to offer that's better than that?'

Anna caught herself nodding. She'd felt it when she'd found out how she could repackage and sell all the bankrupt stock, after the crash. She took a risk and made it pay off and she'd saved the jobs of a lot of the market workers. She was proud of that.

She wondered if she would ever be able to explain how it felt to Dain.

President Wells interrupted Franklin.

'Please come to the point, Guild Master.'

'President, it's this. We entrepreneurs, we're the life-blood of Market World. There's trouble in the city already, strikes, demonstrations, disorder on the streets. It's bad for business. You start investigating people, you'll just make more trouble. You'd be better employed cleaning up all these graffiti.'

He had the handkerchief in his hand. He glanced at it and stuffed it back into his top pocket.

'Remember what happened in the Great Hunger? We took some tough decisions and we saved the city. I don't think you remember that often enough. Do you want to live in the Broken Lands?'

He looked round the table and licked his lips.

'It's our job to make Market World work. If we don't do it, there's no one else who's going to pick up the pieces. People have to trust us. If you're not careful, you'll destroy people's faith in the market, and the whole thing will come tumbling down.'

He waved a pale hand towards the towers outside the window.

'You do that and what have we got? No market, no One Law, nothing. It's not a good life over there, in the Broken Lands.'

Anna saw that the eyes of the council members were on Franklin, the Entrepreneurs on the far side of the table from Anna deferential, the elected members uncertain. They were turning their heads, looking towards President Wells.

'Thank you, Mr Franklin,' she said, her voice neutral. 'You make a powerful case, as always. But there is something else we are forgetting, I think. I do not deny the contribution of our entrepreneurs, but Market World is also a success because we have the One Law.'

She smiled, without warmth.

'The One Law applies to everyone, regardless of status, regardless of whether they are rich or poor. It applies to any one of us round this table. Even to me, Mr Franklin. Or to you.'

She lowered her voice and spoke slowly, deliberately:

'If people lose trust in their traders we face problems. But if people lose their trust in the One Law, if they think that it is one law for the rich and a different one for the poor, one law for the

Entrepreneurs and one for the rest of us, we face even bigger problems. We must have justice by the One Law and we must be seen to have justice.'

She glanced down and touched the report again.

'I will keep this document confidential, but we cannot ignore it.'

She paused again. Anna realised that, despite the ash blond hair and the careful make-up, there was a tiredness in her eyes.

'You will all know of the problems we face in the city. There have been demonstrations, food-riots, that kind of thing. There was an ugly business in the park just yesterday, not an area of the city where people expect this kind of thing. I have to say, Mr Franklin, that your approach to business is not always helpful.'

She spoke carefully, with emphasis, as if explaining something to a student:

'People find it aggressive.'

Franklin stared directly at President Wells. Anna felt her breath coming faster.

The President went on:

'People must trust our Enforcers. They must trust the One Law. And they must trust our traders. Am I right?'

She glanced briefly round the committee. Most of the delegates were looking down at the table in front of them. An entrepreneur on Franklin's right, a dark-haired woman with a sharp triangular face, raised a hand:

'I can speak for trust in the entrepreneurs. I chair our ethics committee. Business ethics. The city can rest assured that we police our own. Let's not call the integrity of our traders into question.'

'Yes,' Franklin broke in. 'You let your Enforcers loose, you start an investigation into the Guild, you'll make more problems than you know how to handle. If it ain't broke don't try to fix it. Market World ain't broke.'

Anna thought of the city she knew. No-one ever tried to bribe her and she never tried to bribe anyone. She knew a few of the traders cut corners, and there were groups of people at the club meetings you had to get in with if you wanted to get ahead. That was why she was so excited to be a member of the Guild.

She knew some of them had a tougher approach to business than others. She'd never connected this to the demonstrations she'd seen outside Franklin's supermarkets, or the way people sometimes suggested she should moderate, as they put it, her wages, or the pavement traders outside the park, or the children she'd seen ferreting in dustbins for food. She paid wages people could live off. Respect for the customer, respect for the staff. That was what Quality Catering was about.

She sat silent, thinking. Dain saw the One Law as duty, not profit. She'd never really thought about it; it was just part of the world in which she lived. The proceedings seemed distant, like the squabbles of the gulls over fish heads in the bins outside the market she'd once watched. Closed bins and a pair of goshawks solved that.

President Wells raised a hand to quiet the argument.

'I can see we are not moving to agreement here. We must have a decision on this matter. We will vote.'

She paused. Anna saw that the president had the full attention of everyone in the room. President Wells continued, raising her voice slightly:

'The motion is that the city continue the investigation into the Old Market cartel.'

She placed both hands flat on the table and looked round the room.

'May I see those in favour?'

Franklin interrupted her, holding up a hand, the handkerchief gripped in it:

‘I believe it is usual to ask for amendments to the motion before the vote?’

President Wells sighed:

‘Yes, if there are any?’

She glanced round the table. No one moved.

‘Very well, let us continue.’

Franklin cleared his throat:

‘I have an amendment: that the city abandon the investigation forthwith.’

He grinned round the table and slowly raised both hands:

‘Any takers?’

All the other traders voted in favour. The President nodded.

‘I see. I believe it is more usual for the President to call the vote. May I see those against the amendment?’

She looked at the representatives of the citizens. They sat with the hands in their laps. No-one met her eye. She raised her own hand.

‘Ten votes in favour,’ she spoke distinctly, with emphasis. ‘Ten abstentions. One vote against. For the record. The amendment is carried. The motion is now that the city abandon the investigation into the Old Market cartel forthwith.’

Franklin slammed a hand into the table. He glared at the elected representatives opposite him.

‘Let’s see the votes for the amended motion. Let’s see who trusts the traders and who doesn’t.’

President Wells stared at him, unsmiling, for a moment. Then she shifted her gaze to stare past him at the towers.

‘I’m afraid the motion, as amended, has been withdrawn. Chair’s privilege.’ She continued to gaze at the towers. ‘No further business. The meeting is now closed.’

Anna watched as the entrepreneurs rose to their feet and gathered round Franklin, talking loudly. President Wells remained seated.

None of the elected members approached her. Some were filing out of the room. Some were talking together, their voices subdued, and glancing back at the President and at Franklin.

Anna thought of something Franklin had once said in a newscast interview:

'It's called competition. I like to win. Don't call me greedy, it's how Market World works.'

She remembered Dain across the restaurant table:

'That's what I defend, the One Law, Franklin's Law. That is my duty. It's all we've got, all that stands between us and the Broken Lands.'

She felt intensely curious about the report that had lain on the table in front of President Wells. What did Dain know about it? The President had been careful to take it with her, tucked firmly under her arm. She rose to leave the room and became aware that Franklin had turned in his chair and was gazing at her. He nodded and turned away.

# PART 3: THE BABY AUCTION

# 24

Anna stared up at the words:

FRANKLIN ENTERPRISES

They were engraved across the façade of the New Market Hall, above them Franklin's symbol, the golden cartwheel, and below, in stark black capitals on a golden banner across the front of the building:

TODAY!
GRAND BABY AUCTION
Your Chance for a New Family!
Don't Miss the Bargains!

She hadn't realised how big the building was. It filled the entire side of the street, towering over the stadium next to it.

She crossed the road and joined the crowd at the entrance. Most of the people were young, in their twenties or early thirties. They were all well dressed, clearly from the richer parts of the city, and in holiday mood. The men wore smart jackets, often striped, and the women's dresses were new and brightly coloured.

Everyone around her was cheerful, people talking loudly about health certificates, of what to look out for, of friends they knew and how they'd got a bargain, about wet-nursing and tutors and waiting-lists for the best schools. Someone was reading out from a list of the top children's names for the year.

The Baby Auction was one of the most joyful events in Market World's calendar. People treated it as a public holiday. The street was lined with stalls from early in the morning, vying for the best positions, mostly offering baby clothes, prams, feeding equipment, health insurance, pushchairs, respite care, prepared meals, nursery enrolment, babycare handbooks, portrait photos of you and your new child, everything you could possibly need.

She'd studied the background to the auction. The official website explained that the One Law permits trading in children, provided certain safeguards are observed. She recalled some of the phrases: *Children are not citizens and do not have the citizen's automatic right to independence and respect. Remember, the city pays a substantial child bounty to compensate you for all the costs of child-rearing.*

Anna had flicked through the videos of babies taking their first steps, of children in a playground, of parents looking proudly on at a student award ceremony, of grandchildren on a beach with their grandmother, of a silver-haired older couple leafing through a family album.

She wished her father had lived, that she could now lead him into the hall to see what she had achieved.

*A child is an investment for you and for Market World,* she read, and of course it made perfect sense. If Market World is to have a future, it needs children and it cost a lot of credits to bring up a child. In the early years the birth rate had plunged. People were too busy earning and spending to waste time and money on parenthood.

The bounty changed everything. It meant that children were worth money to their parents. Once you knew you'd get the bounty when the child grew up, the child became an investment, not simply a cost. Franklin had realised that if children were worth money, they'd always be people who'd want to buy them. He set up the grand annual Baby Auction.

She clicked on the link to the auction pages, a commercial website, faster, slicker, more engaging. Anyone could put a child up for auction (strictly speaking, of any age up to eighteen, but the children on offer were almost always babies) provided whoever was doing so had the certificate of ownership. The child went to the highest bidder, who gained the right to the bounty when the child became a citizen.

Healthy, attractive children commanded a good price but there was always a risk. The Baby Auction website had its own estimate of the likely profit you'd make if you invested in a baby. It showed pictures of the luxury flat in the centre of the city and the once-in-a-lifetime holiday that you might be able to buy once you got the bounty.

While the sellers at the auction were mainly from the poor of the city who needed the money now and found it hard to pay all the costs of rearing the child, the buyers tended to come from the better off groups. They could afford to pay cash down and wait to get the bounty when the child became a citizen. Anna grasped the point and used it to make her pitch.

'Quality Catering may cost a bit more, but everyone knows we don't cut corners and we provide value for money. That's guaranteed, people rely on us, especially the kind of people who come to the Baby Auction.'

She'd pointed out that there was more to the Baby Auction than buying and selling. The success of the auction, the steadily growing population of Market World, the enthusiasm for new citizens that it demonstrated affirmed the value of their way of life.

As President Wells had said in her morning newscast:

'The Baby Auction isn't just another fair, another market place in our city. Remember, in the Baby Auction we invest in our future families, we trade in people's dreams.'

The camera closed in on her face, catching the intensity of the President's gaze. Her voice dropped to the familiar passionate undertone:

'Only in Market World can you buy hope.'

Anna looked up again at the twin banners streaming out from the poles on the corners of the building:

COME AND BID FOR YOUR NEW FELLOW-CITIZENS!
SHOW THEM WHAT THEY'RE WORTH TO YOU!

and

ENTRIES TOP 1000!
A NEW RECORD FOR THE BABY AUCTION!

That was why the crowd around them was so happy, why people were relaxed, anticipating another bumper auction. Quality Catering was part of it all, part of the bright future that Market World offered its citizens.

Anna bit into her sandwich. She always felt a shiver of excitement when she came out on what she called 'informal inspection'. She'd checked the restaurant and the cafeteria, making sure the staff understood that each of them mattered to the success of Quality Catering. Now she was standing at the mobile stall just inside the hall.

It was one of the standard rolls, salmon and cream cheese, but just the right amount of each and that fresh pungent flavour you could only get from fish caught wild. Good quality bread too, just enough crust, and she'd been offered a choice of cheeses, of bread and of garnish.

She frowned and spat the food into a napkin.

'Excuse me!'

She spoke firmly, waving to the stall-holder.

'This bread's stale. I can't eat this.'

The stall-holder turned to her immediately:

'Madam, I'm terribly sorry. I can't understand how that happened.'

He was dressed in the regulation straw boater and red and white striped apron. His plump face reddened:

'I do apologise on behalf of Quality Catering.'

He looked as if he meant it.

'Please let me prepare you another sandwich. Would you like a complimentary glass of wine while you wait? Just two minutes. We have a choice of Valley White, Manor House Red, Southern Rose…'

Anna put up a hand to stop him.

'It's OK,' she said. 'I think I must have been mistaken about that roll.'

She smiled at him and saw his eyes widen as he recognised her.

'Madam,' he stuttered, 'I'm ever so sorry…' he fell silent, his mouth wide open.

'Don't worry,' said Anna. 'Just checking up on things. I want you to know you handled that well. I've noted that.'

She turned and moved away into the crowd before he could answer.

*It's the service that counts,* she thought. *I can make this business work. I can do this better than anyone I know.*

The main hall was the largest indoor space Anna had ever entered. The clamour of so many people trading, talking, babies crying, parents bargaining, of the marshals directing people to the various viewing areas, was almost overwhelming.

Along the sides of the hall, stretching away in front of her, were the triple rows of stalls. Parents and the other dealers were displaying the babies on offer, already negotiating with visitors, presenting health certificates and immunisation records, doing side deals before the main auction started.

She glanced up into the huge transparent glass dome above them all, through which the light of common day shone down, and smiled.

*This,* she thought, *is Market World. And I'm here, at the very heart of it.*

The building was decorated simply, like all Franklin's buildings, the walls painted white, the carpet grey and hard-wearing, a massive cartwheel logo high above the stage:

'Why throw money away?' Franklin always said. 'I don't want people coming here to look at the walls.'

Anna could see the auctioneer standing at the side of the stage. He wore a dinner suit and held an old-fashioned top hat in one hand. He was giving instructions to one of the handlers. They would bring the babies on stage one by one to display them when the bidding started. She stared up at the giant screen to the right where images of neatly dressed infants succeeded each other, in baby-clothes, hand-knitted shawls, dear little mob-caps. All smiled appealingly at the audience.

Anna thought of the child she'd cradled in her arms by the river, the blue eyes gazing up at her, the care with which the rent in the pink bonnet had been mended, the wisp of red hair matted against her forehead. She wondered if the mother was here today, among all the other parents hoping for a sale, hoping their children would go to a good home, to someone who'd give them a better life.

A new thought struck her: why didn't all the people who couldn't really afford to bring up their children, all the mothers like the woman by the river, bring them here? You only paid a fee if you made a sale, a small percentage, and you'd get a good price. It made perfect sense. And yet Anna knew it was only a tiny proportion of the city's poor who would offer their children today. Many others would end up like the children scavenging the dustbins behind Franklin's store.

The bidders who'd paid good money for their family would surely value the children more than the parents would. The bidders were the kind of people who could pay for things, who could give the children a better life, people who could love the children better, people, she found herself thinking, just like herself.

She looked round. She was walking among the stalls, casting her eye along the row. Some of the children were in the regulation clear plastic cots, some even asleep, tucked up in the cream blankets with the Franklin logo printed on the corner, but most of them were in their mother's arms.

Anna saw that most of the mothers weren't holding them out to the customers, but clasping them tight to their breasts, one mother even feeding her child. Anna stood some distance away, staring as the tiny mouth sucked greedily, the starfish hand squeezing at the naked breast.

There was something remote, private in the infant's face. Anna felt herself an intruder. She caught the mother's eye and looked away quickly. The noise of babies whimpering, crying lustily, grizzling, of parents shouting out details above the din, beat against her from all sides. She moved on, her eyes thoughtful.

At the next stall the mother held her child against her breast. She was wearing a traditional village costume, one of the dark blue calf-length sleeved dresses with the machine embroidered insert mass-produced in Franklin's factories. It was far too large, sagging on her body. Anna realised it had been bought to accommodate the pregnancy.

Her husband stood beside her, in a cheap, ill-fitting blue serge suit. They'd hung a cardboard sign on the side of the cot, carefully lettered in biro:

COUNTRY BRED
SHE SLEEPS ALL NIGHT

Anna smiled. The father caught sight of her:

'Come on missus, she's a good girl.'

There was something she couldn't quite place in his voice.

'She's weaned now,' he went on. 'She always sleeps all night, like it says on the sign. She don't want much feeding, we give her bean paste, a few left-overs, mashed potato, toast, that sort of thing. I'm proud of her. You won't find a better child in the building.'

He spoke in the countryside burr, yet, that was it, it was overlaying the distinctive slurring accent of the residence blocks. Anna started to move on. The woman, small, with a lean face and dark uncertain eyes, held the child out.

'Won't you hold her, missus? Her name's Becky, she's a good girl.'

Anna shook her head.

'Please missus. We need the money, there's no jobs, we've got three others at home…'

The woman clasped the child against her breast. Anna hadn't the heart to ask them which village out in the countryside they came from. She knew they were really from the blocks. They thought people would pay more for a country child.

There was a fanfare over the loudspeakers. A ripple of excitement ran through the room. Anna looked up as the auctioneer strode to the centre of the stage.

The auction proper was about to begin.

# 25

Matt stood at the edge of the pavement gazing up at the façade of the New Market. He braced his shoulders, and glanced at Ed beside him. She was dressed in a cheap imitation of the dove-grey suit President Wells often wore to the Council. He and Lars wore dark pin-stripes, cheap copies of the business suits the entrepreneurs wore. His hair was tied into a neat pony-tail at his neck. He couldn't remember the last time he'd worn a tie. Lars caught his eye and touched his own tie-knot. Matt fumbled and pulled the tie tight.

Grisha was dressed in a light blue trouser-suit.

*OK so far,* he thought, *we don't look that different from lots of people who shop in Franklin's stores.*

All four of them were carrying small holdalls, of different designs, because Eve said that they'd attract attention if they all had identical bags.

Most of the crowd had now gone into the auction. Matt could hear the noise of babies and adults from across the street. He looked round him, running his eye along the pavement, checking the traffic.

The pavement stall-holders were relaxing, some of them sitting on their stools. There would be a lull in business until the end of the auction, when the crowd spilled out again with their new babies, ready to spend.

'All right?' He could hear the tension in Grisha's voice. 'Everyone ready?'

He took a deep breath and nodded at Grisha. He wasn't convinced that the demonstration would change anything, but Ed had been keen:

'It'll make a real impact,' she said. 'Selling their babies! People will see what's rotten at the heart of Market World. Can you think of anything better?'

The leaflets certainly had impact. They'd been carefully planned and Lars was good at the art-work. A fat carnivorous Franklin, halfway between a pig and a wolf, leaned over a baby as if he was going to eat it. The parents, dressed in rags, were cringing away to one side, huddled together, the woman in tears, the man protesting. Coins dripped from the Franklin monster's paw.

In the next picture Franklin, a grinning pig, sleek in a suit, offered a terrified baby to a wealthy couple. The man, also wearing a business suit, a bored expression on his face, was handing a thick bundle of credits to Franklin. The woman, slim, dressed in the latest fashion, was reaching out greedily for the child.

*Starvation wages?* read the headline. *Can't feed your babies? Never mind, Franklin'll take 'em off you. No family for you if you ain't rich.*

The text was all about the wage cuts in Franklin's supermarkets, the costs of bringing up a child, the conditions in the cramped flats of the residence blocks, the evidence of malnutrition. Ed wrote most of it. She'd been putting her energy into finding out what went on in the city. Matt became aware that she had a passion to know about how people lived, as for everything else in her life.

Grisha led the way as they crossed the road. They paid and passed along the entrance passage. The hubbub grew even louder and a fanfare blared out, followed by a momentary lull.

Grisha raised her hand.

'Right, masks on, good luck to all of us.'

Matt put on the Franklin mask, the plastic helmet of tangled red hair fitting snugly over his head. He could see Ed holding a President Wells mask in both hands. He helped her fit it on.

She squeezed his hand.

'Take care,' she whispered.

'Take care. I'll be keeping an eye out for you. At least you've got bigger eye-holes.'

A voice behind them shouted out:

'What's going on? No masks in the hall.'

He released Ed's hand:

'Come on, quick.'

They moved fast, into the hall, past the concessions. Matt and Ed veered to the right, Grisha to the left with Lars keeping close behind her. Matt forced his way into the crowd. People swung round to protest, then stared at him, and past him at Ed.

He reached into the holdall and flung a bundle of fake credits up into the air, as far as he could. The brightly coloured notes swirled above them, caught up in the currents of the air conditioning, floating out over the room. Everyone was staring upwards.

He saw more credits soaring upwards on the other side of the room. The crowd eddied around him. People were rushing forward to grab at the money.

'Get the leaflets out,' Ed was yelling.

He turned. She'd already got the packs of leaflets in her hands and was hurling them up too. They floated gently out, opening, like butterflies he thought. The special lightweight paper cost money, but it worked brilliantly.

He pushed his way further into the hall. The auctioneer fell silent, the microphone in his hand, staring out into the hall, an incredulous expression on his face.

Matt felt the crowd was pushing against him. He heard shouting from the baby stalls:

'Look out! Don't shove, that's my child.'

Someone was shrieking on a high wailing note. He couldn't tell if it was a baby or a parent.

He flung up another handful of leaflets, then more. He stared upwards. They were like a flock of birds, floating above him, gliding, wheeling on the air currents, sailing out over the hall.

'What do you think you're doing?' – a harsh, brusque voice.

He felt hands grasping at him. Someone was fumbling at the mask. He swung round pushing them away. A woman in a smart brocade dress tripped and fell. He reached down, grabbed her hand, lifted her up and set her back on her feet.

He couldn't see Ed. He heard the shrill blasts of whistles somewhere outside the entrance passage. He shoved both hands forward, straight in front of him, and parted the crowd like a swimmer parting waves. Ed was there over to the right. One of the security guards in the dark green Franklin uniform had both arms round her and was holding on as she twisted her body, trying to wrench herself free. The guard's hat fell backwards off his head. He was an older man and the light glinted on his silver hair. Matt reached them and slapped hard with the palms of both hands against the guard's sides. The guard gasped and slumped forward, releasing his hold on Ed.

Matt shoved past the guard and seized Ed's hand. The whistles were louder, the sound ringing in his ears.

'Come on,' he said 'we've got to get out.'

She was shouting something at him and pointing to the side:

'Get your mask off. Make for the fire exit.'

Masks off, they pushed sideways towards the line of stalls.

'Just take it easy, like we're part of the crowd,' she said. 'Drop your holdall.'

Matt tried to calm himself. He smoothed down his hair, and looked round, raising himself on tip-toe to see over the crowd. There was a knot of confusion on the other side of the hall. He glimpsed Grisha's masked face between two of the attendants. Lars jerked into view pulling at one of them with all his strength, then someone pushed him from behind and he fell forward.

A shout went up over by the entrance. Matt could see the black uniforms of Enforcers entering the hall. He bent down, pulling Ed down with him and moved forward as fast as he could.

They were at the row of stalls now. They squeezed through into the empty space behind. Matt caught his breath.

'Why are you here?' said a voice he recognised.

He spun round. A woman was standing close beside him - the woman in the yellow dress from the park, her black hair framing her face, her dark eyes vivid with concern.

# 26

Anna stared at the two of them. The whistles were shrill in her ears, much louder now. With a shock she recognised the tall powerfully-built man who'd saved the child from the river. She could just make out the scar on his forehead. She felt she must help him. The other one was the woman who'd passed the bundle, the child, back to her.

The image of the red-haired child clasped against her breast flitted into her mind.

'It's you,' she said softly. 'You're the one who saved the child.'

She could see the Enforcers moving purposefully across the hall scanning the crowd.

'They don't understand,' she said to him, 'they didn't listen to you then, they won't now. You've got to get away.' She glanced back at the entrance. 'Follow me. Look as if you belong here.'

She nodded curtly to the woman.

'Don't hold hands. I'll do the talking.'

Anna led the way towards the entrance, walking along the passage behind the stalls.

'Excuse me,' she spoke loudly, authoritatively. 'The auction will resume in five minutes. I apologise for the delay. Please let me through.'

People stood aside, glancing curiously at the well-dressed woman and her two companions in their business suits. Enforcers were standing across the exit, whips in their hands. She addressed the more senior of them. She could see stubble on his chin where he'd shaved clumsily that morning:

'Officer, I'm Anna Pascal from the Guild of Entrepreneurs.' She showed him her official pass. 'We need to pass through. I have two of my staff here.'

'You wait your turn,' grunted the Enforcer. 'We're checking everyone.'

'If you've any concerns, Officer, please ring this number.' Anna handed him Franklin's business card. 'Every second you delay us costs Mr Franklin money. He doesn't like waiting.'

The Enforcer hesitated, staring at the card, and waved them through. Anna compressed her lips to conceal a smile.

She felt a thrill of excitement. She could do almost anything she wanted. She'd never been anything but lucky. She had to talk to the black-haired man. He was the one who'd shouted at Dain on Celebration Day. What was he doing here? They mustn't be allowed to take him away. He'd saved the child in the park.

She was sure he wanted to do what was right. Images jostled in her head, Dain's face across the restaurant table, his words: 'the One Law, it's all we've got ... that is my duty', the child, dripping wet, saved from drowning, staring trustingly up at her.

You had to follow the One Law, it was all they had. She wanted to make this man understand that. Other thoughts rushed in: the face of the baby wrapped in the woman's shawl in her father's shop long ago, Dain holding the little boy's hand in the alley behind Franklin's supermarket, this man in front of her, looking up at her in the arena on Celebration Day with blood on his face.

The lobby was empty.

'Don't worry about the Enforcers,' she said. 'I can handle them. I must know what you're doing. I want to help you.'

The man threw up his hands and dropped them helplessly.

'My name's Matt,' he started, then in a rush. 'The Enforcers took my father and mother. Long ago, they just took them. There's so much to tell you.'

His eyes were locked on hers. The brown-skinned woman broke in:

'It's simple. We hate Enforcers. They beat people up. They take people's babies away. They didn't care a credit for that child in the river. You saw that.'

The woman had extraordinarily delicate features and greenish-brown eyes. She reminded Anna of a young panther. She glanced round.

'We're wasting time,' she said. 'We have to go now.'

Anna forced herself to speak calmly.

'My name's Anna. Don't worry, you're safe with me.'

She kept her eyes on Matt. She found herself thinking of the ardour in his voice. He spoke like a preacher. She had to help him.

'The Enforcers,' she told them, speaking carefully, 'they're there to look after us, to keep everyone to the rules. Surely you know that. They have to make quick decisions and sometimes they make mistakes.'

She wanted so much to explain things to him, clearly, just as Dain had, so he'd understand, so he'd agree with her.

'Listen to me,' she said. 'What you're doing is wrong. The Enforcers are all we've got. We've got to help each other. Do you want the Broken Lands to come here?'

Matt stared at her. He opened his mouth.

The brown-skinned woman cut in again:

'I hate the Enforcers. They're on Franklin's side. There's a better way to live - read the leaflet.'

Anna realised how young she was, not much more than seventeen. The young woman's eyes blazed with excitement. She thrust a bundle of papers at Anna. Anna took it automatically, not looking at it. She looked pleadingly at Matt. His eyes were troubled. He grasped her hand.

'Anna,' he said. 'Go back. Don't get mixed up in this.'

The doors slammed open. They were surrounded by Enforcers. An older man in the green uniform of Franklin's security guards shouted out:

'She's one of them. Look, she's holding the leaflets. She says she works for Mr Franklin but I've never seen her before.'

He stopped in a fit of coughing. He'd lost his hat.

The Enforcer Anna had shown Franklin's card to was standing in front of her.

'Mr Franklin will have to wait,' he said. 'You will come with us. You are called to account.'

# 27

Dain paced across his room on the eighth floor of the Halls of Law. In front of him the sun was low on the horizon, the towers casting long shadows across the city square, across the Halls, across the residence blocks. The streets were inky-black canyons between them.

His face was calm, but his right hand tapped restlessly against his leg. He strode back across the room and sat at his desk, empty apart from the silver-gilt model of the scales of justice at one corner.

He reached out and touched it, setting the balance bar swinging. It was a prize. He'd received it when he passed out top of his year at the College.

Slowly equilibrium returned to the scales.

He spoke into his communicator:

'Adam. In here.'

He stared at the scales. Justice weighed in a pan.

Adam marched in, turned to face the desk and saluted. As always his uniform was perfect, the scar scarcely visible on his expressionless face.

'Captain Lucas!'

'At ease.'

Adam relaxed, removed his hat and tucked it under his arm. His arms remained straight, thumbs pressed against the trouser seams.

Dain continued:

'This is a serious business at the Baby Auction. They disrupted one of the most important markets in the city's calendar. It's a matter of judgement whether it's free speech or a breach of the One Law.'

He looked up at Adam.

'I am instructed to proceed with charges.'

He placed a faint emphasis on the word 'instructed'. A flicker passed across Adam's face.

Dain continued:

'I will now interview the suspects.'

Adam cleared his throat.

'Yes?' said Dain.

'No disrespect, Captain. If you wish, I can take over that part of the case. In this instance. If you wish.'

Dain looked at him sharply. There was no expression in the light brown eyes, looking over his shoulder into the distance.

'Adam. We've known each other a long time. It's the senior officer's duty to interview the chief suspects. I simply wished to inform you of the situation. That will be all.'

'Yes, Captain.'

Dain watched him salute impeccably, turn and stride from the room.

Anna had never known this place existed. They marched her along a windowless corridor deep in the Halls of Law. The passed along another corridor, up a bare stone staircase and into a lift.

The first Enforcer halted, rapped on a door and opened it.

'In there.'

Light flooded in from a large window, half-blinding her: the sun was setting over the city, behind the towers. She could just make out the figure of an Enforcer seated at the desk in front of her, the surface bare apart from a gilt model of the scales of justice. He was looking down into a drawer. He looked up and slid the drawer shut, his face expressionless. Dain! She made an effort to stop herself calling out his name. She tried to put all her need for him, her desire to help him into her eyes.

'Ms Pascal,' he said, 'Please sit.'

He motioned her to the chair and spoke formally.

'Interview with Ms Anna Pascal, seventh September, year twenty-one, 19.20 hours, Captain Lucas.'

He glanced out of the window at the towers that filled half the view, then at the scales of justice. Then he met her eyes.

'You are aware you face serious charges? Conspiracy to disrupt the Baby Auction. There's a great deal of interest in the case at the highest levels. It comes at a difficult time for the city.'

He paused again, and looked away. He spoke more softly. She had to strain to make out the words.

'You must understand. I'm ... I'm concerned, deeply concerned.'

'Dain, I wanted to help. You don't understand, you can't understand. He's a good man, I wanted to help him.'

'The One Law has no concern with motives. I have a clear record of your actions. You were arrested in company with known subversives. You were carrying anti-market literature. You sought to help other suspects evade arrest.'

He paused, looking directly at her. He was pleading with her. Anna's thoughts were in turmoil. Surely Matt was a good man? How could it be wrong to help children? Dain was still speaking.

'Ms Pascal, Anna, I want to help you. But we must all follow the One Law.'

How could she explain everything clearly? It was too simple and too complicated.

'The Law is sometimes wrong,' she said. 'When he was in the park that day, he saved that child in the river. He's a good man. He was trying to help the babies at the Auction, I know he was.'

So much depended on convincing Dain of what she was saying. She slid her hands across the table, reaching out towards him.

'Don't you want to help him?'

He was staring at the scales.

‘I am helping him,’ he said slowly. ‘Him and everyone like him. That is my duty.’

He spoke carefully, his words measured, but there was passion in his eyes.

‘The One Law. It’s all we have, don’t you see that? We must uphold the Law. You must not let your feelings be the master.’

She couldn’t think of anything to say to him. He was wrong, he must be wrong, but how could she deny all that he lived for? It would be an act of cruelty. Besides, everyone said that the One Law was all that stood between Market World and the Broken Lands.

‘Don’t you remember?’ she said, after a while. ‘Those children in the alley behind the store? That horrible man, Snape? I was proud to be with you.’

Dain was silent. He sat there, not moving, staring down at his hands on the table.

‘Once,’ he said, ‘Once I let my feelings rule. My father always said children deserved a special kindness. Then I remembered the Broken Lands, but that was long ago.’

Anna saw how tender the skin was about his eyes, how slender his wrists were, like a teen-ager’s. She longed to touch him. He continued:

‘Once. There were no witnesses.’

‘But I was your witness, I’d be on your side.’

He looked up at her and gave a faint smile, but his eyes were still pleading.

‘That was then,’ he said, ‘this is now. Can’t you see? Everything we have depends on the One Law. We cannot allow it to be destroyed.’

She took a deep breath.

‘I know that is right. But…’

His eyes were locked on hers. He didn’t speak. She thought of a spring coiled too tight ever to unwind.

'You're a good man,' she said, 'a hero. Why is it so difficult?'

'An Enforcer serves the One Law and no man. That is my duty.'

She gathered her thoughts and spoke more slowly.

'I met the ... accused I suppose you call him, in the park that day.'

Her heart throbbed. The image of the man with wild black hair, a streak of blood across his forehead, her hand reaching out to him in the stadium on Celebration Day flashed across her mind. She smothered it, she was with Dain, that could not be part of her life.

'He was saving the child, surely that was a good thing. There was that misunderstanding, he was arrested, then he ran away.'

Dain glanced downwards, then back at the scales. She felt she had to keep talking.

'When I saw him at the Baby Auction, I wanted to help.'

That was true. That was the most important truth.

Dain spoke tonelessly, as if repeating a lesson.

'But it is for the court to decide. We must trust the law.'

'I knew no-one would understand him. I thought if I could get him away, it would all be all right. I just wanted to talk to him, to make him see why the One Law is so important, what it means for all of us.'

Why wouldn't he look up at her? Why wouldn't he say he understood?

'Now I want to help you. You're a good man, you believe in what you're doing, not like everyone else I meet.'

He remained silent. She could see the pulse beating on the back of his hand. If she could touch him it would be all right.

'All I did was help them leave the hall. I stopped the riot, the disruption. They'd nearly got the Baby Auction back underway when you arrived.'

She took a breath and pressed her lips together.

‘I didn’t want him to be hurt, to suffer. He was trying to help people, that’s all.’

Dain looked back at her. After what seemed a long time he spoke:

‘And the others?’

‘I wasn’t thinking about them. They weren’t important.’

She had never seen his face look so sad, not even when he was talking about his parents in the restaurant. She reached forward across the desk to touch his fingers.

‘You are so precious to me,’ she said.

He reached out and stroked the back of her hand, once, his fingers soft and so very gentle on hers. Then he slowly drew back his hand.

‘Guard!’ he called out.

‘Escort for the prisoner.’

She looked back as she was led from the room. There was so much pain in his face.

# 28

Dain remained seated at the desk, looking out at the night sky dark above the city. The towers stood out clearly against it, gleaming in their own light, but he couldn't make out the residence blocks or the forest beyond.

There was one thing he hadn't said to her, one argument he hadn't used:

'Anna, I love you. I want to protect you and you must let me help you.'

He had kept faith with the One Law.

An image from the Broken Lands filled his mind, his father standing in a village street, dressed in the white robe, his hands held up, barring the way against a troop of men mounted on black horses. Flames rolled up behind them, the fire glinting on their helmets. His mother was dragging him away, pulling at his hand, shouting something he couldn't quite hear. Then there had been the child, trapped against a building on the other side of the road.

He was certain he had done what was right. His love burned inside him, locked away, in the same place that the memories were. His duty to the One Law, the law must govern. One day Anna would understand.

His communicator buzzed.

'Captain Lucas?'

A sharp male voice he didn't recognise.

'Yes.'

'Report to the President's office, top floor. Forthwith.'

He took the high speed security lift, tapped his passcode into the panel and walked along the richly carpeted floor to the presidential suite. He'd only been here two or three times before, always with superiors, most memorably after the convictions in the market cartel case, when he'd been told that he would be awarded the Star of the City. It seemed a long time ago.

The assistant took him straight through into President Wells' personal office. The President sat at her desk reading from a thick paper file with the Enforcer's crest embossed on the cover. She was dressed formally as always. She continued reading for a few minutes.

Dain stood stiffly at attention. Behind her on the shelves were the usual leather-bound law books, and a framed picture of a much younger man, dressed as a lawyer, smiling confidently at the camera. He had the same ash-blond hair as the president, cut severely short. The next photograph showed him wearing a graduation gown, the president next to him, her hand on his shoulder and a smile on her face. Dain saw there were no photographs of a partner anywhere.

President Wells closed the file, looked up and gave him a formal smile.

'Captain Lucas.'

Rebecca Wells was silent for some moments. She spoke with precision:

'I wanted to see you briefly to make certain you understood the gravity of the auction case. It is a matter of deep concern to our leading citizens. My office has been in communication with the Justice Division. The city will press charges for a serious breach of the One Law.'

She paused.

'Madam President, I understand it was a political protest, at most temporary disruption of trading. The auction achieved record sales.'

She raised her eyebrows. He fell silent.

'I hadn't finished, Captain Lucas. You may not understand the situation fully. I have the final report on the Old Market cartel here.'

She tapped the folder in front of her.

'It shows that the matter went much further than we originally suspected. Some of the most senior figures in the city may be implicated.'

She paused.

'We stand at a crossroads. There are people calling our basic values into question. This cannot be tolerated.'

Dain stared at her.

'Yes, Madam President. We must impose the law, but, if I may say so, we must make sure that charges are supported by evidence.'

She made a chopping gesture with her hand.

'I have been talking to Franklin and to other members of the Guild. The auction is a major public event. Any attack on it, any challenge to the principles on which it is based is an assault on our way of life. There is unrest in the city. We cannot permit any further incitement.'

She rose to her feet.

'Captain Lucas, you have distinguished yourself at a young age. You may yet attain the rank of Commander or even Commissioner. We are in urgent need of new blood at the top. I am confident that I may let this matter rest in your hands.'

'But Madam President, we cannot proceed beyond what our witnesses have told us.'

'Let me be honest with you, Captain Lucas.' She moved closer to him. 'I have been concerned about the Enforcers for some time. There are too many officers who do not understand that their first duty is to the city.'

She paused again.

'We must ensure that there is respect for the One Law. The people need to be able to trust their Enforcers. I place my trust in you.'

Her eyes remained fixed on him and she spoke slowly, emphasizing the words:

'We have decided that the matter will be treated with the utmost gravity, in the interests of all the people. We must, we absolutely must, defend the One Law. It must be absolutely clear that the Law applies to everyone, men and women, rich and poor, even ordinary citizens and,' she stressed the word, 'Entrepreneurs.'

Dain had nothing to say. He watched her move away from him, back behind the desk. She continued:

'That will be all. I leave it to you.'

She glanced down at the file.

'I have equally pressing matters to attend to.'

She turned to the window, her back to him, and stared out over the lights of the city, the great towers, illuminated from top to bottom. Dain could see Franklin's tower rearing up directly in front of them, its small square windows sparks of light. The street-lamps shone out more dimly below them. The grey bulks of the residence blocks were barely visible in the distance.

He saluted again and left the room. He thought of Anna, her face turned away from him, hunched on the chair; Anna looking up at him, her eyes full of tears, Anna's words:

'I didn't want him to be hurt, to suffer. He was trying to help people, that's all.'

Back in his office, he reached out to the scales of justice on the desk in front of him. His fingers trembled slightly. He took a deep breath.

He thought of the expression on President Wells' face as she confirmed what he had begun to suspect, that the corruption in the city extended beyond the market case. He wished he could talk to Anna openly, somewhere away from here, where he could make her see that she was wrong, that his duty to the city mattered more than any one person; where he could help her understand that sometimes your heart says one thing and your reason another, that the One Law was all they had, the only defence that lay between the city and the Broken Lands.

The faces of the children in the alley by the supermarket came into his mind. He knew he'd done the right thing. Somehow it was because he'd been with Anna that day. In any case it was of minor importance. There were no witnesses. An attack on the principles of free trade at a major city event such as the Baby Auction was a different matter.

He reached out and picked up the tiny scales and blew on them. The balance swayed from side to side. He set them at the corner of his desk, lifted his laptop from its drawer, opened the template for a charge sheet and started tapping at the keys.

In his report he summarised the evidence: four of the suspects had prepared disguises and materials, had gone to the Baby Auction intending to carry out a political demonstration and had done so; the fifth, Anna Pascal, had visited the Auction in the course of business and had been caught up in the incident. Statements from the Enforcers on the hall doors indicated that she had removed the trouble-makers from the Auction. She stated that she had done so in order to calm the situation. The evidence pointed to charges of temporary disruption of trading for the first four, a minor breach of the One Law. For Ms Pascal, he recommended that the court find no case to answer.

He glanced at the scales. The beam was hardly moving at all.

# 29

Anna watched the early morning sunlight slanting through the high-arched windows, catching the motes of dust that sifted slowly down through the courtroom air. She glanced round her. She stood in the dock in the main hall of the Halls of Law. The room was capable of seating several hundred people in rows on wooden benches. On the dais at one end, behind a long oak table, stood the high-backed chairs of the judge and the two assessors. Above them she could see the crest of the city, the scales of justice and the words:

PROPERTY, EQUALITY, DIGNITY, TRADE

picked out in gold on the light oak panelling. *Justice would be seen to be done,* she thought: *a lesson for the people.*

She knew the trial had attracted great attention. She had already noticed some of her fellow traders in their business suits, sitting at the front, staring at her. She ignored them. Behind them were other citizens, smartly dressed as if for an outing. The press box to the right was packed. She could also see a contingent of students, glancing nervously about them, and, right at the back in the cheapest seats, ordinary people from the residence blocks in their blue work clothes, sitting there, silent, their eyes on the richer groups in front of them.

Most of the noise that surrounded her came from the middle of the hall, from the people with comfortable incomes. She knew they'd come for entertainment, just to say they'd been there, chattering, gossiping and bargaining, always bargaining. *They made me a Hero of Enterprise,* she thought. *Now I'm on trial. Those people just wanted to help the children, why can't everyone see that?*

She looked round to her left. In their separate boxes and slightly in front of her were the other accused. Ed was nearest to her, then the pair she'd only glimpsed at the Baby Auction, Grisha and Lars, with their strikingly pale hair, and furthest away from her and obscured by the others, Matt.

She leaned forward. She had to see his face. He was staring at her. He inclined his head. His expression was one of regret.

The noise ceased abruptly. The judge and his assessors entered and took their seats. The judge was an older man, dressed in the sleekest business suit Anna had ever seen. It was almost a caricature of a suit, so well cut it fitted him like a second skin. He wore a gleaming white shirt and a tie that proclaimed unobtrusive good taste. His silver hair was brushed back and reached down to his collar. His face was thin, lined, his mouth turned down at the corners, his nose prominent and hawkish. He ran his sharp blue eyes along the accused, pausing briefly at each one, as if to fix their faces in his mind, and then turned to address the hall.

'Citizens, we have two cases to judge today. The first is of the utmost gravity. It concerns a conspiracy to carry out a demonstration at the Baby Auction. I will go so far as to say that the offence strikes at the heart of Market World, of the One Law and of our way of life. The charge sheet refers to a temporary disruption. The offence is much greater than that and I shall treat it as such. It is clearly an attempt to undermine support for the principle of free trade. It is hard to imagine a more direct and heinous attack on the One Law.'

Anna stared at him. A whisper ran round the courtroom. This would be a test-case for the One Law. She could see the traders at the front glaring at her, as if she wasn't a person but an obstacle in their way. She shivered. She thought of Dain, of the pain in his face as the guard had taken her out of his office.

The judge glared at the court.

'Silence!'

His eyes scanned along the benches. He spoke with an exaggerated clarity.

'If there are any more interruptions, I shall clear the court.'

He glanced down at his notes.

'The second case concerns a less serious charge, but it also merits our undivided attention.'

Anna's grasp on the rail in front of her tightened. The judge paused again and regarded his audience keenly. There was absolute silence in the hall.

'I will dispense with the normal introduction. Matt Torman, Grisha Christan, Lars Brand and Eden Carmel. You are called to account for conspiracy to subvert the One Law. How do you plead?'

Anna saw Ed glance hurriedly at the other three. She turned to the judge, and started to speak. Matt cut in:

'Not guilty: we were just trying to help those poor children.'

Anna felt a wave of relief. He was telling them the truth, surely they'd understand.

She saw Lars waving his hands:

'No! Don't listen to him. We're guilty as charged and we did right! Down with Franklin! Down with the One Law! Down with the Baby Auction!'

Ed was shouting too:

'Yes, guilty on all charges. We hate Market World!'

Grisha was leaning forward, shouting something at the judge. A ripple of excitement ran through the audience. Anna could see one of the journalists was already speaking urgently into his communicator, shielding his mouth with his hand, like a schoolboy talking in class.

She strained forward to catch sight of Matt. He was standing upright in the dock, staring straight in front of him.

The judge slammed his gavel down onto the desk in front of him.

'Silence!'

His eyes roved round the room sharp as needles. Anna watched as he pointed to the journalist.

'You sir! You are barred from my court. Serjeant, escort him.'

He turned to the accused:

'Now we will start to hear the evidence. I remind the court that this is a serious matter. We will treat it with the utmost gravity.'

Anna felt herself completely alone in the courtroom. The other four were arguing about the plea. Only Matt seemed to make sense to her. The image of Dain in his office with the scales on his desk, his words 'That is my duty', and the pain in his face as he said it blotted everything out for a second. She shook her head.

The judge had his eyes fixed on the accused like a hawk at a snake. Anna watched as a series of witnesses were brought into the court and examined by the judge. The assessors sometimes asked brief questions to clarify what was being said. She felt numb, unable to believe she was part of the proceedings.

The story unfolded quickly. Evidence was brought about the purchase of specialist light-weight printing paper, the masks, the clothes and even the hold-alls. There were references to a secret organisation standing behind everything, a threat hanging over the city. Various door-keepers, members of the public, participants in the auction and security staff had seen the four accused enter, don masks and fling the fake credits and the leaflets up into the air. She wanted to break in, to tell them it hadn't been like that, that Matt had held back the crowd from the line of babies, that he'd helped the woman who'd fallen in the crush.

The final witness was one of Franklin's security guards, in uniform, his arm bandaged. He gave his name as Beckman. Anna recognised him: the silver-haired man who'd picked her out in the lobby.

'He grabbed me from behind. I was hanging on to her, that one.'

The guard pointed to Ed.

'Then he got me, the one they called Torman, and they were off. He broke my hand.'

He lifted up the bandaged hand, showing it to the court.

'They nearly got away, but I saw them later. They were in the lobby. They were with that one there.'

He fixed his eyes on Anna.

'That's her, she had the leaflets. They were all talking together. Look at her! Thinks she's better than the rest of us. I bet she's behind the whole thing.'

Anna could feel the eyes of everyone in the court on her. She looked round and then remembered her role. She felt the pulse pounding in her throat. She knew she must remain calm, cast her eyes down and look submissive. *But if they blame me, maybe they won't think it's all Matt,* she thought. Then: *but Dain's right about the One Law, he must be.*

The guard was still talking:

'She tried to say she worked for the New Market, but I've been with Mr Franklin for forty years, I know everybody and she's never been in the Hall before. She was trying to get them out, but she didn't reckon on me.'

He stared at her, his eyes glittering with triumph.

'I see,' said the judge. Anna felt his glance on her, keen as a blade. 'Thank you. You may go.'

He paused and looked round the hall, waiting until the murmur of conversation had died down. He glanced sharply at Anna.

'The court will rise.'

# 30

No-one spoke to Anna when they escorted her down to the holding cells. She sat at one end of a bench bolted to the floor. The windows in the white-washed walls were high up, so high she couldn't see out of them. She counted five bowls of bean stew on the steel table

After a moment, she heard footsteps and the others entered. Grisha glanced at her, nodded, said something to Lars, and they both sat at the other end of the bench, their heads close together, and started eating. Matt came over to her and stood there, looking down at her, his eyes warm, his face troubled:

'I'm so sorry it's turned out like this. They should have left you out of it. We all know you were just trying to help.'

'I'm sorry too.'

Anna looked up at him. She could see where the wound on his forehead had healed. She wanted to stroke the hair back from the scar.

'Sit down,' she said. 'It looks worse for you than it does for me. That judge is out to get you.'

He shrugged.

'Hi Anna,' said Ed, and sat herself the other side of Matt, very close to him, Anna thought.

She watched as Matt took a mouthful of stew. Ed started talking to him:

'Why didn't you plead guilty back there? It's our only chance to say something against Franklin. We've got to show everyone there are people who hate the One Law. Otherwise they win. They always win.'

After a moment Matt put down his spoon.

'Yeah, maybe I should have. I don't know. They should treat the children better. And those Enforcers are thugs.'

He thought a bit. Anna watched the big capable hands wrapped round the bowl.

*He's the only one who talks about the children,* she thought. *But Dain's an Enforcer and we have to have the One Law. It's all there is.*

'Ed,' he said, lowering his voice, but Anna could still hear him, 'I wanted to look after you, too.'

'Yes, but you're the one needs looking after.'

Ed squeezed his hand. Her face shone like a star.

Anna felt the distance between their lives and hers.

The recess ended. The judge entered the courtroom and took his seat.

'Now I will take the second case,' he said. Anna felt his eyes on her. 'This concerns someone who is perhaps known to many of you, at least by reputation: one of the city's most successful young Entrepreneurs, Ms Anna Pascal.'

He paused and glared at the press box.

'This court enforces the One Law on all without fear or favour. We are no respecter of persons. You may report that.'

Anna knew everyone in the court was staring at her. She was wearing the same clothes in which she'd been arrested. She hoped the stain on the cream blouse wasn't too noticeable. Everything seemed distant, a game being played out by others according to obscure rules, and at the same time so close she didn't know how to protect herself.

The judge spoke directly to her, his voice harsh:

'I see no charge is recommended. Now, however, there is evidence to indicate that you are also a member of the gang. You are called to account for conspiracy to subvert the One Law. How do you plead?'

Anna hesitated:

'Not guilty,' she said finally.

The judge's eyes rested on her a moment.

'I see. We will consider the evidence. It is not necessary to recall Mr Beckman. We have his statement that you were talking to the other defendants as fellow conspirators. First witness please.'

Anna stared at the witness box. Her chest was constricted; she could hardly breathe. She was gripping the guard-rail so tightly her wrist hurt. Dain Lucas mounted the steps and stood at attention, his cap under his arm. She noticed he wasn't wearing the Star of the City. He glanced swiftly at her, then turned his attention to the judge.

'Captain Lucas. You are the arresting officer. Please tell the court what the demeanour of the accused was when you arrested her.'

Dain glanced back at Anna, then at the judge.

'She was…confused,' he said softly.

'Speak up, we need to hear you.'

'She was confused. She did not seem to understand what was happening.'

He glanced at a notebook.

'She said: "All I did was help them leave the hall. I stopped the riot, the disruption".'

He glanced at her.

'I am confident she understands the value of the One Law.'

Dain paused, and stared out across the court:

'She indicated the accused, Torman. She said: "He was trying to help the babies at the Auction, I know he was".'

The judge continued to stare at Dain, watching him carefully, as if, thought Anna, he was an enemy.

'How exactly did the accused indicate Mr Torman?'

'She was standing close to him.'

Dain hesitated and glanced again at Anna. She could not read his expression. The judge continued:

'Please answer the question.'

'She was holding his hand, she pulled at it.'

'I see. Does that indicate any kind of relationship, to your mind?'

Dain was silent. Anna willed him to understand: *He took my hand. He wanted me to go away, not to get involved.*

'Captain Lucas?'

'I apologise. An Enforcer sees so many things. I don't know what kind of relationship it indicated.'

Dain took a deep breath and continued:

'I keep an open mind.'

Someone laughed at the back of the court. The judge glared at the audience and continued.

'What was she holding in her other hand?'

'Her other hand? I'm not sure.'

'It's here in the station officer's notes and also in Mr Beckman's evidence.'

'Oh, there was something. Some papers. No-one was paying any attention to them.'

The judge raised an eyebrow. Dain paused and glanced downwards at his notebook. There was a moment of silence while the court waited. He went on:

'I believe it was a leaflet, there were many of them in the hall. She may have picked it up.'

'A leaflet. I have it here. It is subversive literature. It defames one of our most respected entrepreneurs, Mr Franklin, the President of the Guild. It also attacks one of our most respected institutions, the Baby Auction. The accused was holding it in her hand. I understand from the evidence that she had several of them. In fact, seventeen.'

The judge indicated a small pile of leaflets on the table in front of him.

'There were many leaflets in the lobby and in the hall as you say. Perhaps the accused picked up seventeen of them. Then again, perhaps she dropped them there? Thank you. You may go.'

Dain stared at him. Anna knew with absolute certainty that he would do anything he could for her.

'But…there are witnesses who state that Ms Pascal was there for commercial reasons, unconnected with the demonstration. She held the catering contract.'

'Thank you, Captain Lucas,' the judge's voice cut in. 'I am conducting this trial. You may go.'

Dain interrupted, nearly shouting:

'Your honour, I must intervene. Anna, Ms Pascal, stopped the riot. The leaflet was nothing to do with it.'

People were talking all across the courtroom. Anna could see that several of the journalists had their communicators to their mouths.

The gavel rapped into the table.

'Captain Dain, you have been dismissed. Go or you will be removed. Remember. Your duty is to the Law.'

The judge stared hard at Dain. He glanced at Anna and opened his mouth to speak. The gavel slammed down again. He turned and walked slowly down the steps. Anna felt as if she was in an empty place without a guide.

The judge tapped the gavel on the block for no obvious reason.

'I will now retire to confer with my assessors. The court will remain seated.'

Excited conversation burst out all round her. Anna stared across at Ed, who nodded to her and looked away. Behind Ed, Lars and Grisha were talking softly. She could just see Matt. His face seemed resigned. Then he looked up and gave her a smile of comradeship. Warmth flooded through her. She gathered herself and smiled back at him.

The judge and the assessors returned after forty-five minutes, and took their seats. The judge surveyed the courtroom. He fixed his gaze on the accused. After several seconds he spoke in a loud voice:

'I find the accused guilty on all counts.'

A babble of noise broke out on all sides. Anna could see the journalists talking into their communicators. Two were already in the aisle, walking as fast as they dared towards the exits.

The gavel crashed down. Anna flinched.

'Silence! Return to your seats. Do not treat my court with contempt. Perhaps I must explain the function of this court, since there are those present who fail to grant it the respect that it merits.'

His eyes flashed.

'This court is the first and last defence of Market World. Here we enforce the One Law, without fear and favour, simply according to the facts. Without us, you have the Broken Lands.'

He glanced coldly at the witness box, now empty.

'The President has her Enforcers. They bring the cases to us. And it is for us to decide them according to the One Law. We are justice.'

He paused and surveyed the court.

'The facts of the first case are simple. There are many witnesses to demonstrate that the accused entered the building where one of the most important events in our city's calendar was taking place. They were in disguise. They distributed leaflets and false credits in a manner calculated to obstruct trading and to bring the principles on which the Auction is founded into disrepute. Mr Torman chose to plead not guilty, his privilege. The court has seen through that.'

He narrowed his eyes. Anna felt that the judge was taking pleasure in his words. *You're my enemy,* she thought.

'There was some uncertainty about the facts of the second case. The accused may have entered the building on a different pretext, it doesn't matter what. It is certain that she assisted the escape attempt of two of the accused after their crime. On her own admission she helped them leave the Hall. It has been alleged that she was motivated simply by concern for the children, that she was not party to the conspiracy. However, we have established that she was seen holding hands with one of them. To my mind that signifies a ...' he paused and a rustle of sound went round the courtroom, '...relationship.

We have established that she was deep in conversation with two of them. We have established that she was carrying seventeen subversive leaflets when arrested. She may have distributed others.'

He let his eyes range along the rows of people packed into the room.

'There has been a suggestion that she might face a lesser charge, perhaps, I do not say certainly, because she is acquainted with leading figures in the city.'

He smiled, showing his teeth.

'This court, as I have said, is no respecter of persons. We respect only the One Law. We find her equally guilty.'

He slammed the gavel down for the last time.

'Anna Pascal, Matt Torman, Ed Carmel, Grisha Christan, Lars Brand, you are called to account. You have sought to obstruct trade and to destroy one of our leading institutions. You have failed.'

He paused.

'You have damaged us. More than that, you have cost us a great deal of money. We do not forgive debts. You will repay what you owe to Market World through forced labour. You are exiled for a period to be decided by your conduct. North Colony.'

A ripple of indrawn breath, almost a gasp, fanned across the courtroom. The judge glared round, as if daring anyone to object.

'Clear the court.'

Anna felt Matt's eyes on her. She stared at the steps down which Dain had left. She felt as if a tiny sliver of ice had entered her heart.

# 31

Dain stood behind his desk. He straightened his back.

'Adam,' he said. 'How long have we known each other?'

Dain saw a flicker of surprise pass across Adam's face. He paused before answering:

'Nine years, Captain. Since the first day you came out of college.'

'Nine years,' Dain kept his eyes on Adam's face. 'I've never asked you how you got your scar.'

'That?' Adam grinned briefly. 'Long time ago. It's the reason I joined up.'

'Yes,' said Dain. 'When you knew where you were, when the One Law meant what it said.'

He glanced across at the Towers outside the window, the sunlight reflected bright off a million plate glass windows. *Like eyes,* he thought, *staring out over the city.*

Adam cleared his throat.

'I watched the trial.' His eyes seemed softer. 'With some of the men. We were surprised at the verdict. I wanted to let you know that.'

'It's the verdict of the court, Adam. Not our business. Our duty is to the One Law.'

'Yes, Captain. But we were surprised.'

Dain turned his eyes to the Towers. *Windows that stared out at you. How could you look inside those windows?*

'You know people in the force, I suppose?'

'Yes quite a few. And the men respect you. They want you to know that. What you did in the Old Market was ...' Dain heard him stumble slightly over the unfamiliar words, '... unparalleled. True leadership.'

Dain became aware that Adam had half-turned beside him and was also staring out at the Towers.

'I suppose you must know people in the Information Division?'

'A few but they're very tight. People always say ID knows more about you than you do yourself. Sometimes it's true.'

Dain kept his eyes on the Towers.

'There's a report, Adam. It was prepared for President Wells at the top level. It's about the Old Market scandal.'

'Yes, captain.'

Adam had turned to face him again.

'You could say I'd be interested to know what's in it.'

'Will that be all, captain?'

Adam saluted crisply and turned to go.

Dain thought for a moment and sat down at his desk. Anna, her eyes dark as oil staring at him across the courtroom; Anna, her faced turned away as she was taken from the building. If only he'd been able to say more, to make the court understand. He shook his head. He must not think of her, she was convicted, she'd broken the law. But she just wanted to help, she had done what she thought was right.

He reached out and touched the scales of justice. He thought of the intensity in President Wells' eyes as she said:

'We must, we absolutely must defend the One Law.'

The crime in one pan, punishment in another. They balanced perfectly. He blew gently and the balance beam quivered, setting the pans swaying.

He hesitated, then slid open the bottom drawer of his desk. He reached to the back and touched the book lying there, a battered leather-bound prayer book. A man in a white surplice smeared with blood kneeled in the dirt of a village street, holding the book to the lips of a woman who lay there, reaching up to him.

*The Broken Lands,* he thought. *You believed you could change them, with your faith. You failed. There is only one defence against chaos. That is the One Law. Your heart may say one thing but reason says another.*

He picked up the scales and carefully placed them next to the book. He thought for a moment, rose, crossed the room and opened the cupboard which contained his dress uniform. He unpinned the Star of the City from the jacket. It hardly seemed to weigh anything. He set it down in the drawer next to the scales. They were lying on their side, the balance pans tilted awkwardly on the chains. He shut the drawer and locked it, and put the tiny key in an inner compartment of his wallet.

He picked up his uniform cap and held it between both hands in front of him. He stared at the badge. He could just make out the scales and above them the motto: 'Property, Equality, Dignity, Trade'.

He rose and placed the cap neatly on his head, glanced again out of the window towards the towers, turned smartly and left the room.

# PART 4:
# THE NORTH COLONY

# 32

The truck lurched over another rut, throwing Matt against the colonist next to him. The sun would be coming up over the low hills lighting up the valley outside, but here only a pale half-light penetrated between the flaps in the canvas cover. He looked round at the others. Most of them seemed to be asleep or half-asleep. The green-uniformed guard by the tailgate was nodding, then jerking awake to glare at them. He could feel Ed leaning against him on the other side.

He hated the Colony, the endless roll-calls, or audits as they called them, the stupid green overalls, the managers continuously telling you how much you owed Market World, most of all the fact that he could only be with Ed when they were sent out on a work-party, like today.

*Re-education? It's a prison,* he thought, *they just want to punish us.* Ed snored gently. *At least she's out of it,* he thought. He'd seen Lars and Grisha in the Colony, but they were together at the other end of the parade ground and he hadn't been able to get near them. They'd taken Anna away after the trial.

He thought about the trial. It seemed so long ago. He'd tried to do his best, to help Ed. He felt a surge of warmth for her. She'd always do her best for him. Anna was so different, she'd wanted to help, but sometimes she seemed to think buying and selling everything, even babies, was normal.

He remembered the child in the river, how he'd held her against him and passed her back to Anna. He remembered Anna at the trial, her face wretched. That Enforcer was on her side, anyone could see that, but it didn't make any difference. They'd taken her somewhere else, Matt didn't know what had happened to her. He hoped he'd see her again one day, but her life was different from his, she'd always had money.

His bones ached, but he was too cold to sleep. He'd given Ed his jacket. She wouldn't take it at first.

'I've got warm blood,' he said, 'I keep having to take it off. Do you more good.'

He wrapped it round her and swung his arms to show how he kept himself warm.

That was on the parade-ground, before they'd been lined up and counted under the arc-lights, and loaded onto the trucks. The manager was there, thin, with gold-rimmed glasses and dressed in the same grey suit he always wore, however cold it was. He was reading something out about how much the trial cost, how much the Colony cost, how much they'd all cost Market World, how much they'd earn on the work-party, how much they'd have to pay off. There was a lot about credits. It was called 'balancing accounts'. Ed stood there ignoring the cold, her eyes fixed on the manager as if he was trying to take something from her, something precious.

The manager finished talking.

'What was that all about?' Matt whispered.

'The usual stuff. We owe them, we've got to work harder,' she replied. 'But he said something at the end: we've got a chance to earn a bit extra today.' Then he said "Make sure you do your best," and he smiled at us. It's crazy.'

It was bitterly cold and the guards couldn't get the tally right and kept shouting at them. Matt managed to keep next to Ed.

'Get yourself moving!' bellowed a guard, 'Onto the truck.'

Matt reached down to help Ed up. The guard slammed his club against the tailboard.

'Keep moving!' he snarled at Matt. Matt fixed his eyes on him. Ed scrambled up.

'Come on,' she said, her voice low. 'Don't make trouble.'

He heard the creak as they opened the gate in the razor-wire fence and the truck lurched forward, revving hard.

After a long time, the truck swung hard to the left and stopped. Matt was thrown forward. He got an arm round Ed to stop her falling off the bench. The guard wiped a hand across his face. Matt heard someone shouting outside:

'Everyone out! Let's see the film stars for today.'

Matt kept as close as he could to Ed. The wind cut through his shirt. The guards were wearing greatcoats, standing in a circle round the prisoners with their clubs ready. The sun was now above the horizon and he could see fields in front of him, stretching into the distance.

*The sea of grass,* he thought, *no-one's looking after the land. If they don't do something soon they'll never get the weeds out. They should have ploughed it weeks ago.*

'Right,' a voice boomed out. Matt looked round. A short man with long black hair and a red-patterned silk scarf tied round his neck wearing a creased safari suit was standing in front of the colonists, holding a megaphone to his mouth. Everything about him gave the impression of frustration, from his sudden violent movements to the compressed rage in his voice. Thick black eyebrows shielded his eyes and he had full red lips.

'I'm your director, Des Riddell. Pleased to meet you. Today I'm going to make you into film stars.'

He paused.

'Don't know much about films, do you? Otherwise you'd be telling me how proud you are to be working with me.'

He glowered at them.

'But you don't know anything. You're just here for Re-education. You're Colonists. You've got to earn the money to pay your debt to society, right? You've cost Market World a lot of credits and you're going to work to pay them back. Fair's fair. That's our motto,'

He pointed to the slogan on the truck behind him:

FRANKLIN CORRECTIVE ENTERPRISES

arched over the cartwheel and below it, in larger capitals:

FAIR'S FAIR

The director glared round belligerently:

'Well you're going to earn some credits today. We're making a film and you're the extras. Now, anyone here can use a plough? I thought not. What's the point of sending me you lot? I need people I can work with.'

Matt shrugged: 'I can plough,' he said loudly.

'Ah. We've got a star,' said the director. 'Step forward. What's your name?'

Matt patted Ed's sleeve and moved through the crowd.

'I'm Matt.'

The short man looked him up and down.

'Big guy, huh? You'll do.'

He raised his voice to address the colonists.

'Today Matt's going to show us how it's done. It's an agricultural scene. The rest of you are peasants. Peasants!' he shouted at them, 'Make like you're peasants, you know, like you're from the country, like you're stupid. Shuffle your feet! Hunch your shoulders! Let's see those mouths sag! Make me proud.'

He staggered from side to side in a clumsy dance, his mouth twisted, his eyes dull.

Matt could see the guards thought this was funny. He stood there, the director in front of him, the mob of colonists behind him, milling about, staring vacantly. The guards stood round in their green uniforms, swinging their clubs, mocking them. He felt the anger hot inside him, against all of them, all of Market World.

They had a law against normal kindness and they had to sneer at the people who grew their food.

He saw Ed, right at the front, the only one not moving. Her face shone with concern for him. She didn't think peasants were fools. She'd worked her way through the crowd. He ached to put his arms round her.

Des squinted up at the sun.

'Come on. We're wasting good daylight. Work to do.'

Matt could see a group of technicians gathered round a camera mounted on a trolley to his left.

'Where's the plough?' he asked. 'Where's the tractor?'

'Don't try and make a fool of me,' shouted the short man. 'It's in front of you. We got it specially, don't break it, it's a period piece, it cost money.'

Matt stared. A rusty hand plough, the handles bent to the right, lay on its side on the edge of the field. He heard a neighing and looked up. A young man in a felt jacket, corduroy trousers and leather boots was leading a heavy horse round the end of the trucks. He looked round and immediately started towards Matt, the horse swaying its head nervously from side to side.

'You're the only one here who looks as if he knows what he's doing,' he said, his voice soft with the burr of the countryside. 'You take care of him. He gets scared when there's too many people. His name's Frankie. Frankie Franklin. He always gets his own way. Reminds me of someone.' He winked.

Matt reached out and stroked the horse, running his hand firmly down the soft brown coat. He felt a shiver in the flank.

'Easy there, easy,' he murmured stretching up so he could talk in the horse's ear. 'Easy Frankie, easy old fellow. We've just got a bit of work to do. You'll be fine.'

The horse turned his heard towards Matt, the brown eyes focusing on him. The breath snorted warm, moist on his hand.

'Recognise that accent,' said the young man. His face was pale, pinched, eager. He looked as if he didn't get enough to eat.

'My family's from Fernhill,' said Matt. 'A while back, when I was a kid.'

The man smiled broadly: 'I know Fernhill. They had a horse fair once. They know their horses. Know how to bargain too.'

'He'll be OK,' said Matt. 'I'll bring him back to you.'

The horse shifted uneasily and stamped down with a giant feathered hoof. The director backed away.

'Easy, Frankie,' whispered Matt, stroking his hand along the side of the head, gently over the nostrils, so the horse could smell him.

'Enough of that,' shouted the director. 'You're wasting the light. Let's get on with it.'

Matt realised the short man was holding one of the guards' clubs, gripping it uncertainly with his fingers. He prodded towards Matt with the end. Matt turned to the young man.

'Come on.'

Matt took the reins from him and led Frankie towards the field. They manoeuvred the plough into position and he started buckling the traces, checking that they didn't foul each other. Frankie stood patiently, obviously used to the harness. Matt patted his way along the warm flank and attached the long driving reins to the bridle.

He took his position grasping the handles of the plough, the reins gripped in his left hand. He stood tall, leaning back slightly, the sun warming his face. He ignored the sound of the crowd behind him. He felt calmer than he had for a long time.

He pulled the rein taut and flicked it upwards with his wrist, sending a ripple along it.

'Get on, Frankie,' he said, speaking firmly, not shouting. The horse started forward, the shoulders bending to their task, the massive hindquarters swaying from side to side, the plough running smoothly forward. Matt leaned to the side with all his weight, angling the ploughshare downwards, feeling the resistance through the handles. He stepped forward onto the board at the back of the plough, forcing the blade further down and keeping it stable.

The share bit into the earth, a brown wave of soil turning smoothly over and crumbling to the right. He sent another ripple along the rein and felt the tug as Frankie strained forward, leaning into the harness, hauling the plough onwards, into the rich ground.

*We'll get a good crop out of this,* he thought. *It's been fallow for quite a while.*

He found himself grinning at the horse's hindquarters.

*This is what I can do,* he thought. *I was made for it.*

He relaxed the reins slightly.

'Easy old fellow,' he said, 'we've got all day. Take it steady.'

# 33

Matt became aware of someone running clumsily alongside him, his feet slipping in the rough soil.

'What do you think you're doing?' yelled a voice. The director glared at him, doubled forward, his breath coming in short gasps.

Matt eased back on the reins.

'Whoa, Frankie,' he said to the horse.

The director had now recovered enough to talk. He was leaning on the club.

'We haven't set up yet. I need to check the light levels.'

Matt felt confused. Frankie was shifting his hooves, eager to move on. Matt had to haul on the reins to keep him where he was.

A voice sounded out from behind them:

'It's OK, Des. I got the face shots. He's a natural, looks like a real countryman.'

'But I'm from Fernhill,' Matt started to say, then realised that no-one was listening to him. He moved slowly forward, keeping the reins taut, until he could stroke Frankie's neck to calm him, long gentle strokes. He wished he had something he could rub him down with.

He stared back across the field. The director, Des, had started to tramp clumsily back towards the crowd of colonists. He caught a flash of sunlight from the camera lens as it panned across the scene. He could see the colonists were bunched together in a tight group with the trucks parked in a rough line behind them and the guards round them. He thought he could make out Ed at the front. He wondered if she could see he was smiling at her. He hadn't realised how far he'd come across the huge expanse of land.

He leaned into the horse, smelling the rough sweat and the leather of the harness, stamping to keep his feet warm, stroking

Frankie as tenderly as he could. He didn't know how long he stood there for. He could see a group of men in jackets round the trolley doing something to the camera. Occasionally sunlight flashed off the lens. He shivered, pressing himself against the warmth of the horse.

After a while he saw the director wave his arms violently and lift the megaphone.

'OK everyone, to your places.'

He pointed at Matt.

'You, ploughboy, you've got to come towards us, keep it slow, make it look like you're working at it. Everyone else, you're just watching.'

'OK, Frankie old fellow, your star turn,' Matt muttered and slipped back to the plough. He heaved it upright, shook the reins and pulled with all his weight to the right, easing backwards off the board, letting the plough ride up, over the ground. Frankie started to turn. He leaned hard over, bracing himself, putting his weight on the rein, bringing the horse slowly round. He looked along the horse's flank, along the line of the furrow, judging when to haul back, then urge the horse forward and put his full weight onto the plough to force the blade down again, into the soil.

*Not bad,* he thought, *lined up pretty straight.* He glanced at the colonists. *Bet none of them can tell the difference, not even Ed. She could set a ploughshare though, I've seen her do it in the workshop. Not Anna's world, this.*

Frankie snorted and shook his head, setting the harness jingling. Then he leaned forward against the collar and forced the ploughshare into the soil, cutting down until Matt pulled back, adjusting the pressure on the plough-board. The smooth wave of turned soil flowed evenly out to the right, where it should be, along the line of the first furrow. He glanced up at the group of people round the camera ahead of him. They fell silent, watching the plough draw nearer. The camera crew ducked down, he could see them angling the lens upward at the horse's head as Frankie loomed towards them. He was glad to see Ed in the front row, his jacket clutched round her, her eyes fixed on him.

The director was shouting something:

'Come on! Closer, closer, really close, this has to be real. We want to feel the plough.'

Matt eased on the reins. He could feel a new quivering running along them. Frankie wasn't use to crowds of people. He was shaking his head nervously. Just then someone snapped on an arc lamp. A blaze of white light flashed into Matt's eyes. Frankie plunged forward. Matt hauled back on the reins with all his strength.

'Whoa, boy, easy!' he shouted.

He heard a crack and felt the left hand trace suddenly go slack. The plough canted over. Frankie swivelled sideways, straight at the camera, snorting loudly. Matt caught a glimpse of the crew diving sideways, of Frankie rearing up and crashing down with the full force of his hooves at the lamp, of the lad who'd brought the horse diving through the crowd to grab at the broken rein. The crowd swirled backward, eddying out to the sides.

Together Matt and the young man brought Frankie under control. They turned the horse back towards the ploughland, pulling back on the reins. Matt got to the other side of the bridle and spoke soothingly:

'Frankie, old fellow, take it easy, they're not from the country. They don't know anything.'

He felt the breath coming hard in Frankie's nostrils. The horse turned his great head to him, the eyes panicked, questioning. After a while Matt felt Frankie growing calmer under his fingers and handed the reins back to the young man. The great horse stood there, shivering slightly.

The guards were glaring at him, their clubs at the ready. The other colonists were herded together. He was aware of the director and the camera crew, doing something to their machinery, to one side. Ed slipped through and he felt her hand warm in his.

She pressed herself against him:

'I'm so glad you're OK, Matt. He's huge, that horse, I've never seen anything like it, when he came at us.'

He smiled at her.

'His name's Frankie. He's just a heavy horse. You have to know how to handle them. Not like that idiot.' He nodded at the director. 'He spooked him.'

A harsh voice boomed out at them. Matt put his arm round Ed to protect her.

'Right everyone, entertainment's over. Back in the wagons.'

It was one of the guards speaking. Matt saw he'd got hold of the director's megaphone. The director was waving his arms about, shouting at someone who had taken the side off the camera and was poking at it with a screwdriver longer than his fore-arm. The other guards were pressing in on them, herding the crowd towards the trucks. Matt could see some of the guards prodding at the backs of the people in front of him with their clubs, as if they were cattle. He patted Frankie's flank.

'See you again old boy, you did well.'

He nodded to the lad from the village:

'He's a good horse, he showed 'em something. And I brought him back OK.'

# 34

Matt watched the guard walking along the rows of colonists, his club swinging by his side. He squeezed Ed's hand and released it. The manager was obviously annoyed. He was shouting something about how much the camera cost to fix, how they'd all ruined their big chance to earn more credits. He kept jabbing his finger towards them. The arc-lights glared down at them in the darkness and it was colder than ever. The roll-call had gone on much longer than usual. Matt could see the guards were tired of it all and angry with the colonists.

The manager shouted even louder, the arc-lights glinting off his glasses:

'OK, it's the big scene tomorrow. This is your last chance. Get this right and you'll get something off your accounts. This is your last chance to shape up. Dismiss.'

'What's all that about, Ed?' he asked.

'Keep your voice down,' she said.

The guard at the end of the row swung round, gripping the club. He was burly with crew-cut red hair. Matt could see he was spoiling for trouble.

'Who's talking?' His eyes fastened on Matt. 'It's you. You're the one who smashed the camera. You need a lesson.'

He pushed his way through the colonists.

'Leave him alone!' yelled Ed. 'It was me, I was talking!'

Matt could see other guards making for them.

'Stay out of this,' he muttered to Ed, then shouted 'It was nothing to do with her'.

He dropped his arms. The guard grinned:

'Too bad.'

He raised his club to smack at Matt's shin. Matt braced himself, then flinched back as Ed threw herself in front of him. She grabbed the club with both hands and clung on screaming: 'Leave him alone!'

Matt flung himself forward, covering Ed, and took a blow across his shoulders.

'Ed! Get down!' he shouted, hunching over her.

A voice rapped out, sharp, slightly hoarse:

'What's going on? Leave them alone. You know we have to compensate for any injuries. Besides we need all the extras we can get. Big day tomorrow.'

Matt looked up. The guards were staring at someone to the side. The manager. It was the first time Matt had seen him close to. He had shrewd light blue eyes and lines reaching down at the corners of his mouth.

He pushed his glasses up onto the bridge of his nose, and took a breath. He'd been running, Matt guessed.

'We can't have this,' said the manager. 'We're behind schedule today and we must do the village scene tomorrow.'

He paused and gave a slight nod.

'You can settle the account tomorrow. Get them to the dormitories.'

Matt stretched out his hand to Ed and felt the touch of her fingers. Then she was wrenched away and disappeared among the prisoners as the guards led her off.

'Come on, you, we'll sort you tomorrow,' grunted the guard who'd struck him, jabbing his club into the bruise on his back to urge him forward. Matt straightened his shoulders. It would take more than that to make him wince. Ed was on his side and she was worth all of them.

# 35

Matt flexed his back. The pain was OK, a dull ache when he moved it. He could tell the trucks were going somewhere different today. Ed was beside him on the bench again. He had his arm round her. She'd have let those guards beat her and she'd done that for him. He let the thought trickle slowly through his brain. She'd done that. She smiled at him, and then leaned against his shoulder. He felt he could face anything.

The truck ground slowly up a rough incline and slowed to turn a sharp corner. He couldn't see outside, the canvas covers were pulled across. He realised they were on a zigzag, climbing a steep slope. He heard another truck following on behind them, changing gear clumsily for the corner. Maybe the others are in that one, he thought.

There was a sudden gust of wind and the canvas flapped open. He looked down at the Colony below them in the valley, three ugly grey concrete blocks surrounded by pine woods. He could just make out the six-metre wire fence and the floodlights on their columns at the corners.

He leaned towards Ed and muttered:

'I bet there's ways out of those kennels they've never thought of.'

She turned to him and grinned.

'No talking!' The guard thumped the metal floor of the truck with his club. He scowled at Matt and pulled the flap shut.

Matt thought about the Colony. He'd seen that it was in a valley. There was a river running next to it and the ground rose up the other side. The trees thinned out and he'd glimpsed blue sky over the ridge. There were no roads except the one running up the valley and no sign of any other buildings.

*Once you were in those woods,* he thought, *they'd never track you down.* He glanced round. *Not this lot, they're all from the residence blocks. Bet they've never been in a forest.*

The truck lurched over the crest of the ridge and kept going as the ground levelled out. After a time, Matt couldn't tell how long, they turned and stopped. A guard pulled the canvas open at the back of the truck.

'Everyone out. Move it.'

Matt started to rise, and felt Ed's hand on his arm.

'Take it easy,' she muttered. 'Don't be so keen, let's keep at the back. They're making films again. We've seen films like these before at Celebration Day.'

The guard jabbed his club towards her and she fell silent.

They followed the others out, ducking under the flap. Matt shielded his eyes against the light. It was full day outside the dim cave of the truck. The others were standing in a group, the guards round the edges with their clubs, their faces expressionless. In front of them was a village, but not like anywhere Matt had seen before. The houses were made of close-woven branches, covered in clay. He could see the wood underneath where the clay had come off.

All right for a barn he thought, but no-one ever lived in a house like that. The wind comes straight through. If you've got clay and straw, any fool can make bricks. That's how they think we live, those people in the city. Like animals.

Someone was shouting at them from the front. It was the director, Des. The Franklin Enterprises truck was drawn up behind him, the sun gleaming on its smart paintwork. The technicians were bringing a camera trolley down the ramp at the back. A pick-up truck with a camera mounted on the back stood beside it. Matt looked away, he didn't want to be singled out again.

He sniffed. Country air, everything overlain by the diesel from the trucks, but there was something familiar in it. He caught it again, the rich, warm smell, half like a compost heap but with the sharpness of horse-pee in it. Some way away, but there were horses, quite a few of them. There must be a stable. He liked horses. He wondered if he could get Ed and him a job working there. Then he remembered what Ed had said about Celebration Day. They'd been horses in the films on the big screen in the arena. He wished he'd been paying attention more that day, but it hadn't seemed to matter.

'OK everyone.'

The director had the megaphone in front of his face again. 'Day two of our epic. We're doing the village market today.'

He paused and waved a hand upwards.

'Look, the sun's on our side. Cue for a song, join in everyone.'

He started to sway from side to side, shouting the words out at them through the megaphone:

'The sun has got his hat on,
Hip hip hip hooray!'

He gestured to them, his arms outspread, appealing. Those in the front row started to sing along, a ragged mumbling chorus.

'The sun has got his hat on, - louder! Louder!
And he's coming out to play!'

The noise died away. The colonists glanced round at each other, at the guards, who just stared at them. The camera crew hadn't joined in. They were watching, grins on their faces.

'Let's do it again! Everyone this time, join in!
The sun has got his hat on....'

This time all of them joined in, shouting out the words. Matt expanded his lungs, sucking in the fresh air and sang out, trying to drown out the megaphone. It was a good feeling, a bit like when he'd first started school in the village. He remembered what Ed had said. He glanced round at her and gripped her hand tight among the crowd. The others had grins on their faces. A ripple of laughter ran across the group.

The director had a smile on his face too.

'Right, today's a holiday – not for you lot, but for the village. You've all got your best clothes on and you're going to have fun. I want to see you strolling down the street, chatting to your neighbours, waving to each other, just like it would be in the old times. Maybe there's someone you fancy, now's your chance!'

He looked round at them.

'It's a happy day! There's a market, you're all going to the market. You're going to trade, to buy and sell, just like we do in Market World, only we don't have credits here, you just have to pretend. That's the best part - everything's for free.'

He waved his arm round to include all of them, the guards, the whole of the village:

'For one day only, forget about the One Law! Nothing has to be paid for. It'll be fun and you'll be villagers, getting all the things you can't make for yourselves: clothes, food, wood carvings, maybe musical instruments. Can anyone play a pipe or a drum? Well now's your chance. It's the village holiday.'

He gestured at some tables set up alongside the van.

'There are your outfits. You're actors now, bright-coloured holiday clothes. Some lovely dresses there for the ladies: brocade, silks and satins, it's all artificial, but this is make-believe. Don't be shy, men, now's your chance to wear tights. And hats, they went in for hats in those days. Come on, everyone get changed, ladies to the left, men to the right.'

Ed gripped Matt's elbow:

'Keep at the back. Remember the films on Celebration Day? There was the village market with people having fun, then there were horsemen riding through it, smashing everything, beating people down, riding over them. They said it was the Broken Lands. Maybe they made it here, with colonists.'

'I didn't really look at the films. It's the guards settling accounts we've got to worry about, like that manager said.'

Ed looked uneasy. One of the guards was watching them, weighing his club in his hands.

'We've got to find a way out of here.'

Around them the others were rushing forward. They rummaged through the clothes, exclaiming over the colours, the material, the styles. Matt understood that many of the colonists had never had the chance to wear clothes they chose for pleasure before. It had always been work overalls or the cheap mass-produced stuff in Franklin's stores. Everyone hated the green colony overalls. This was a real holiday. Matt watched the men elbowing each other out of the way for a bright blue doublet or parti-coloured tights, the scrimmage around the codpieces, the jokes over the hats. He thought of Celebration Day, of the images on the giant screen of the market, the villagers in the time before the Great Hunger.

'Keep at the back,' he grunted.

She'd got black tights on, a quilted red and black jacket and a black felt hat with a red band. He thought of the joker in a pack of cards.

'You look good,' Ed said. 'Tights suit you.'

Matt sniffed the air. Something came to him over the smell of the village and the cloth and leather of the clothes, the bodies of the colonists. He could make out the aroma of meat, meat-pies, and fruit from somewhere in front of them, then faintly from further away, a familiar odour he'd known from the village. Horses. Suddenly everything came back to him, the film on the big screen, the market, the horseman riding full tilt into it, the whips flailing down.

He glanced at the guards.

'Ed! I can smell horses, not so far away. The smell carries in the air. We've got to keep at the back.''

She sniffed: 'Can't smell anything, except people and clothes.'

'It's there. No-one recognises it, they're all from the city. Look out for the others.'

One of the guards took a pace towards them. He dropped Ed's hand.

She started to speak, then the megaphone cut in and he couldn't hear her. The pick-up truck was in position, ready to lead them down the village street. The director was standing on the back, gripping the hand-rail, the camera set up beside him, pointed directly at them. Matt ducked back, away from the gaze of the glass eye.

'Everyone ready? Another chorus of the 'The sun has got his hat on?' No? Everyone keen to get on with the show?'

The director checked his watch and glanced up the street.

'Right, let's see if we can do this in one take. Everybody's happy, it's market day. No work today, we're all off to have fun. I want to see you all enjoying yourself. That's it! Wave to your neighbours.'

He gave an exaggerated wave to one of the guards, sweeping the megaphone through the air. The guard ignored him.

'Never mind, get in the spirit of things. They'll be a good meal in it for you. Most of the stalls offer food, and it's all for real and all for free. Think of that! Let's see you tuck in, you deserve it.'

He banged down on the roof of the truck, and it moved slowly off, the camera whirring. The crowd of colonists thronged the narrow street behind it, delighted at the prospect of a free market. Matt looked up. He could see another camera on scaffolding behind one of the houses, panning to follow the parade.

The street was just mud, stamped down hard in places. He made out a hoof-print. The green-uniformed guards were lagging behind, ducking into the alleys between the houses out of camera shot.

Matt glanced round. There were no guards near them. Most of the colonists were in front, following the pick-up, eager to get to the market-place, the lens scanning across their excited faces. The noise of chattering voices rose up. Someone was playing a pipe, just three notes, repeated.

The crowd spilled out into a square. There was the market, right in front of them, the stalls with brightly coloured awnings, striped yellow and red, white and crimson. He thought he recognised Franklin's black and gold. The tables were heaped high with all sorts of goods. He grasped Ed's hand.

'It's the market, just like the film,' he whispered. 'Keep at the back.'

People were rushing towards the stalls, some of them almost running. Matt couldn't see Lars or Grisha anywhere. He heard the stall-holders shouting out their wares over the din:

'Apples, Fresh cherries!' 'Meat pies!' 'New cloth, it's from the city!' 'Come and taste my cakes! Baked this morning!'

He spotted Grisha in the distance, her milk-white skin standing out against a flamboyant full-length blue and gold dress. He waved at her but she was intent on the stalls.

He caught sight of the camera truck sliding into a side-alley on the other side of the square. Everyone was round the stalls now, some of them already eating. He could smell fresh baking, the aroma of cooked meat and over it, caught by a gust of wind, the rank smell of horses. It was much stronger now. He looked round again.

'Come on, there's no time,' he grabbed Ed by the arm. 'Quick, down here.'

He dragged her into a side alley. A guard stepped out from behind a pillar, his club raised.

'What are you doing here? Get back on the set.'

Matt tried to look sheepish.

'Just having a look round.'

He straightened and punched the man in the face, as hard as he could. There was a sharp pain across his knuckles. The guard grunted and fell backwards.

He caught the faint creak of bridles, the noise of horsemen jostling in a narrow street. The unpaved street! He realised the sound of the horses' hooves would be muffled. None of the others would hear anything over the uproar in the market.

Ed was bent over the guard. Matt could see he'd broken the man's nose. Blood was trickling from one nostril. The guard had pale skin and prominent freckles. He hadn't shaved that morning.

'He's out of it for a bit.' Ed's voice was business-like. 'Come on.'

They ran down the alley and glanced round the corner of a cross-street. Matt caught a glimpse of the horsemen, black horses, red sashes on their jackets, the sun glinting on metal helmets. They were crossing the end of the street no more than fifty yards away. He pulled Ed back against the wall of a house.

'Keep your voice down.'

He felt the wall behind him give. He realised it was plywood. He pushed against it and felt it bow, tearing away from the nails at the corner.

'Give us a hand. Push there.'

He pointed to the bottom corner. Ed shoved at the wall for all she was worth. Matt leaned against the top of the plywood panel, braced himself, and heaved. The panel tore loose and angled inwards. They were through.

Matt pushed the panel roughly back into place and looked round. The building was just a simple wooden frame with wattle and daub panels nailed on at the front and painted plywood at the back. The main source of light was a single window in the front wall, unglazed, looking out over the market. There was no door and no ceiling. He could see blue sky through the thin thatched roof above.

He gripped a wooden upright. The whole structure rocked slightly. Dust and straw sifted down from the crude thatch roof. He pulled Ed down onto the floor at the back. *Beaten earth, just like the street,* he thought. They looked out over the market, at everyone gathered round the stalls, trading away, most of them with food in their hands. He noticed some of the stall-holders were eating their own wares, gesturing to the colonists to get more. Someone was playing the pipe, more musically now and there was a drum and some kind of stringed instrument.

Ed glanced up at him, her eyes wide. They both heard a horse snort, and shake its bridle, so close to them it seemed just the other side of the wall.

# 36

Matt pulled Ed against him and wrapped his arms round her. She felt so vulnerable.

'The scene from that film. I never believed they'd do it.'

Ed's eyes were huge in the darkness.

'Oh Matt, it all makes sense. First they shot the film of the ploughing – the golden time. Now it's the attack on the market. They use the colonists as the villagers and they pretend it's the Broken Lands. Everything we see at Celebration Day is fake, and we believed it, everyone believed it.'

The horse snorted again and stamped, very close. Matt saw one of the women on the edge of the crowd in the square swing round, a meat pie halfway to her mouth. She screamed and the sound cut through the hubbub in the square. The pie fell from her hand and burst on the ground in a brown stain of gravy.

The horsemen swept in from the left, a black wedge, right into the heart of the crowd. People were running in all directions, tripping, sliding about on the muddy ground. Some were still clutching their purchases. A stall went down, then another. The horsemen were lashing out with their whips, bringing them hard down like flails. The flicked out the thongs so that the knots cut across faces, necks, legs, anything in front of them.

A horse reared up, the rider braced back in the saddle tugging, pulling at the whip to bring down another stall. He saw a fat man hurl a pie at the horseman in front of him and duck down, his hands raised, the bright green bonnet swept away from his balding head. The horseman smacked the butt of the whip down hard. The man disappeared under the horses' hooves.

The screaming had stopped. The only noises in the square were the clatter of hooves, the grunting of the riders, the sound of feet running, sliding and the crack of the whips. Some of the colonists were crowding into one of the alleys opposite. Their costumes stood out against the dull buildings. An eddy ran through the mob, as if it had met a sudden blockage. Matt could just see the director still standing in the back of the pick-up with one hand on the camera, waving the truck forward. A line of guards with linked riot-shields in front of him were forcing the people back into the square. The black eye of the camera panned across all of it: the faces distorted with fear, the imploring hands reaching out, the wreck of the stalls, the horsemen, the whips cracking down, down, the peaceful village houses beyond.

Matt held Ed so tight he felt she was part of him. For several minutes neither of them moved. All he could hear was the noise of the screaming, the cracking of wood, the trampling of the horses and, over it all, the slashing of the whips.

'Franklin,' murmured Ed, so softly he could hardly hear her against the clamour. 'Franklin's world.'

Outside the frenzy was dying down. The guards were surrounding a group of dishevelled colonists who were huddled together against the buildings on the far side of the square. The colonists stared round at the destruction as if they half-believed it couldn't be real. Matt recognised Grisha. She was holding Lars cradled against her. There was a streak of blood down one side of his face.

Colonists lay crumpled amid the wreckage of the stalls. Some of them were crying out for help, waving their arms or trying to pull themselves to their feet. One of the technicians was taking close-ups with a hand-held camera, shouting directions to an assistant with an arc-light. Matt felt sick.

Most of the horsemen had dismounted. Some of them were chatting with each other, pointing at the stalls. One of them picked a pie out of a box on the ground, bit into it and spat in disgust. Others were tending their horses, loosening the saddle-girths and preparing to lead them back the way they'd come. Matt stared at the director on the pick-up truck across the square. He was talking to a horseman who was still mounted and gesticulating towards the stalls, clearly excited by the scene he had filmed.

Matt stood up and looked at Ed. She was still sitting there, staring out through the window, horrified. He pulled at her arm.

'We've got to get out of it. Now, while we can. Come on.'

She looked up at him, her eyes wide and bright in the darkened room:

'Market World,' she murmured, 'Everything's faked. And they did that, in the square.'

Matt levered the corner of the plywood back and peered into the alley. There was no one there. He was aware of confused movement back in the square and a noise of horses, men talking, a truck revving its engine. He couldn't hear anyone calling out now. The air stank of pies, horses and the tang of blood. He felt suddenly cold.

He helped Ed through the gap. Her hand quivered slightly in his. They moved swiftly, keeping close to the buildings. They came to an area where the whole street was just a plywood facade. He paused to listen. Everything was still quiet. The smells of the square were fading. He caught the rich scent of grasslands and, more faintly, the resinous odour of pine trees.

Ed squeezed his hand.

'I guess we're clear,' she said.

He realised she was shivering. She looked up at him:

'Oh how I hate Market World. Everything's fake, even the Broken Lands are a lie.'

# 37

Matt put his hand on the plywood façade of the last row of buildings and peered cautiously round it. He motioned Ed forward. In front of them stretched meadow-land, like that he'd ploughed the day before. Here it had been let run wild, the grass and weeds had grown nearly waist-high. A gust of wind blew sharp in their faces. He could see the wave running through the grass behind it. *A country for horsemen,* he thought.

'There's a wall over there,' said Ed, 'We can get behind it.'

Bending low they ran for the wall. It was built of undressed stone, roughly mortared together. Matt hauled himself over it, dislodging the top stone. He reached back to help Ed.

Once on the other side she crouched next to him and peered back over the top:

'It's OK, no-one's following us.'

He didn't answer. She turned and sank down slowly beside him. In front of them the grass was shorter. There was an empty space, then rows of black wooden posts stretched out to another wall in the distance. In front of each of them the ground was humped up.

Matt felt overwhelmed, as if he couldn't take in what he was seeing. He wrapped his arm round Ed and they huddled together in the lee of the wall.

They sat there for a while. The sun rose higher in the sky. He listened to the grass rustling in the wind.

'A graveyard,' Matt said slowly. 'It's a graveyard. Hundreds of them, there must be hundreds.'

After a time, he didn't know how long, he got up and walked to the nearest post. He pulled the grass away from it. A name was scratched on it and a date. *Alison Fenger*. Who was she? And the date was earlier this year. Someone should be remembering her. Someone should be looking after her grave. There was just a wooden post, that was all.

He moved forward, away from the wall. Ed followed, keeping close to him. Sunlight shone down bright all around, but the wind chilled through him.

They moved slowly between the graves. After a while Ed broke the silence:

'Look at the dates. They must start at the far wall. We're back five years now. So many of them, under the ground. This colony's been here a long time. People who make trouble, they send them out here. They never come back.'

She slipped her hand in his.

Matt didn't answer. He kept moving forward, pausing to scratch at one of the posts and inspect a date every now and then. He caught the sound of a lark breaking out into song, high above them. He nodded slowly:

'Sing on, little feller.'

He halted and looked out across the posts, over the stone wall, across the grasslands. Was that the salt of the sea he could smell in the air? Ed was behind him, scratching at the moss on one of the posts.

'Here we are. Twelve years back,' she said.

He thought of the sea. You could find a boat, and you could travel far away from here, maybe beyond the Broken Lands. The wind would take you, you wouldn't have to steer. You could forget all about it, about everything that had happened in Market World.

Ed had pulled most of the moss off the post.

'They're so rotted you can't make out the names.'

He looked back at her.

'We'd better find out,' she said. 'There isn't really anything else to do.'

He took her hand and interlaced her fingers with his. He looked down at the posts around them.

'Posts,' he said. 'Just wooden posts.'

He pulled at the moss on the nearest one. Shards of wood fell away from it. He let go of her hand and moved further down the row.

'This one's a bit better. They used a decent bit of wood. Carved it properly too.'

He scraped the moss carefully off the wood and bent down to read the writing. He took his hand slowly away from the post and touched it against his forehead, his heart and his lips. She watched him sink slowly to his knees.

'Matt!' she said, 'what is it?'

He didn't respond. She moved closer and stooped down. He listened to her reading out the names:

*Marcia Torman* and next to it *Alder Torman* in clear script, incised with the point of a knife. Someone had scratched something below it. She read the words: *Food to the Hungry*. Behind the grave he could see further markers, each with its overgrown hump, stretching away to the distant wall.

Matt felt Ed kneeling beside him. She put her arm round his shoulders and he leaned on her. A cloud covered the sun and moved on.

'We know what happened now.'

Matt spoke at last, softly, his words clear.

'We've found them, here on the grasslands, beside a broken village, here's where their journey ended, at the Colony.'

He looked up at Ed.

'Dad and Mum. I've found them.'

He saw her eyes were filling with tears.

'I'm so sorry,' said Ed. 'Re-education. Settling accounts. This is how they deal with subversives, anyone who makes trouble. They send them out here and they never let them come back. Some they use in the films.'

She sighed.

'I guess my parents are here too, somewhere among these graves. Maybe they're not marked.'

She pointed to the corner of the graveyard. A mound of earth, twenty yards long and as many wide was humped up. She touched her forehead, her heart and her lips. He realised she had been crying soundlessly for some time. His heart went out to her.

'Ed,' he said. 'I'm so sorry.'

Beyond the mound was another pit, newly dug, raw earth next to it. Ed wiped the back of her hand across her eyes. Ed nodded:

'I guess that's for the film shoot today. Maybe you and me, when they'd settled our account.'

She looked across at him.

'We have to get back to the city. We have to tell everyone.'

They sat there for a long time, holding hands, listening to the song of the skylark far above them. Matt thought about the past, about the Enforcers coming out of the woods, how they'd dragged his father from Duke's back, how his mother had held him, how she'd gone to the city and never returned. He heard truck engines starting up in the distance, the vehicles turning and then the sound diminishing as they moved away. He thought of Re-education and of Ed and of the day she'd turned and smiled at him in class. Never owe more than you can pay. It wasn't about paying.

The larks were now silent, huddled in their nests among the grass. The light of common day faded in the west and above them the stars came out, hard and bright in a clear sky. The family in the stadium on Celebration Day came back to him, the way the little boy had looked up at him when he'd been standing there with Ed.

'It'll be a cold night,' said Ed. 'We ought to get moving. They'll miss us at audit if they haven't already, though they'll be a few names short after today.'

Matt looked at her:

'We've got to get the others out. Lars and Grisha. We can't leave them.'

Ed was already on her feet, her hands hugging the doublet to her. He wished they'd let her keep his jacket.

'It's too risky. How will we do it?'

'I don't know, but we've got to. Looking after others, helping people, that's what they don't understand.'

He could see her eyes gleaming in the dark.

'It's the last thing they'll expect us to do, the very last thing.'

# 38

Matt and Ed lay on the top of the ridge looking down into the valley. The grass was soft under his chin. The Colony stood out as an island of light amid the darkness of the pine forest. He could just see the thin silver ribbon of the river snaking down beside it to disappear among the pines. The road zig-zagged down to the left in a cleft in the forest. In front of them were the first trees. The scent of the pinewoods was almost overpowering in his nostrils.

Two yellow eyes stared at them from the edge of the wood. Whatever it was turned away and slunk off. *Black shadows in the forest,* he thought. *I've seen worse.*

He shivered, and pressed Ed's arm gently. They rose, scrambled over the skyline and moved fast, down into the trees.

It was quieter here. The branches muffled the sound and they seemed to be walking on a bed of pine needles. The scent was almost over-powering. He paused and breathed it in.

'I was brought up in a village amongst pine woods,' he said, half to himself. 'It was a long way from here'.

They were deep among the trees now, on a path going downhill. He guessed some animal had made it. He had to hold onto the trunks where it got steep. Ed sometimes slipped behind him and once he caught her as she slithered down. They kept onwards, always downhill. The moon rose and light filtered among the trees. He turned and looked up at Ed, sliding between the trunks, both hands out, holding on where she could. He slowed his pace.

Ahead of them he could hear water. There was a dampness in the air. They must be getting near the river. A light flickered among the trees.

He turned to warn Ed and he heard a noise, metal on metal, the slam of one of the truck doors, not very far away.

'Down,' he whispered, 'something's happening.'

The truck's engine started, then spluttered, started again and caught. People were talking but he couldn't make out the words. The truck engaged gear and started to move slowly. Someone shouted and it stopped. He heard another sound, a dog barking and someone cursing it. He hunched down, closer to the earth.

More noise and the truck moved off, the engine revving. The headlights swept through the forest, lighting up the tree trunks, passing over them and fading off to the left. He could hear the noise of the engine diminishing, then louder again and above them.

'They're going up the zigzag,' Ed whispered. 'They've got dogs.'

'Yeah,' he said. 'They're hunting us, but they didn't think we'd come down here. That dog knew something was wrong, you could hear in the way it was barking.'

He touched her shoulder.

'We've got a chance. They don't know dogs.'

After a few minutes they made their way forward. Matt peered through the last row of trees. Beyond it was the wire fence, and then the parade ground where they had the roll-call, lit up like day-light by the arc lamps.

'No-one around,' whispered Ed. 'They're all in the guardroom. They don't reckon on anyone wanting to break into this place from outside.'

There was a light in the guardroom next to the gate. The sign next to it was floodlit. Matt read:

NORTH COLONY
FRANKLIN CORRECTIVE ENTERPRISES

arched over the emblem of the cartwheel and below:

YOUR RE-EDUCATION, OUR VOCATION

and the slogan:

FAIR'S FAIR

The gate was chained shut. The arc-light glinted on the razor wire strung along the fence posts.

'Let's try round the side, where the river is,' he whispered.

They circled back through the forest until they came to the river bank. He heard the stream tumbling over rocks in front of them, no more than a foot deep.

'If they come after you, run in the river. It'll confuse the dogs.'

'Yeah, everyone knows that. I'll keep my feet dry for now.'

He followed her along the bank of the river to where it ran next to the colony fence.

'They obviously gave this job to the cheapest contractor,' she said, 'Franklin's Fencing Fuck-ups, cheapest quality polished ferrous wire.'

She'd crept forward and was lying along the foot of the fence, just where the spray from a fall in the river splashed up on it.

'It's rusted, look.'

She pulled hard against the wire, working it up and down where it was nailed to the post. There was a snapping noise and the bottom strand sagged. They ducked down. Silence.

'Don't think they heard over the noise of the river. Anyway they should have used galvanised.'

She showed him her hand, palm out. A gash ran across it where the end of the wire had torn the skin. Matt took her hand stroking it, suddenly filled with tenderness for her.

'It's OK,' said Ed. 'You do the next one, you've got the muscles. But keep it quiet.'

# 39

Matt surveyed the compound, shielding his eyes against the lights. Nothing moved, except the insects dancing in the beams. He listened. Nothing. Ed tapped his shoulder:

'There's only the ones in the guardroom,' she whispered, 'the others have all gone with the dogs. They think we're out on the moors trying to get away.'

He nodded. The light glared down, bleaching everything white. He could pick out every pebble, every blade of grass. He rose to his feet and inched his way forward around the edge of the parade-ground towards the dormitory blocks, his hand stretched out in front of him. Nothing.

Ed strolled casually past him to the main entrance and made to twist the handle on the reinforced metal door. She couldn't move it.

Matt touched her lightly on the arm.

'Keep watch.'

He took a firm grip with his right hand, wrapping it round the handle, and covered it with his other hand. He took a deep breath, raised himself on his toes and pushed downwards with all his weight. He felt the strain in his wrists, up along his arms and across his shoulders. The handle wouldn't move. He glanced back across the compound.

He realised that they'd put the hinges outside so the colonists couldn't get at them. He slid his fingers up against the bar that secured the hinge to the door, braced himself and pushed upwards, ignoring the pain in his finger-tips. The door lifted. A final heave and he had it off the pivot, angling out from the doorway on the tongue of the lock.

He moved carefully backwards and laid the door down on the grass.

He felt Ed's arms tight round him.

'Brilliant!' she whispered. Her breath was warm on his cheek.

'If you can get the door to the women's block open, I'll get Grisha. I know where she sleeps. You get Lars, OK?'

He flexed his shoulders, moved across to the women's dormitory and lifted the door up and off the hinges.

*Easy from outside,* he thought, *but you'd never do it from inside.*

Inside the building it was pitch dark. He reached out to the right and felt the rough concrete of the wall, faintly gritty under his fingers. He moved cautiously forward.

Light from the arc lamps trickled faintly round the edge of the shutters. He could just make out the bedsteads ranged along each side of the room. The snores on his left were suddenly interrupted. He froze against the doorpost. A sigh and the sleeper rolled over and started snoring again.

There was enough light to see Lars's face. He looked so young lying there, Matt thought, just like a schoolboy with his freckles, his hand clasping the pillow next to his face. He laid his hand gently on Lars's pale cheek. Lars stirred, rolled half-over and awoke, abruptly, halfway through a snore. Matt could see his eyes, open wide, bright in the darkness. He laid his hand across Lars's lips.

'Shh! It's me, Matt. We've got to get out of here.'

He grabbed Lars's clothes and half-pulled him out of bed. Lars leaned against him and shook his head. There was blood on the side of his face.

'Matt! What's going on?'

'Come on, we're going out.'

'Not without Grisha.'

'Ed's looking after her,' he muttered. 'Get your clothes on, you'll need them. And keep the noise down.'

He grasped Lars's hand firmly and led him towards the door. Lars's hand felt soft in his.

He stepped cautious onto the parade-ground. Everything was still quiet. Ed pushed past him, followed by Grisha leading Lars by the hand. Grisha took a pace forward and stood under the arc lamps, staring round her. She seemed dazed.

'Lars,' she said slowly. 'I'm so glad you're safe. I couldn't find you after they put us on the trucks. I thought... I thought I'd lost you.'

She hugged him to her, so tight it seemed to Matt that she'd never let go.

'Come on,' he said. 'No noise.'

He thought he heard something far away. He raised a hand. Ed cocked her head to one side.

'I can't hear anything.'

Matt stood there listening, his muscles tense. On the wind, clearly now, he could hear the baying of a hunting dog when it scents its prey. Under it, a truck engine revving hard. It must be coming over the crest of the ridge.

They'd all heard it. He saw them looking at each other, caught in the white light of the lamps. There was a clamour of voices from the guardroom and an oblong of light as the door was flung open.

'Under the wire, quick.'

Ed was crouched by the fence, holding up the bottom strand. Grisha threw herself flat on the ground and crawled through. Lars stood where he was, staring at the guardroom. Matt heard the baying again, louder, much nearer now. They'd let the dog off the leash. They'd be racing down the slope after it, swearing, tripping over tree-roots, sliding on the path. He saw torches flashing wildly between the trees. Then the truck roared up to the gate, its headlights swinging across the parade-ground. Matt heard a voice yelling:

'Get the gate open, you fool!'

Matt shoved Lars towards the fence. He nodded, grunted something and crouched down. Grisha seized his hands and pulled him through. They disappeared into the darkness.

Matt was gripping the wire, tearing at it, trying to widen the gap. He heard the splash of water and barking outside the fence and the dog was on them.

Matt could see its teeth, gleaming white in the arc lamps, saliva flecking the muzzle. The eyes blazed at him as it crashed against the fence and then gathered itself to force its head through the gap. Ed sprang back, the jaws snarling up at her. The dog was straining to tear at her legs. Matt let go his hold on the wire and the fence sagged back. The broken wire caught in the dog's collar, holding it there. It twisted from side to side, slavering at them, unable to free itself.

Matt heard the crunch of boots just behind him. He pulled Ed backwards and whirled round. The guard was nearly on him, raising his club to smash it down. Matt bent low and hurled himself forward, driving his head into the guard's stomach and forcing him to the ground. The others were all round him, beating at him with their clubs. He glimpsed Ed trapped between two of the guards, throwing herself from side to side in an effort to escape.

Three of the guards grabbed hold of him and hauled him to his feet. He pulled one of them against his chest, then lunged forward and thrust him backwards into the others. Two of the guards were dragging Ed towards the truck. He fought his way towards her. Someone pulled a coarse black canvas hood over his head from behind and yanked the draw-string tight round his neck. He gasped for breath, choking and they let go of his arms. Someone was sniggering just next to his ear. He blundered sideways, off balance. Something smashed into the back of his head and he fell forward into blackness.

# PART 5: FRANKLIN'S GAME

# 40

Anna paced across the cell. She didn't know if it was daylight outside or night-time. The air smelt musty, as if no-one had disturbed it for a long time. She thought of the trial, of Dain shouting out to her, to the court, to all of them: 'Ms Pascal stopped the riot. The leaflet was nothing', of the judge silencing him.

Four paces. Dain believed in her. She wished desperately she knew where he was now. He'd thrown away his career for her. She touched the unfinished grey concrete, rubbing her hand down the wall, feeling the grit rasp under her fingers.

The judge had given them all the same sentence: North Colony. She had no idea what it meant, but she'd seen the shock eddy across the courtroom. Why weren't they together?

They'd been led down from the courtroom together, Ed and Matt at the front, then Grisha and Lars, then herself. She wondered if she'd get a chance to be with Matt in the transport. She wanted urgently to talk to him, to make everything clear, to explain how she was trying to help. She watched him, Ed beside him and a guard just behind. Matt bent and whispered something to Ed and she glanced up, a smile lighting her face.

They'd been brought out into a courtyard in bright sunshine. A truck stood waiting. She edged forward, towards Matt. Two of Franklin's security guards in their green uniforms, but with leather belts and boots like the Enforcers, were talking to the guards. The taller one was writing something on a piece of paper. He handed it to the guard, and said:

'OK, it's the woman we'll take.'

She just caught Matt's startled expression, his arms wrapped tight round Ed, holding her close against him. The two guards from the court moved towards him, one on each side, their whips raised. Then Franklin's guards seized her by the elbows and forced her back through the doorway into the corridors.

They'd taken her down iron staircases deep into the building, then into a long brick-built tunnel lit by bulbs every few yards, so that you walked between the pools of light. They didn't talk. She felt they were taking her away from the Halls, out under the city. They made her change into green overalls, already stained. Then they took her along a corridor between great iron-bound doors, pulled one of them open and shoved her in here.

She looked round the cell. The floor was paved with stone slabs. A dim light-bulb behind a plastic cowl was the only form of lighting. There was a wooden bed with a rough mattress. She inspected the walls. Someone had scratched the initials: 'A T' and a date twelve years ago next to the door. It meant nothing to her. That was when she started pacing. Four paces between door and end wall.

The door was metal-faced with a small spy-hole and was studded with rivet-heads. The hinges were on the outside. There was a metal shutter, about two inches high by six inches wide, at the bottom. She pushed at it with her foot. It didn't move. She thought about the trial, about the Baby Auction, about the river.

She reached the wall, turned, paced back, turned, paced, pressed her hand flat against the wall, turned, paced to the door, turned, paced back, pressed both palms on the wall and halted. Her thoughts flowed on:

*What will they do to Dain? They'll find a way to get rid of him. Insubordination? Faking evidence? Maybe he's in a cell here, the other side of this wall. Maybe he has his hand against it, just here.*

She stroked her hand gently down the wall, turned and continued pacing. Maybe they'll send us both to a Colony somewhere, maybe we can be together.

Later, there was a noise from the door. She watched as the shutter rattled briefly and flipped open. A brown plastic tray was pushed through, with a slice of grey bread and a bowl of thin bean stew on it. It smelt of nothing. There was a slip of paper in the corner. She picked it up and read:

'Franklin Colony Enterprises. Your Re-education is our Vocation. One hearty vegetarian stew accompanied by a thick slice of artisan bread: only five credits debited to your account. Have a good day!'

Five credits, she thought, I could do a gourmet meal for that, two meals, with wine. And they've left the dumplings out. And there's no spoon. She felt suddenly hungry.

She sat on the bed and ate the stew, using the bread, then tipping what was left down her throat. She licked the last drops from the bowl, wiped her hand carefully across her lips and licked it. She put the tray by the shutter. It was abruptly withdrawn.

She didn't know how long she spent in the cell. She paced between the walls. Occasionally the shutter would rattle, the empty tray would be whisked through and a new one pushed in. Always the same stew, the same invoice. She did exercises: press-ups, sit-ups, squats, jacks. She thought about Dain, his face as he left the courtroom, what they would do to him. She thought about Matt, his arms round Ed, holding her close against his body when he thought they might take her away. She thought about Grisha and Lars.

She lay on the mattress thinking of Dain, of his calm grey eyes, of her fingers running through the grey streak in his hair, of the gentleness with which he'd held the little boy's hand that day behind Franklin's supermarket, of the litheness and beauty of his body. She knew with absolute certainty that he mattered to her more than anyone. After a long time she slept

# 41

In Market World, Celebration Day was more than two months past. Fallen leaves carpeted the City Park. It was early morning and the sun was just above the horizon, hidden in cloud. The first chill of winter was in the wind blowing down Central Boulevard. No-one in the squad of Enforcers standing in the shadow cast by the Residency building allowed himself to shiver.

Dain glanced round at them. He could trust them, the same team he'd taken on the Market raid. *Anna,* he thought, *this is for you.* He tensed as a dark limousine entered the square. Franklin's car. A wave of excitement ran up his spine. He knew Franklin had called an early breakfast meeting in his tower, timed to make it clear to the other entrepreneurs that they met when it suited Tower Enterprises. Dain compressed his lips. *It's convenient to me,* he thought, *the fewer people about, the better.*

Dain gestured with his left hand to the squad behind him. They moved swiftly to their positions, covering the short distance from the Residency to the tower opposite in a few seconds. A second group ran silently ahead of him up the steps to guard the tower entrance. No-one must go in or out.

He moved smartly alongside the car as it drew to a halt at the foot of the steps and opened the rear passenger door.

'Good morning, Mr Franklin. You are called to account, charged with the crime against exchange.'

He continued in a calm, firm voice: 'You have full commercial rights to any confession you choose to make.'

Franklin's head jerked up and Dain saw him grimace.

'What the hell are you talking about?'

Then he grunted and mastered himself. He spoke in more cordial tones:

'Captain Lucas, forgive me, I forget myself. A pleasure to see you so early. May I ask what brings you here at this time in the morning?'

'Mr Franklin, you are called to account.'

'Is this some kind of a joke? I'm sorry, I've got something urgent just now, but we could meet briefly in forty-five minutes. Please feel free to wait in the executive lounge. May I offer you coffee? Breakfast?'

Dain did not smile. He felt completely confident.

'Your meeting has been cancelled. You are under arrest and speak under caution. You will come with me.'

'No. This is intolerable.' Franklin's eyes glinted. Dain saw him signal to his security team in the lobby of the Tower. 'I don't have time for this. You are making an expensive mistake.'

Dain raised his left arm and touched his communicator: 'Adam. Full back-up. Now.'

He smiled at Franklin. The Enforcers had blocked all the exits from the lobby and Franklin's men were no match for them. Two black jeeps drove fast into the plaza, their engines loud. They halted, one in front of the limousine, one behind, trapping it. He gave a second signal and watched Franklin half-turn and suddenly lurch forward. An Enforcer had entered the car silently on the far side, swung across the seat and already had Franklin's wrists bent back for the cuffs.

Franklin gasped. Dain saw his cheeks redden with anger.

'This is an outrage. You over-reach yourself.'

Dain swung himself into the car and sat beside Franklin. He breathed out, relaxing his shoulders. He was beginning to enjoy himself. He watched as another Enforcer pulled the driver out of the car and took his seat.

'To the Halls of Law. Secure Entrance. Don't worry Mr Franklin, we'll make sure no-one sees you being taken into the building.

Oh, Adam, no need to bother with handcuffs. I should have mentioned that earlier.'

Fifteen minutes later Franklin sat in Dain's office, glaring at him. Dain looked out over the city. The sun had risen above the cloud-bank now and the towers were casting deep shadows over the streets. Franklin ran a hand through his hair. He did not raise his voice, but spoke with an incisive edge.

'I demand to see my legal team. You exceed your powers. The compensation will bankrupt you.'

'Calm yourself. This is a breakfast meeting.'

Dain smiled with his mouth, keeping his grey eyes directly on Franklin.

'I don't do breakfast so I'll come straight to the point. You're a busy man. So am I. In the course of my investigations I came across a report into the background to the cartel scandal.'

He placed a thick file on the desk between them. *I owe Adam,* he thought.

Franklin reached towards the file. Dain pulled it away from them.

'You'll get access to all information when you are charged. This is an informal meeting. You are helping us with our investigation. You will be compensated for your time.'

He took a pile of credits from a desk drawer and put them next to the file. He counted six from the top and set them in front of Franklin.

'Standard hourly rate. Same for any citizen. Sign the receipt.'

Franklin grunted.

'I don't see where this is going.'

Dain pursed his lips:

'The file contains information on meetings between the senior Entrepreneurs, chaired, we believe, by yourself. Meetings that do not appear in any official records.' He leaned forward. 'I'd very much like to know what went on in those meetings.'

Franklin waved a hand.

'I don't remember.'

'Indeed? Here is a list of dates. Here are photos of you entering and leaving. I have witnesses who saw you. Secret meetings, to talk about matters of mutual interest, no doubt? What could that be? Fixing prices? Agreeing everything beforehand, sorting out the bribes, just like the Old Market case? Is that how Market World works?'

'Secret meetings? So secret I've never heard of them,' Franklin smiled briefly. 'I don't think your witnesses will have either by the time we get to court.'

'Here's an interesting thing. Each of those meetings took place just before a major movement in the market. A court would find that interesting.'

'OK. So charge me.' Franklin glanced at his watch. 'We've been here half an hour. That phone'll ring in about ten minutes. Tell you what, I'll put money on it.'

Dain kept his eyes fixed on Franklin.

'Perhaps. But this is an informal meeting. Let me tell you something. When we break up a price-ring, a cartel, anything like that, it's always the same. We move in and the smart ones see us coming. They queue up to give evidence against their friends. They hope we'll be grateful.'

He smiled at Franklin.

'We only need one of them. If it's someone authoritative that's a bonus.'

He lifted the file and dropped it with a thud.

'I've just shown you the list of meetings. It's a thick file. What else do you think there is in it?'

He watched as Franklin narrowed his eyes.

'I don't know. You tell me.'

'That would take the risk out of it. Maybe it's the rates you all agree in advance – wages, prices, everything. Maybe it proves that Market World is just a big con-trick. Maybe it isn't.'

Dain paused. He glanced out of the window, at the towers, and back at Franklin.

'You're an entrepreneur, aren't you? I thought you liked risk. Let's be clear what we're talking about. The question is: Do you want to be first in the queue? I'm offering you the chance. And if you don't, there's another question: How much do you trust your friends and associates? How many of them will be in the queue to talk to me?'

Franklin stared back at him. He said nothing for a while, then smiled as if to a friend:

'You don't understand business, do you?'

He had his handkerchief in his hand.

'My duty is to the One Law.' Dain said. 'That law lies at the heart of business in Market World.'

'Business is about winning. It's not about duty and the law. I like to win. Remember that.'

Franklin licked his lips.

'Think of it like this. Everyone competes. Sooner or later they'll be someone out there who does it better, cheaper, faster. Then everyone goes to him, right?'

'That's the risk you take.'

'So what do I do, what do I think about in my Tower? I'll tell you. Nobody really likes risk.'

He grinned.

'It gives you ulcers, you can't sleep when you're worrying, that's what they say. I wouldn't know. Because what you do, what I do, is get the other guy, your competitor on side. You do a deal with him. No risk for him, no risk for you. Everybody's happy, well the two of you are happy. That's business.'

He shrugged.

'In Market World, things work. People like me make them work. If you'd prefer another way, try the Broken Lands. Sometimes people get upset. The thing is …'

He thrust his body forward towards Dain, his eyes glinting:

'Don't be on the losing side.'

He glanced at the phone.

'Oh, this is off the record isn't it?'

Dain nodded, watching him. Franklin went on.

'If it isn't, I'll deny it anyway. And no-one will say anything in court, because they all like it how it is. Bet you.'

He leaned back in his chair.

'I'm telling you all this so we don't have any misunderstandings. You do your job, I'll do mine. Oh, one last thing. How much do you earn? My security chief earns more in a month than you do in a year.'

Franklin's eyes were sharp as knives:

'You're a capable man. Perhaps you could replace her?'

The phone rang.

'Aren't you going to answer it?' Franklin said.

Dain ignored him.

'I think you should. Might be someone important.'

Dain looked past him and called out:

'Adam!'

His deputy entered.

'Shall I answer the phone, Captain?'

'Take the accused downstairs and hold him for further instructions.'

The phone continued to ring. Franklin shrugged and moved towards the door. On the threshold he turned:

'Another thing. I just remembered. Where do you think Anna is, Captain?'

Dain's throat tightened. The noise of the phone beat at his ears.

He directed his attention to Adam.

'That will be all.'

The door closed. Dain grabbed the receiver, holding down the rest with his other hand, so that the call was not yet connected. He thought: *What would Anna want me to do?*

He took a deep breath, released the rest and answered.

'I'm sorry. I've just come into the office.'

'No doubt.'

A soft imperative voice. President Wells herself! He stiffened in the chair. The President continued. Her voice had an edge to it.

'I thought you'd have more sense than to conduct raids without my authority, after everything that's happened. You've made a fool of yourself and you've disgraced my city.'

'Madam President, Franklin and his collaborators are criminals. They fix the entire market. This is a conspiracy against the people.'

'Do you think we don't know that, here on the top floor? The One Law! A trap for the simple-minded, baited with chocolate cake. Willing buyer and willing seller. Fair exchange. Who cares? We must have trust in Market World, we must have order. Do you want to bring the Broken Lands here to the city?'

'But…'

She cut in.

'I had great hopes for you. You're a hero to many people. I was willing to keep you even after that fiasco in the court. You will be replaced by someone who understands how to protect the people. It will be best if you remain in office until we can arrange a suitable transfer. You will not under any circumstances initiate further actions. Is that clear?'

Dain stared out at the great towers in front of him. He thought of President Wells, twenty stories above him, gazing out over the same view.

'You will bring the file to my office immediately. That includes all copies. Everything.'

The phone clicked and he was listening to a dead line, the receiver still pressed hard against his ear. After a while he replaced it. He opened a desk drawer and pulled out his uniform cap. He sat there, holding it with the badge facing him. He could just make out the motto 'Property, Equality, Dignity, Trade' in tiny capitals arched above the crest.

He'd sat in this chair when he interviewed Anna. She'd reached out to him, across the desk: 'The Law is sometimes wrong,' she'd said. And: 'Don't you remember, those children in the alley behind the store? I was proud to be with you that day.'

He knew he'd helped the children because of Anna and because of something his father had once said. And then she'd said: 'You are so precious to me,' and fixed her eyes on him as if he was all that mattered to her. Market World. His duty.

The phone rang again. He ignored it. Time passed. He was roused by a tapping sound. Adam was standing in the doorway, rapping lightly on the open door.

'Captain Lucas, I thought you'd like to know. Mr Franklin has left. Lawyers. They had all the papers signed personally by the Minister. I delayed them as long as possible, but I had no alternative. He left this envelope. Said it was compensation for the time you wasted this morning.'

Adam handed him a sealed envelope, his name scrawled on it in blue ink. Dain dropped it on his desk without looking at it.

'Thank you Adam. Just put the contents through the shredder would you, bag them and bring them to me.'

'But you haven't looked …'

'Adam, as I say.'

Adam returned in a few minutes. Dain poured the thick wad of shredded credit notes into an envelope, sealed it and pushed it across the desk.

'Mail that to Franklin. Recorded delivery. And thanks, Adam.'

'It's my duty. To the One Law.'

'One other thing. All the papers on the Franklin case. They require them upstairs.'

He fixed his eyes on Adam.

'No copies.'

'Certainly Captain, I'll get on to it.'

'Remember: no copies.'

Adam's eye flickered so swiftly Dain could not tell if he had imagined it.

Adam saluted, turned smartly and marched out of the room.

Dain picked up his cap and left the building. He looked up at Franklin's Tower reaching up into the midday sky, and wondered if Franklin was looking down from a high window, if Franklin could see him far below.

# 42

Anna heard the click of the spy-hole in the door. She could just make out the light glinting on the eye the other side. She stared at it, then slowly moved forward and put her hand over the hole. Silence. Then the bolts rattled back and door swung open.

A small rounded man with a worried frown in a neat dark blue business suit stood there, blinking at her.

'Ms Pascal?' he said. 'Come this way.'

He seemed both old and young at the same time, with a lined face and chubby cheeks. Anna noticed he had a thick pink file under his arm.

'Come on,' he said. 'We mustn't be late.'

'Where are we going?' she asked him, but he was already striding ahead of her with short nervous steps along the corridor.

Anna followed him along a passage, up some metal stairs, then into a service lift. He pressed the only button and grinned uneasily at her. The lift rose for what seemed a long time.

'Try to smile a bit,' he said. 'You want to give a good impression.'

The lift halted and the doors opened onto a more spacious thick-carpeted corridor leading to a panelled door, with the word 'Boardroom' on it in gilt letters. Anna caught a faint scent of polished wood.

The small man motioned her forward.

'There you are,' he said. 'Good luck! Oh, don't forget the file.'

He handed it to her. This time the grin was definitely intended to be encouraging.

She walked slowly forward and opened the door. What else was there to do?

'Come in, Ms Pascal, or should I say Anna?'

Franklin sat at the centre of a large oak table, placed lengthways across the room in front of her. He was polishing his glasses. There were others on each side of him. She recognised some of the Entrepreneurs, including the dark-haired woman from the City Council meeting who chaired the Ethics Committee. At one end was a portly man in full Enforcer's uniform. She realised it was the Chief Inspector from the Old Market. There was someone else sitting back from the table, his face in shadow, at the opposite end.

Behind the table the sun streamed in through a plate-glass window the full width of the room. Anna could see the city spread out below them, the lesser towers, the residence blocks, the silver serpent of the river and beyond, fading into the haze, the green of the forest. Somewhere below them out of sight were the Halls of Law. She gasped.

'Nice isn't it?' Franklin remarked. 'On a good day, you can see the sea. Maybe the Broken Lands – at least that's what I tell people, and they believe me. Anyway, the file.'

He held out his hand. She dropped it on the table in front of him. He opened it, pushed the glasses onto his nose, read briefly, then looked up and smiled.

'To business.' He waved a hand to each side. 'I think you know everybody, doesn't matter if you don't.'

Anna knew she must speak calmly.

'But I believe that gentleman is in the North Colony, three hundred miles from here.'

She pointed at the Chief Inspector. Franklin looked swiftly down the table, then back at her, frowning.

'No, he can't be. He's here, isn't he? Perhaps the judge changed his mind.'

Franklin nodded to the figure at the other end of the table, who leaned forward into the light. Anna recognised the sharp eyes and aquiline nose of the judge from Dain's trial. She lifted a hand to her mouth.

'That is a possibility,' the judge remarked. 'I believe the gentleman in question is at liberty, pending an appeal. These cases ...'

Franklin cut in.

'We'll move on. My meeting.'

He smiled at her. She forced herself not to recoil. The important thing was to find out how to help Dain.

'Think of this as an interview, Anna. I expect you've been to many interviews on the other side of the table, but now we are interviewing you.'

He paused and glanced at the folder.

'An interesting CV: CEO Quality Foods, Hero of Enterprise, Young Trader of the Year, Youngest Ever Member of the Guild... Oh, I'm sorry, it says here "stripped of these honours, and now a colonist in the North Colony" – but you're not there either, are you? What will you do next to surprise us? Maybe you'd like to get your titles back.'

She met his eyes.

'I have no interest whatsoever in having anything to do with the Guild or the Council or your lying organisation, Franklin, or any of you.'

The sun lifted over a low bank of cloud. She felt suddenly magnificent, the others reduced to shadows before her in the blaze of light.

'You lie, you cheat, you bribe. I believed in Market World. You destroyed that. I've seen how you forge evidence, how you corrupt judges, how you bring down anyone who's honest, how ...' She was shouting at them: 'What have you done with Dain?'

Franklin shrugged.

The chair of the ethics committee had had her hand raised throughout Anna's speech.

'It's simply a matter of ethics.' She spoke severely, as if Anna was wasting her time. 'You must understand, the greatest good of the greatest number. You say we lie and cheat. Would you rather have the Broken Lands? Now in Market World . . .'

'Enough of that.'

Franklin cut in, silencing her without seeming to raise his voice.

'We're not children. We haven't done anything to Dain yet. Anna, you've seen some of Market World. We've given you plenty of time to reflect. We're grown-ups here, so we're not going to feed you rubbish about the Broken Lands and anarchy and Market World as the pinnacle of civilisation. We're going to make you a proposition. Fair's fair. I like you, Anna. Don't you remember I once offered you a job?'

The handkerchief was hanging down from his top pocket, he must have mopped his forehead, thought Anna.

He slapped his hand down hard on the table.

'There are no Broken Lands.' He smiled, showing his teeth. 'Haven't you realised that?' He dropped his voice to a stage-whisper. 'Don't tell anyone, it would just make trouble.'

Anna shook her head wildly.

'No! I don't believe you. Dain told me, he's been there. . .'

'Yes, Dain. He's been there. To be sure there were areas of disorder in the old days. Things were ...' Franklin waved a hand as if dismissing it, '... unsettled at one time. But that was then, this is now. We had to give the people something to explain why it was so bad in the early stages, the Great Hunger and all that. Nasty stories to frighten children.'

He gave a snarl of laughter and glanced swiftly along the table. Anna could see that the entire board was intent on him, apart from the judge whose gaze was fixed on Anna, as if she was a criminal.

Franklin continued smoothly.

'We came to an understanding, just to keep everyone happy. We'd tell stories about the Broken Lands. We'd say they were everywhere, all round us. We'd tell people how lucky they were to be in Market World, the only safe place in a continent of carnage, slavery, rape and destruction.'

He waved again. This time his gesture included the table, the building, the window and all of Market World, stretched out before them.

'They lapped it up. Everyone loved it. They all cheered Market World. And they worked so much harder, without anyone having to make them do it.'

He nodded to the dark-haired woman.

'You'll excuse me stealing your line, but I do like to hear the sound of my own voice. It's business ethics, the greatest good of the greatest number. It makes everyone happy, well everyone who counts.'

He smiled modestly and dipped his head.

'And it's all down to me.'

Anna hated him.

'But the films on Celebration Day … I've seen it, the warlords, the riots, the massacres, the endless toil, the horsemen smashing the market. I've seen the Broken Lands too.'

'Of course you have. So have we all. Not bad films are they? I made them, well one of my companies did. We use actors, stooges, stand-ins, call it what you will. The sets are pretty impressive, aren't they?'

He looked seriously at her.

'We're updating them now. All that stuff about warlords, it's old hat. Strikes and demonstrations are the real problem these days, urban disorder. It's becoming a serious issue. People have to know it's the protestors who are the real enemy.'

He smiled.

'So now we'll have films of the demonstrators smashing things up, attacking ordinary people. Then our gallant Enforcers crush them and restore order. Everyone'll believe it's true, you'll see.

And then it will be true, more or less. If you're going to tell a lie, make sure it's a big lie.'

Anna felt anger flooding through her. She wasn't going to shout at them. She was going to remain calm:

'Dain fought all his life. That was his duty. To stop the Broken Lands coming here. To make order in the world. He did that for you.'

'Of course. We come to Dain. Dain is making trouble. That's why we've brought you here. He wants to re-open the investigation. He's making accusations against senior Entrepreneurs. Yesterday he tried to question me.'

Franklin's eyes flashed.

'That grated. Not a problem of course, we've dealt with people like him before, but it comes at a bad time. As I was saying, there's a lot of trouble in the city these days, and some people think he's a hero.'

Franklin's eyes were on her, chill as midnight. Anna realised the whole Board were staring at her. *What were they going to do to Dain?*

Franklin leaned forward slightly:

'So here's our proposition: we'd like you to talk to Dain, explain things to him. Talk him round. He has a great career in front of him if he shows sense. If not, he's nothing. He'll end up like his father – tell him that, he'll know what I mean.

You could be very helpful, Anna. I'm sure we could arrange an appeal, errors in the evidence, fresh witnesses, no case to answer, generous compensation, that sort of thing. My friend on the right understands all this.'

He lifted a hand to the judge.

'No need to comment, judge. Anna, you've met the inner circle. You're a talented young woman, you could do well, very well out of this. Maybe one day you could join us on the Board. And

Dain, who knows? I want you to think of this as a growth experience. We've all had them haven't we?'

His gaze ranged along the Board. Anna saw that none of them could meet his eye. The former Chief Inspector shifted in his chair. She felt the anger inside her like a beast she must master. She spoke firmly, emphatically, as if to someone who might have difficulty grasping what she was saying:

'There is absolutely no way I could lie to Dain, no way I could make him your servant. He would hate me. He's worth fifty of you. And so are his parents, and Matt and Ed and Grisha and Lars and all of them.'

She fell silent. She had nothing more to say. She had done exactly what Dain would have done, if he'd had the same offer. She would never betray him.

Franklin stared at her for a full minute. Then he slowly closed the file and slid it off the desk.

'I see. No go. I liked you. You've let me down.'

He glanced swiftly along the table.

'We're agreed I think. You've wasted our time. You could have been an entrepreneur. Now you're just an escaped colonist. Maybe they'll send you to the North Colony. That's where we make the films. Have you ever met anyone who's come back from the North Colony?'

He rubbed a hand over his face.

'I used to like you Anna, you … forget it. I'll give you a chance.'

He gestured to someone behind her

'Throw her out with the rubbish.'

Hands grasped her by the shoulders and dragged her backwards to the door. Franklin stared at her for a second and then closed his eyes, ignoring the attempts of the business ethics chair to attract his attention. The last Board member she saw as the door swung shut was the judge, a thin smile on his face, his eyes still fixed directly on her.

# 43

Anna got slowly to her feet and put out a hand to support herself. The metal door slammed shut behind her. She was leaning against a brick wall some three metres high with rubbish piled against it. She looked up at the tower above her reaching into the evening sky. She was in an alley somewhere behind Franklin's castle. She had to get away before the Enforcers came. She started walking, then she broke into a run. She rounded a corner and halted abruptly. *Don't draw attention to yourself!* She stood out like a neon-sign, a young woman in filthy convict's overalls. The wind chilled her.

She felt alone, an outcast, hated by every honest citizen. She walked smartly as if she had somewhere to go. It was a quiet middle-class residential street. Evening was drawing on, she could see the windows lighting up. She imagined families returning home after work, the evening meal, conversations about the day's doings, putting children to bed. She had no money. If she asked anyone for food, they'd call the Enforcers. She wrapped her arms round herself. There was a much larger road at the end. She could see people crossing and hear the rumble of traffic. There would be shops, maybe Enforcers patrolling. She ducked into the first side-alley she came to.

The alley was so dark that at first she could see nothing. The walls reached up above her, at least four stories high on each side. Dim light filtered past shutters on some of the windows. She moved forward, her feet scuffing through rubbish, and turned a corner. Another alley stretched in front of her, a larger road at the end of it. She turned right, then right again, deeper into the maze.

There were smells all round her. Rotting fruit she recognised, sweat and foul water, but there were other smells, sharp, pungent overlaying them. Something scurried round a corner, perhaps a small animal in the rubbish. She moved quickly into another alley, tripped on some rubbish and fell forward, her right palm landing on something sticky. She got to her feet and rubbed her hand down the wall.

She heard footsteps behind her. She paused. The footsteps came to a halt. She ran blindly, dodged through an archway and stumbled down steps. Her feet slid, she grasped the wall to keep her balance and stood there, trying to quiet her breathing. There was silence, only the noise of water running somewhere nearby. She moved on more slowly.

She thought of Dain. She must tell him about Franklin, about everything. She kept the thought of him there within her, as if he were a tiny flame of warmth. Someone would find her soon. Then they'd send her away. If only she could get to him first.

There was a fresh noise, a whistle. She couldn't tell if it was human or an animal or a bird. It seemed to be behind her. She rushed forward, panting. The whistle came again, in front of her. She took three paces back and then took a side-turn into yet another alley. The whistle was closer. She rushed across a tiny square, past a sudden burst of light from a shop-front, then down another alley. She crouched in an angle of the wall. She stayed there for a long time. She could see movement in the darkness. She willed herself to keep still. She felt a warm tongue licking her fingers. She ran her fingers through the fur. After a while she heard purring and felt the pulse of the tiny throat.

Finally the cat gave a sharp animal cry and was gone. She straightened up, listened and sniffed the air. Everything quiet. The people who lived round here worked hard and went to bed early.

She was completely lost. She moved on, down the alley. The clouds must have moved away. There was a faint light from the sky and she saw that she was now in a more respectable area. The alley grew slightly wider and then narrowed so that she could only just squeeze through the gap. After a short distance, the path opened out into a larger square, with a park in the middle.

She glanced both ways and waited unseen while a man in a thick overcoat passed by. Then she ran across the road. There were trees in the park, tall elms. She found that it was slightly warmer underneath the branches. A small wooden hut stood in a corner next to a heap of leaves. She tugged at the door. It was locked. She looked round in all directions. A few streets away, reaching up over the blocks she could just make out the unfinished tower of the cathedral. She remembered the tiny silver cross on the chain around Dain's neck.

There was no-one in sight. She bent down and burrowed into the leaves. She was too cold to sleep. Maybe she could hide for another day, but after that someone was bound to find her. She lay there staring up, wondering if Dain saw the same sky, wondering about Matt and Ed and Grisha and Lars, wondering what stars shone down on them.

# 44

Dain walked on towards the Plaza, aware of the lesser towers rising up around him. Central Boulevard stretched out in front, lit up by the glow of the shop-windows. It was mid-morning, a watery sun and a chill wind in the alleys. The people on the street walked fast, their shoulders hunched, eager to get inside, out of the cold.

*Market World,* he thought, *my parish. It's rotten at the heart. I tried to heal it, to do my duty. President Wells is against me. They've thrown me on the scrap-heap.*

He kept walking without thinking consciously about where he was going.

*Anna loved me, and I couldn't find a way to help her. She was a trader, a member of the Guild. Was she part of Franklin's world?* He shivered. *How many of these people, walking between the towers are part of it? What are they carrying in those briefcases that matters so much?*

He turned a corner, and another. Now he was among the better class of residence blocks close to the city centre, a district of tree-lined squares. There were private gardens in front of the blocks, with railings and locked gates. The buildings were faced with stucco here, and had much larger windows than further out, where the poorer people lived. He knew they had lifts and that there were underground garages and private gym clubs. All of them had security systems. Some even had hall porters, staring out at him from behind plate-glass doors. He noticed them turning away when he glanced at them.

The wind had stripped the trees. Gardeners were raking up the leaves. A bonfire burned in one corner of the square, the wind whipping the thin stream of smoke away. He passed close to one of the gardeners, an older man with a prominent nose pinched white by the wind, dressed in a muffler and heavy jacket. His eyes were shielded by the flat cap he wore pulled down over his forehead.

'Good morning,' said Dain, 'Chilly day.'

The man grunted and turned away, busying himself with the leaves. Dain realised the other gardeners had already moved away and had their backs to him.

*Do they all hate me? The black uniform. Don't they remember the Old Market? Don't they understand that without Enforcers they would have no Law?* His mind went back to his words on Celebration Day: 'Only one man may stand outside the market. Only one man does not sell to the highest bidder. That man is the Enforcer.'

He walked rapidly on. He was aware of someone in an alley to the right, but when he looked up they were gone. The strikers' song: 'Franklin, Franklin, show you care, Franklin, Franklin, pay us fair' was chalked up in fading capitals on the end wall.

He would soon pass the last of the towers, still unfinished. It was half the height of Franklin's, a framework of massive girders with the pods for offices, meeting rooms, residences and leisure facilities slung between them. There was plenty of space for new pods. He could see the lifts crawling up among the struts.

His eye was caught by something white fluttering high above. Birds used to cluster round the market until the hawks drove them away. Now he could see a whole flock of them, wheeling and plunging downwards, riding on the eddies in the air round the building. The wind caught them and they were driven towards him. He realised they were leaflets, hurled from a high window.

One slanted downwards, circled above him and fell, flapping open on the pavement. He picked it up. He'd seen it before, the cartoon graphics from the Baby Auction, Franklin taking the children from the poor and giving them to the rich, the leopard grin on his face, the rolls of credits stuffed into the pockets of the business suit straining over his fat body. Dain flipped it over and glanced at the back of the piece of paper. He saw there was new text here, more crudely printed:

NOW FRANKLIN HAS THE ENFORCERS ON
THE PAYROLL!

*What happens if you demonstrate against Franklin Enterprises?*
*You get a free one-way ticket to the North Colony*
*and you don't ever come back.*
*That's what happened to the Baby Auction Five*
*just because of a peaceful protest*

The text went on, about poverty wages, the trial, free speech and food prices, about Anna and Matt and Ed and the others and the arrest. There was a cartoon of Franklin handing a bulging briefcase, credit-notes bursting out of it, to an Enforcer in Captain's uniform, the Star of the City on his breast.

Dain stared at it, horrified, then crumpled the leaflet and forced it into his pocket. At the exit of the square he glanced back. The gardeners were huddled together. They had one of the leaflets. One of them glanced at him, then turned away and snatched the leaflet into his pocket. He quickened his pace.

*The One Law is the only answer. I have always believed that. Anna will understand.*

He thought of the Broken Lands, of his father in the village, of his mother standing there, left behind on the moonlight shore. They'd thought they could make things better by kindness, by sharing, by helping people. They were wrong.

He had no idea how far he'd walked. He was chilled to the bone. He turned corners at random, threading his way through the city. His mind was full of images: Anna's face luminous with joy, whirling in his arms at the Residency; Anna sitting at Franklin's table; Anna with the child in her arms, the river water staining her yellow dress; Anna in his office after he'd arrested her, shaking her head, unable to accept that she'd done anything wrong; Anna who wouldn't let him help her find a way out; Anna standing there alone in the courtroom. He thought of the others with her when he'd arrested them all at the Baby Auction. They stared at him, Ed with her shock of brown hair and Matt with his puzzled eyes and open face.

He turned a corner. He thought he saw someone slip into a side-turning. He quickened his pace. The alley opened out into a square. The cathedral, still half-built, rose up in front of him. He knew they'd run out of money three years ago. He halted, and stared up at the façade, an array of rough concrete columns, bunched together so close you couldn't see the gaps between them, rising to the golden cross at the apex. The stub of the tower behind had a spider-work of scaffolding round it. They hadn't even started on the spire that would top it.

*My father's world,* he thought, *duty to god, whoever he is. Oh, why didn't you run away with mother and me, why did you try and stop the horsemen?*

He was aware of someone behind him. He turned sharply and glimpsed a figure ducking back into the alley. He followed. The residence blocks here were so close together that he felt he was walking into twilight after the square.

A hand reached out of a side-turning and grasped his wrist, the fingers cold as winter ice. He whirled round.

'Dain. I have got to talk to you.'

'Anna!'

He pulled her forward. The drab denim overalls hung loose on her body. There was a rent in one sleeve and dark stains across the chest. He wrapped his arms round here and held her close against him. She was so thin! He plunged his face into her black hair. Then he tilted her head back and pressed his lips against hers.

# 45

They kissed for a long time. Anna's could think of nothing but the simple fact that Dain was there with her.

'I was so desolate,' she said, the words tumbling out. 'I thought they'd taken you away somewhere, to a Colony.'

He wrapped his jacket round her and held her gently, warming her.

'I'm so happy you're here,' he said. 'But how did you find me?'

She nestled against him.

'It was the cathedral, I just thought you might be somewhere near the cathedral, if you were unhappy.'

*I found him,* she thought. *I know he'll believe me.*

'There's so much to tell you,' he said. 'Now I know the truth. Franklin's a traitor, he's betrayed the One Law. I arrested him. They let him go.'

He pulled her tight against him, the familiar body against his.

'Listen to me, please listen,' she said. She reached up with both hands and held his face.

'Everything's a lie, the Broken Lands, everything. I know it is. I've got the proof. Franklin told me to my face.'

Dain stared at her for a second and then nodded. She went on:

'They kill people; no-one ever comes back from the North Colony. After the trial they didn't send me there with Matt and Ed and the others. You must understand. They'll kill them, all of them, I know they will. We've got to save them.'

Dain led her across the square and along the grey stone flank of the cathedral, to a side door. He took her inside and she stared up at the huge empty hall, the great columns reaching up to the roof far above them. There was a glow of light about the altar and a great golden cross above it but everywhere else was in darkness. The sounds of workmen echoed around her.

'Sit down', said Dain. 'I come here to think. You're safe here. I won't be long.'

He kissed her again. She wrapped the jacket tighter round her, smelling the scent of him from the collar, and leaned back on the bench.

In a few minutes Dain returned holding a bowl and a mug of coffee. She smelled bean stew and realised how hungry she was. He grasped her hand, warming it between his.

'Tell me what happened,' he said. 'I know they rigged the trial, they wanted you out of the way.'

She took a large spoonful and swallowed it.

'I was so proud on Celebration Day, sitting at the front of the prestige stand with a ticket for the reception in my pocket.'

She smiled up at him.

'That's when I fell in love with you,' she said. 'You were so real, everything about you was splendid.'

'I couldn't take my eyes off you,' he said, 'standing there at the front of the stand, with your hand in a salute. I nearly forgot to give the order to march on.'

She leaned forward and kissed him full on the lips. She held him to her, as tight as she could.

'I love you,' she said softly.

His arms were round her, embracing her. She remembered the warmth that would suddenly come into his grey eyes, like the sun glancing on deep water, the grey streak across his stiff dark hair, the way he'd been there, on her side, in the courtroom.

'I love you too,' he said.

She ran her hand gently down his face from forehead to chin.

'Then that man ran out,' she said. 'It was Matt, and Ed was there trying to help him. But he isn't a trouble-maker. He saved that child in the river. He just wants to help people.'

Dain spoke gently:

'I was trying to do what was right. My duty, but I was wrong all the time. It seems a long time ago. President Wells is against me. They'll throw me out of the Enforcers as soon as they can find an excuse. They don't want a scandal.'

'Those films they show us about the Broken Lands,' she said. 'They're fakes. They make them in the North Colony. Franklin's behind it. He's got a film crew, they make the colonists dress up and they film them. The Broken Lands are a lie, it's just a trick to make people think Market World is better than anywhere else. It's horrible, Franklin laughs about it. He thinks it's a joke.'

She felt his body go tense.

'My parents…' he said.

'He laughed about that too. Said I should tell you. There were places where there was chaos, local warlords, but it's gone now. He said your parents were nothing.'

Dain spoke slowly.

'They gave their lives for what they believed in. And I gave my life to the One Law.'

He fell silent.

'I know you did,' she said. 'You did that because you wanted to help. You're worth fifty times what he is. So are your parents. I told him that.'

Her eyes glowed with passion. She dropped her voice.

'You know how the film ends, the soldiers sweeping into the market-place, riding everyone down, wiping them out. Matt and the others are still there. They'll kill them.'

Dain stared at her. She could see tiny images of herself reflected back from deep within his eyes.

'Come on,' he said. 'I'll take you somewhere safe where you can rest. Then I'm going to take a trip north.'

# 46

Matt shook himself awake. He was lying on a mattress in the corner of a small brick room, in the grey light of early morning. His whole body ached. He could feel the bruises down his left side where they'd kicked him.

When the hood had come off he'd been in the guardroom by the gate. He'd braced himself, but they'd just shoved him into the holding cell next to it. He sat there thinking of Ed, remembering her face as they dragged her away, twisting her body furiously as she struggled between two of the guards. *If I'd moved faster, she'd have got under the wire. I've got to get out of here, I've got to find her.*

He'd been in the cell for a couple of days. He could hear the voices next door when they changed guard on the gate. *They're taking that seriously now,* he thought.

'Get this lot on.'

He realised he'd been woken by the noise of the door opening. He recognised the crew-cut guard who'd beaten him on the parade ground earlier.

'What have you done with Ed?' he demanded.

The man grinned at him.

'You'll find out.'

He threw down a pile of clothing and slammed the door.

Matt got to his feet. He held up the jacket and felt the cloth: good quality, in fact the kind of outfit that would once have been worn by a respectable villager, a miller perhaps or a blacksmith, on market day. It was a wool mixture, green and yellow with tiny flecks of orange. There were some boots, again well made, leather, worn but carefully mended and resoled, and a cloth cap with a peak. The cut was traditional, a style that people would have thought of as old-fashioned when he was young.

He held the suit against his face and smelled it. There was a faint odour of outdoors. He caught heather and the aroma of the pine trees.

He was still dressed in the market clothes, the tights, ripped when the guards overpowered him, and the velvety doublet, the brightest thing in the cell, purple and yellow. He took these off and put on the clothes, sliding the shirt carefully over the bruises. He wondered if Ed was still in her party clothes.

After a few minutes the key scratched at the lock and the door swung open again. A guard stood on either side.

'Out you come,' the taller one said. 'No tricks.'

They both held cattle-prods, the points towards him.

He walked out into bright daylight and looked round, blinking. He was on the parade ground in front of the colony buildings, the dormitory block to his left. Green-uniformed guards stood in two lines, wearing full body-armour and gauntlets, their visors down and the spiked goads in their hands. At the far end was the truck, its awning flapping. He could hear its engine ticking over. After the confinement of the cell, the smell of the pine trees was almost overpowering. He glanced at the fence where Grisha and Lars had crawled through. Razor wire had been strung across the gap. He could see the rust on the other strands of wire from where he stood. There was no sign of Ed.

'Eyes front. Get in the truck,' the voice ordered.

Someone shoved him and he lurched forward. The guards raised the cattle-prods towards him. Matt felt the muscles in his arms tense. The guard behind him shoved him again.

'In the truck!'

Matt moved slowly forward. He could see the guards closing in behind him out of the corner of his eye. He was suddenly grasped and hoisted over the tailboard. The awning was pulled shut and laced by one of the guards in the truck before he could turn and look out. He got to his feet. There were three of them, with helmets and body-armour.

'Special treatment for you, you're a film star,' said one of the guards. 'Got your own limo.'

'Where's Ed?'

'That's her name, is it? You'll find out.'

The truck's engine revved and it jerked forward, causing all of them to sway. He sat on the bench staring at the guards in the half-light. He felt the cloth of the jacket between thumb and forefinger. Hand-sewn. Made by a village tailor, maybe forty years ago.

# 47

Matt sat there, thinking about Ed and the clothes and what the guard had said. He was aware of the truck swinging round the bends of the zigzag, and swaying at the top of the ridge. *It's moving faster than before, I guess it's a lighter load.* He eyed the guards in their green uniforms. There were three of them, all alert, all glaring at him. The engine settled to a high-pitched constant whir. He guessed they were running fast across the grasslands. The truck slowed, swung to the right and came to a halt.

'OK, time to get out,' grunted one of the guards, reaching up to unlace the canvas. The other two kept themselves behind him.

One of them prodded him with the club:

'Move it.'

He stumbled just before he reached the tailboard, then straightened suddenly and sprang over it. Two guards grasped him, one from each side, just as he landed.

'Watch yourself.'

Two others were standing nearby with cattle-prods, the spikes towards him. All of them had their visors down. In front of him he saw more canvas, white this time, blue sky above it. He realised it was a large tent. One of the guards lifted the flap. Matt just had time to catch a glimpse of the market village away to one side before they thrust him through. It took him a second to adjust to the dim light inside the tent.

'Take it easy,' said a voice he'd heard before. Des Riddell, the director, stood there, dressed in his shabby safari suit, hands on hips, his full lips grinning. 'I don't want my star to hurt himself.'

'Where's Ed?'

Riddell nodded. She stood there held tightly between two of the guards. She wore a calf-length dress with long sleeves, light yellow sprigged with posies of flowers, a holiday dress for a villager. Her hair was pulled back under a matching narrow-brimmed bonnet. She stood in front of a trestle table, paperwork stacked high on it, a film canister acting as a paper-weight, a telephone and upright chairs in a half circle behind it.

'Ed! Thank God you're OK.'

'Hi! I'm glad to see you. You had me worried last night.'

He started towards her and found that the guards from the truck were standing each side of him, holding him by his arms. They had their visors up so they could see inside the tent. He tried to twist his body forwards but there were other guards grabbing at him. Anger flamed within him.

'Let go of her!' he shouted.

Des rushed between them waving his hands:

'Take it easy, save it for the set. Now listen to me you two, you're my stars. It's the time of the Great Hunger. You're leading a big demonstration, it's for one of the trade unions they had before we banned them. You're holding the banner, one of you each side.'

He looked from Matt to Ed.

'You will behave yourselves won't you? You're film stars for the day. Everything depends on you. You're young, in love and you're together, you're leading the people. Everyone's cheering, everyone's on your side, just keep hold of that.'

Des had clasped his hands together. There was something strange about his eyes. Matt realised he was trying to look up at them winningly.

'Ed, are you all right? If any of them…'

'I'm all right, but I was really scared for you. Oh, do what he says. Don't let's have a fight here, we've had so many of those. Let's be film stars together, just for a day. You know me, I always mean what I say, don't I? Every time?'

She nodded, then she gave a little shake of her head.

Matt nodded and relaxed his shoulders. He felt the gloved hands loosen their grip. He let his shoulders slump, then wrenched himself suddenly forward. He had his arms round her before any of them reacted. Somewhere he could hear Des's shrill voice:

'That's what I want to see! Raw passion! It's so authentic! Get the camera in here!'

The guards had their hands on him. They were heaving him backwards, away from Ed. She whipped up her right arm and punched hard over his shoulder at someone behind him. He jerked his head backwards with all the strength in his body and he felt his skull smack into something soft. Another guard was running at them, the goad held like a spear in front of him. He swung Ed out of the way. A black-uniformed figure stepped forward and tripped the guard.

A voice spoke with the firmness of accustomed authority:

'That's enough.'

Everyone looked round. Matt saw a figure in the black uniform of the Enforcers standing there, staring calmly at them, a grey streak across his black hair. The other Enforcer picked up the cattle prod and inspected the tip. Matt saw that he was an older man with greying close-cropped hair. A scar ran from the corner of one eye to his mouth.

The Enforcer inverted the cattle prod, gripped it with both hands and stabbed the spike down through the wrist of the sprawling guard, pinning him to the ground. The guard shrieked. His arm twitched. Matt felt the others release their grip on him. One of them was rubbing at his face, blood trickling from his nose.

'Stand back,' said the younger Enforcer. 'These two come with us.'

Matt noticed the three silver stars at his collar and recognised him: Captain Lucas from the trial.

The guards looked to one of their number, who pushed up his visor to show a youthful face, startlingly blue eyes and a broken nose. He dropped his hand to touch the club at his belt:

'Who the hell are you?'

'We're Enforcers from the City Guard. That's all you need to know. I know you: Jerry Knowles. Dishonourable discharge for selling the One Law. I wonder if Mr Franklin is aware of that. You do well to stay out of the city.'

The guard hesitated then stepped back and motioned to his men to down their weapons. Matt felt Ed relax against him.

Lucas pointed to Matt and Ed: 'You will come with me.'

'They're my stars!' shouted the director.

The older Enforcer turned to him:

'Des Riddell you call yourself, but you used to be Dickie Farran. The Farran Adult Movies Scam? Everyone a film star? We've got a file on you too.'

The director backed away:

'I've paid for that. I work for Mr Franklin now,' he said, his voice uncertain.

Matt watched the director's backside collide with the table. It tipped up and the top slipped sideways off the trestles. Papers cascaded down and the phone clattered on the floor. The film canister rolled towards the door of the tent. Dain leaned forward and scooped it up.

'I'll take that.'

'But there's a week's work there,' yelped the director.

'Don't worry, Dickie, it'll be watched. You'll get compensation if you ask for it. With proof of identity.'

The older Enforcer stepped over to the phone and stamped on it twice, crushing it to black plastic shards. Captain Lucas turned to Matt and Ed.

'Come on.'

Matt didn't move.

'Where are we going?' He kept his arms firmly round Ed. 'I don't trust Enforcers. You tried to help Anna at the trial, but you did nothing for the rest of us.'

Dain stopped and looked at him for a moment.

'I serve One Law and no man. It's these thugs who work for Franklin. Anna escaped. She told me what's going on here. She told me the truth. That's why we came for you.'

Ed glared at him. 'I don't trust Enforcers.'

Adam turned to face her.

'The Great Hunger,' he said. 'That's when I got my scar. I had faith in the One Law, then. It was against the black marketeers, the profiteers who wanted to make money out of starving people, did you know that? We fought them and we won. Franklin has betrayed us.'

He pulled his tunic open. Matt saw a mass of scar tissue, pink welts and ridges running across one side of his chest from waist to shoulder. Ed gasped. Matt stepped forward and hesitated.

Adam zipped his tunic up.

'Franklin.' He spat on the ground. 'Come with us or stay here.'

He led them out of the tent. Once in the open, Matt glanced round. None of the guards had moved from where they were standing. A brand-new jeep with the Enforcer's insignia on its pennant was drawn up next to the tent. The paintwork was glossy black, spattered with mud from the journey. Dain got into the front passenger seat.

'Coming?' he said.

Ed jumped up onto the bench seat. Matt followed her.

Adam started the engine. The senior guard had followed them. He laid a hand on the windshield:

'What about the receipt for the prisoners?'

Dain pursed his lips.

'In the post,' he said. 'Oh, I forgot. Here's your compensation, citizen.'

He flung a handful of small change hard in the younger man's face. Matt winced as the guard clutched at his eyes and staggered backwards.

Adam let in the clutch and stamped hard on the accelerator. Dain turned to him and said clearly, above the noise of the engine:

'Guess that's the end of my career.'

Adam nodded.

'Yup.'

# 48

Ed braced herself against the back of the seat in front and glanced sideways at Matt. He put his arm round her and she leaned against him, half asleep. She was comforted by the soft regular movements of his breathing.

Adam drove fast, and soon they were past the Colony buildings. They drove on through the forest, onto a cobbled road and down the main street of a small village. The blare of the jeep's exhaust echoed from the buildings. She couldn't see many people around. They seemed to shrink back when they caught sight of the black Enforcer's jeep. Adam accelerated on the road into the forest. The trees seemed thinner here. She saw daylight between them.

The sun slid down the sky and the trees to the right cast long shadows across the road. She realised they were heading south. After a while Adam switched on powerful headlights. He turned the jeep onto a straight two-lane highway without slackening speed and pushed the accelerator to the floor.

The only other vehicles she saw were slow-moving timber lorries. Adam reached under the seat and pulled out a bag which he passed over his shoulder, his eyes still on the road. She smelt bread and cheese, and bit hungrily into the sandwich Matt passed to her. He'd slipped his arm out of the jacket sleeve and pulled the cloth round over her. She nestled against the warmth of his body, with the cold air racing past outside. She could feel his pulse somewhere in his neck. She looked upwards to where bright stars, unimaginably distant, shone down on her, on Matt, on all of Market World.

She was awakened by the sound of traffic. The first thing she saw was Matt's face:

'Wake up,' he said, 'We're in the city.'

She saw that the jeep had stopped on a deserted street outside a residence block that seemed semi-derelict, the front wall seamed with cracks. A buttress of wooden beams supported it. There were no street-lights. She couldn't see Dain anywhere. Adam turned on a powerful torch and led the way up a darkened staircase. Ed was aware that Matt kept glancing round, checking the doorways and the stairwell.

'Safe house,' said Adam. 'Whole area's due for redevelopment. No-one'll trouble you here. Food in the fridge. Bolt the door, don't go out. We'll join you here as soon as we can.'

He handed her the torch.

'You have to trust people.'

He closed the door and she heard him run down the stairs and start the jeep. The noise of the engine faded as the vehicle passed rapidly through the empty streets.

She glanced round the living room. There was a grey sofa and carpet and a television set hinged to the wall. A plastic-topped table and two upright chairs stood in one corner. Everything came from one of Franklin's stores, everything the same as in a thousand other flats. She could see a kitchen leading off on one side with green walls and an obsolete gas stove. There was another door, closed, opposite it.

She watched Matt as he slammed home the bolts on the door. She took one of his hands in hers and drew him towards her.

'We made it. We got away from of the Colony, and Dain knows we're telling the truth.' She reached up with her free hand to push back the hair from the side of his face. She ran her hand tenderly down his cheek.

'And I'm here with you.'

She slid her hand to the nape of his neck as he bent forward and kissed her. Her heart was so full she felt it would burst. She was completely certain that this was the one she wanted, the one she had always wanted, would always want.

She gazed up at him, at his face, his eyes, blue as gentian. He opened his mouth to speak. She lifted her hand and laid her fingers gently across his lips.

'Shh,' she said 'No more talking.'

She took his hand, turned and walked the three paces to the bedroom door, his hand grasped in hers. She led him through and closed the door behind them.

# PART 6: FINAL SETTLEMENT

# 49

Five days later Matt stood at the back, in the cheapest area of the stadium. He was wearing a badly-fitting business suit that he'd found in the wardrobe at the safe house. He felt out of place, like a birthday present no-one wanted. He glanced at Ed beside him, dressed in the clothes that had hung next to it: an imitation silk shirt and a matching jacket and trousers in dark blue with a faint orange stripe. Tenderness flooded through him. *How confident she looks, at ease with herself - and she's here with me.* She glanced up at him. He slipped his arm round her.

He knew it was Jobs Mart Day, the other big festival in Market World's calendar apart from Celebration Day. The others would be doing the difficult stuff. Their part was to make sure the leaflets got out.

They'd all met at the flat a couple of days ago. Adam had brought Dain and Anna.

Matt stared at her:

'We didn't know what they'd done with you. We were really scared.'

Her eyes were dark as indigo.

'I'm here,' she said, 'and I've learnt the truth about Franklin.'

There were explanations about how she'd been held in the city and how she'd had the meeting with Franklin. She was the one who'd told Dain about the Colonies and the film-making.

'It's you we must thank for saving us, Ed and me,' Matt said. 'That was wonderful.'

She bowed her head to him, and smiled.

She stood so close to Dain that they were constantly touching each other. Matt felt happy for her. It was the first time he'd seen Dain smile. Matt felt Ed's hand slip into his and pressed it fondly.

Everyone was talking at once. There had been a big file of papers and a lot of talk about Franklin and Market World. Anna seemed to take the lead. He remembered her saying:

'I never wanted to hate anyone, but I think I hate Franklin. I used to love what I did, I thought I was helping people. He destroyed that, and a lot more.'

There was a controlled fierceness in her face.

Dain was spreading sheets of paper across the table. He looked round at them gravely.

'We have to take action. Adam has interviewed a number of the weaker Entrepreneurs, with some success.' Adam nodded. 'Anna knew the best people to talk to. Robert Collis was very helpful. We now have a full picture of Franklin's operation. It's breath-taking.'

His face hardened.

'They made a fool of me, of all of us. Market World is a complete fake. It's not a market at all. All the wages, all the prices are rigged. They have secret meetings and decide what they want to pay and what everything's going to cost. They do secret deals between each other. There's no real competition. They talk about fairness and equality and respect. That's all lies. They scare everyone with talk of the Broken Lands. Now we know that's all a forgery too. It has to stop.'

He paused. Anna and Adam nodded. The rest of them were silent.

'There's no point in going to the courts,' he continued. 'We know there's no such thing as a fair trial. We know the President won't do anything, she just wants to keep the lid on things. So what are we going to do?'

Adam spoke for the first time.

'They've always used the Enforcers to keep things under control. They tricked us too. I've been talking to people in the barracks. They're asking questions. Everyone thinks the Captain is a hero, they shouldn't have thrown him out like they did. There are more strikes, more demonstrations in the city all the time. They've put the rents up again. Next time there's serious trouble, the Enforcers will stay in the barracks.'

That was when Matt joined in.

'Ed and me know people who'll maybe help us,' he said. 'They call themselves the Commonwealth.'

Ed smiled at him and he felt suddenly delighted.

Matt and Ed stood against the boundary wall. In front of them were crowds of people, all dressed in their best. Most of the men wore suits, some of them old-fashioned, cleaned and pressed for the occasion. The women wore the mass-produced dresses from Franklin's stores, but carefully washed and ironed. All of them had children with them. He could see new citizens, just out of school or college and desperate to find jobs. They were mostly standing with their parents but straining forward to see down into the arena.

Just in front of him was a family group. The daughter had her hair neatly combed and clipped back on one side. She was wearing a grey jacket, obviously new, and a matching skirt. She was slightly overweight, with pink cheeks and face. The pressure of her parents' expectations showed in the tense lines around her mouth. Matt saw how her mother glanced proudly at her from time to time. He smiled.

He couldn't remember much about the stadium from when he'd been here before, it seemed so long ago. When he tried to think of it, images of his father and of the Enforcers in their black uniforms marching at him like automatons, rank after rank, expressionless, filled his mind. Ed had saved him. He squeezed her tight against him.

Today, everything looked different. He couldn't see the podium from where he was standing, but he noticed that the giant banners towering up on each side of it displayed simply the cartwheel, gold on crimson. He read the Jobs Mart catchphrase on the banner draped between tall flagpoles above the giant screen:

TODAY'S THE DAY!
THE DAY WHEN YOU COME TO MARKET,
AND THE MARKET COMES TO YOU.

The message on the screen was simpler:

TODAY'S THE DAY!
JOBS MART DAY
THE JOBS YOU WANT AT THE RATES WE CAN PAY
THE FAIR WHERE FAIR'S FAIR

He continued to gaze at Ed.

'Ready?' he said. 'Think anyone recognised you?'

'No chance. No-one would look twice at me in these clothes.'

She lifted her free arm, clad in the neat blue material. Matt said simply:

'I would. I think you're beautiful.'

She smiled at him and pulled him against her. He felt the warmth of her, the delicacy of her bones and the strength in her fingers. She nodded towards the arena:

'We'll have to start with the leaflets in a couple of minutes. We've got to get the timing just right. Everything depends on it.'

# 50

Anna felt Dain's arm round her, holding her against him. She glanced up at his face and her heart went out to him. He'd always been in uniform before, now they were the same as any other couple in the crowd. He was wearing a dark grey suit, very slightly too big for him, the cheap fabric of the jacket already showing creases. He still had the same air of authority in his grey eyes. She'd felt it when he led her to their places about halfway down the stand, people glancing at him, then standing back to let them through.

She stared out over the stalls at the arena in front of them. She guessed everyone was in place. Ed and Matt would be somewhere behind them. She almost felt in a holiday mood, to be here with Dain. Then she caught sight of the podium, and thought of the party on it, smug as vultures, ready to con all of them, to rig everyone's wages for another year.

She thought about how she'd once been proud to have won her seat in the Premium Stand, how the entrepreneurs had nodded approvingly at the 'Heroes of Enterprise' chain on her breast, how her mind had been filled with the Residency reception, how she had wanted to be part of it all, to help make things work in Market World, and she thought she had succeeded. Franklin had destroyed all that. He'd tricked her, he'd cheated her, he'd made a fool of her. Then she'd found Dain that day near the cathedral. Dain had believed her, he'd known she was telling the truth. Now it was Franklin's turn.

She thought how she'd first seen Dain at the head of the Enforcers on Celebration Day, leading the City force into the stadium. How vital he'd seemed, how alive; the man who stood outside the market, watching over all of them. She gripped his hand more tightly, and felt an answering pressure from his fingers.

Today felt different. The podium was smaller and she could see there were fewer people on it. She fixed her eyes hard on Franklin in his sleek business suit at the centre of the group, with his red hair already ruffled. The others she'd seen before, senior Entrepreneurs, the whole gang of them. President Wells was traditionally absent from Jobs Mart. Wages were a bargain struck between employer and worker. Employers hired and fired who they wanted.

The music that had been echoing round the stadium, a piece she nearly recognised, uplifting, with strings and a flute solo, came to an end. She felt a sudden tension run through the crowd as Franklin in close-up replaced the slogan on the giant screen. He had a broad smile on his face and his blue eyes were twinkling. The camera tracked back to show both his hands raised, palms open, acknowledging the applause of the audience. Anna watched him as she would a snake.

Franklin leaned forward and spoke in the familiar rough voice:

'Today's the day!'

His glance ranged round the stadium, including all of them.

'Yes, today's the day! The day when we're all gathered here to watch Jobs Mart in action.'

He gestured at the brightly painted stalls lined up in front of the podium and continued in the residence block accent:

'I know many of you are here because your children are here. You've invested a lot in them and we've paid you the bounty. But there's more to it than that.'

His grin included all of them.

*You're so full of it,* thought Anna. *Your turn now.*

'Now your children are citizens, and what do citizens need?'

He put a hand to his ear. The answer came back in a great bray of sound:

JOBS!

The word echoed around the stadium, drowning out everything, though Anna heard someone nearby shouting:

FAIR PAY!

'That's right,' said Franklin, 'and here, at Jobs Mart you'll find them. You all know what happens. You join the queue for the job you want and there's the two-minute interview. The screen shows the rate of pay. If there aren't enough workers, up goes the pay. All determined purely by supply and demand.'

Anna stared at him.

*I know you. All through that meal, in the Residency, you were lying to me. Everyone equal, everyone treated with respect. You thought you could use me. Then you tried to buy me off, and when I wasn't for sale you threw me out like garbage.*

Franklin was gesturing at the crowd. He seemed suddenly to stare straight at her.

'If there are fewer people after the job, we pay more. What could be fairer than that? When we've hired all the people we want, the market closes.'

He jabbed a finger at the slogan above him.

'Competition in action; the fair where fair's fair.'

Franklin paused again. His eyes roved round the stadium.

'But I think some of you are here for a different reason. You're not here for a job for yourself, or for your children. You're here to,' he emphasized the words, 'bear witness. There: you didn't think I said things like that, did you?'

Again the inclusive gesture, arms flung wide, as if he wanted to embrace all of them.

'You want to be part of Jobs Mart Day. You want to be here when the market closes. You want to see how competition works. Because that's what Market World is. It's you, the citizens. Market World works, for all of us, because we all believe in it. It's our faith in the market that makes us different from the Broken Lands.'

He was shouting out the words now:

WE BELIEVE IN MARKET WORLD

His mouth remained open. He was laughing. *It's a joke to you, a three-card trick.* A ripple of puzzled amusement ran round the stadium. He went on:

'Enough of the sermon. On with the show! Don't forget: today's the day!'

Anna touched Dain's arm.

'Today's the day.' There was an edge to her voice. 'Today we settle accounts. I'm ready.'

Dain looked gravely at her and nodded.

'Yes, Anna. I'm ready.'

# 51

Ed watched from the back of the stand as Franklin put a metal whistle to his lips. He puffed out his cheeks and blew hard. The shrill blast resounded from the loudspeakers, deafening her for a second. She saw Franklin on the screen spread his arms yet again, as if to embrace the stalls and shout out, his voice amplified fifty-fold:

I DECLARE JOBS MART OPEN

She felt the crowd press forward all round her. At the front of the stadium she could see people springing up from their seats, first a trickle, then a flood, running for the most popular stalls. Lars was there, right at the front. She recognised him by his short fair hair. He looked back and gestured to some of the others as if encouraging them. She felt a wave of relief. She leaned towards Matt and whispered:

'It's going to be OK. The Commonwealth have turned out.'

'Right,' he said. 'Get ready.'

The screen picked out an individual among the mob of runners, a girl, her hair braided back, her face twisted with effort, her arms pumping, running for all she was worth. She dodged round a dark-haired broad-faced boy who stood there confused, glancing at one stall then another.

The cheers of the crowd beat against her ears. Most people were on their feet, calling out to their children:

'Go for HealthCorp – look they're going up!'

'No, it's TrainCo now.'

'GamesBiz!'

'Forest Futures!'

'Truth TV! Truth TV!'

The camera had moved on to a red-haired lad, shorter than most of the competitors, using both arms to burrow his way into the mob round one of the stalls. The music on the loudspeakers had started again. Anna felt her ears ringing.

Most of the runners were teenagers, girls and boys. They were dressed in their best clothes, jackets and ties for the boys, the girls in skirts, everyone running in black polished shoes. Their hair was neatly trimmed, their faces eager, straining with the effort of forcing themselves forward, past the others. The camera picked out one of the leaders, a blond athletic boy, with the crest of one of the most expensive academies on his jacket. He slipped and fell, then pushed himself upright and dabbed at a smear of mud across his sleeve. Ed heard the groan of the spectators, and caught the chuckles of one or two.

She noticed a few older people on their second or third chance, their clothes slightly shabby and their faces grimmer. The camera focused on a young woman in a wheelchair, her arms working up and down like ram-rods. Anna heard the crowd shout their applause as she swung in front of the blond boy and made it to the head of the queue for the accountancy internships.

People were still pushing their children forward, most of them aware that the richer parents had paid for the most expensive seats at the front of the stands to get their own children at the head of the queue. On the screen she saw a wiry lad in glasses, his hair dishevelled, wrap his arms round the plump dark-skinned boy in front of him and shove him out of the HealthCorp queue. All round her people were booing. The fat boy slapped at his attacker. Ed saw the glasses go flying. Others were joining in, then Grisha ran in from the side. She neatly tripped a slim young man in a well-cut business-suit so he fell onto the fat boy, and dodged out of camera-shot.

'Did you see that?' she whispered to Matt, 'It's starting.'

She saw an older man, perhaps a parent, running towards the fat boy, a stick in his hand. The green-uniformed security guards, their batons drawn, had left their positions behind the stalls. They were making for the scrum around the HealthCorp stall. She saw Lars in the crowd, fighting his way towards Grisha. There were others with him, three or four, then ten, then twenty, more. Once you realised they were the Commonwealth you could pick them out. They were slightly older than the job-seekers and not so well-dressed and with a hard determination on their faces. She could see more and more of them right across the stadium, signalling to each other, running, joining up.

*I never realised there were so many,* she thought. *It's an army.*

The giant screen now displayed a grid, company names across the top, job titles down the side, pay rates in the cells. The rates were continually shifting up and down as people joined one queue, then another. She could see that Franklin's had the longest queue. The apprentice pay rate had started high but was now plunging. People seemed to think it would bottom out soon. There they were, still joining the queue.

'Come on!' She squeezed Matt's hand and released it. 'We've got to get the leaflets out.'

She glanced at him. He already had the first batch out of his satchel and was handing them to people. He pushed through the crowd towards the side of the stand and flung a handful over. She watched them spread out, caught up by a gust of wind, spiralling on eddies of air, fluttering down towards the front of the stadium. People were looking up. She saw the pink of their faces and their hands reaching out.

The leaflets were simple, just one page, with no cartoon, and only on one side. She'd written most of it with Dain and with suggestions from the others:

FRANKLIN'S ROBBING YOUR CHILDREN!

SO YOU THINK JOBS MART'S FAIR?
THINK AGAIN!
IT'S ALL A CON-TRICK
ALL THE WAGE-RATES ARE RIGGED
WE CAN PROVE IT

HERE'S WHAT THEY'LL BE WHEN THE
MARKET CLOSES

The leaflet had a grid on it, just like that on the giant screen, with the names of the corporations across the top. Only here the numbers in the boxes were printed in bold type: the pay rates that the Entrepreneurs had decided in advance, the same numbers that were in the files Robert Collis had handed over to Adam once he'd stopped blustering and admitted everything.

The leaflet finished:

HOW DID WE KNOW THAT?
SIMPLE!

FRANKLIN RIGS THE RATES BEFORE JOBS MART
THEY'RE ROBBING YOUR CHILDREN
WE FOUND OUT THE TRUTH

TRUST US – WE'RE THE COMMONWEALTH

YOU'LL KNOW WHO TO TRUST,
US OR FRANKLIN,
WHEN YOU SEE THE RATES AT THE END OF THE DAY

YOU CAN'T TRUST MARKET WORLD!

She threw a mass of leaflets upwards so they spread out over the people at the back of the stand and started to push her way forward.

# 52

Ed snatched up a bundle of leaflets in each hand. It felt glorious, hurling them up in the air above her, shoving them into people's hands, shouting out:

'Franklin's robbing our children! Read it here! We can prove it!'

On all sides people were turning to her, staring. She paused for breath.

Out of the corner of her eye she saw Matt smiling at people, encouraging them to read. She flung another bundle up, out over the crowd.

'Free leaflets! They're worth money! Go on, you've got to read it. They're robbing your children!'

'Don't talk daft. My kid's down there.'

A woman in a green hooded coat clutched at the paper.

Ed felt someone bump into her from behind. She swung round. People were twisting round and looking upwards, at Franklin's New Market building that rose up so close to the stadium that it seemed to tower over them. Matt grabbed her hand.

'Look!' he shouted, pointing. 'Everyone – look up!'

Ed's first impression was of the light glinting on the plate-glass windows high above her. A window had been opened near the top of the cliff of glass. She could just make a cluster of white specks against the grey of the clouds, floating outwards like seagulls, whirling in the flurries of air around the building. She watched them as they soared out over the stadium, and started to float downwards. Another window opened and more leaflets were flung out, then another window and another.

She felt her hand grasped. Matt was beside her.

'They've done it!' he said, 'I knew they would. It's the Commonwealth! Eve said it's always the same: they screw down the wages so everyone hates them, then they give the keys of their buildings to the cleaners.'

She grinned at him and nuzzled her cheek against the rough cloth of his coat:

'It's brilliant. Now people have to believe us. Market World is a fake.'

She shouted it out:

'Market World's a con-trick! Franklin's robbing your children!'

Her face glowed with excitement. All round them people were seizing the leaflets, reading them, looking up at each other, across at the giant screen. In the stadium the crowds of jobseekers were still massed round the stalls. She could see the security guards striking out with their batons. They were breaking up the fights and shoving people back into line.

Someone thrust a leaflet at her:

'Have you read this?'

She saw it was the woman in the hooded coat who'd pointed up at the leaflets in the sky.

'Yes,' she said. 'It's all true. They've rigged Jobs Mart. They're robbing our children.'

The woman stared at her as if she couldn't believe what Ed was saying.

Suddenly the music came to an end with a blare of trumpets and she heard Franklin's voice booming out over the stadium:

'Everybody ready? Here we go!'

She yelled up at the giant screen:

'You're a con-man! You're a thief!'

She heard other voices, the Commonwealth she guessed, shouting out the same thing.

Franklin started the count-down. The numbers flashed up on the giant screen in the space above the grid, the pay rates still shifting as last-minute job-seekers fought their way to the front of the queues.

10

9

8

7

Ed could hear people taking up the count all round the stadium. Franklin was at the front of the podium, waving a hand up and down, conducting them, the handkerchief flapping in his fingers. But there were other voices too in the crowd:

'Franklin's a thief!'

'It's all a con!'

Look at the leaflets!'

Right in front of her, in the arena, the first banner was up:

FAIR PAY, NOT STARVATION WAGES!
DON'T LET FRANKLIN CHEAT YOU!

Grisha was holding it up on the edge of the crowd, waving it from side to side. Ed could see Lars there with her, then other banners went up, over on the other side of the arena, just in front of Franklin's own stall, back by the podium, on all sides.

'Matt, they've done it! It's all working!'

The Commonwealth were everywhere. Ed had never known there were so many of them. All those strikes, all the actions on the streets, always defeated by Franklin. All the people in the residence blocks, forced into poverty. At last they could fight back at everything that made their lives so hard.

Ed saw some of the Entrepreneurs turn in their seats to whisper to each other. Franklin glanced down and gestured urgently to the security guards in front of the podium. He squared his shoulders and went on counting down:

6

5

4

More voices were calling out:

'Look at the leaflets!'

All around her Ed could see people glancing anxiously at the paper, then up at the screen. The banners were moving forward, converging on the platform. People were joining in behind them, shouting. She saw the pink-cheeked girl, her face angry, her hand drawn back to throw something.

3

2

1

Franklin thrust his head forward, defying all of them. He held up both hands:

'That's it! Close of Market! Close of Market! Competition in action. The pay rates are on the screen. What you see is what you get! Everything determined by the great gods Supply and Demand. Slogans don't make any difference. You can shout til you're blue in the face: you can't buck the market!'

The grid appeared with the numbers frozen. It was headed by the slogan:

JOBS MART: THE FAIR WHERE FAIR'S FAIR

Ed could see everyone around her holding the leaflets and looking up at the screen. They were checking the numbers, glancing at each other and starting to talk, their faces anxious, some of them angry. The jobseekers in the stadium had the leaflets in their hands too. They were talking in groups, looking at the screen, the stalls, the podium. The young people from the Commonwealth were there among them, all of them dressed like ordinary working people, most of them undersized from years of poor food, vulnerable, all of them talking urgently.

Someone was passing one of the sheets up to the platform. She saw Franklin seize it, look down at the crowd, and start towards the microphone, his arms outstretched.

He yelled something about the Enforcers. Then a great roar of sound swept across the stadium, beating at her ears, drowning out the loudspeakers. She was shouting with them, for all she was worth:

CHEAT! CHEAT! CHEAT! CHEAT!

Beside her Matt was shouting too, his voice deep, powerful, like a preacher she'd once heard:

'You starve our children!'

Franklin was speaking into the microphone but no-one could hear a word he was saying. Everywhere around them people were shouting, forcing their way forward, raising their fists. The Commonwealth formed a solid wedge at the front, linking arms, shouting, shoving the security guards backwards. Ed made out words:

'They fixed the rates!'
'You've rigged it!'
'It's not enough to live on!'

and, louder than anything, more and more people taking it up, so the words rose into a great barrage of sound:

'CHEAT! CHEAT! CHEAT! CHEAT!'

Grisha was standing on something, probably part of the HealthCorp stall, talking urgently to the crowd, her back to the podium. Lars stared up at her, his face rapt. Security guards were forcing a way through to her from behind, lashing out on both sides with their clubs. One of them pushed into the crowd, shoving people aside. He stabbed at her with a spar of broken wood torn from one of the stalls. Ed saw her jerk forward, then Lars had his arms round the guard and was forcing him to the ground. The crowd thrust forward and all she could see was the mass of people shouting, hurling stones, bottles, lumps of wood, punching, jabbing, stamping, and the banners, and the guards being slowly forced back.

She felt Matt's arm tight around her, holding her against him as he forced his way towards the front. She twisted under his arm and grabbed hold of his hand. The crowd rushed forward and they were all running down the steps towards the arena. All round them the chanting grew louder. She sensed the fury in the sound.

'CHEAT! CHEAT! CHEAT! CHEAT!'

She caught a glimpse of the woman in the green hooded coat, her face snarling. She was hurling something, a half-eaten burger, towards the podium. More people were pressing onto the steps, some of them forcing their way over the benches. All of them were heading down into the arena. She glimpsed Dain, at the front of the crowd. Anna was just ahead of him. They were running along the side-wall, making for the main exit from the stadium, the place where Exchange Avenue left the arena. She waved at them, but they didn't look round.

Everyone in the stadium was on their feet. The crowd surged forward towards the stalls, slipping on the grass, shouting, shaking their fists. A great howl of rage went up, out, over the city.

The employers had abandoned the stalls. The younger ones were already sprinting down Exchange Avenue, glancing back at the crowd, their faces terrified. The great mass of people flooded after them, hurling bits of wood broken from the stalls, bottles, drink cans, anything they could find. The Commonwealth led the charge, making straight for the podium.

Ed saw a flicker of red and yellow flame run up the side of the first stall and then blaze out above it. The next stall tottered sideway into the first and burst into flame. She saw a thickset young man rip an upright off the burning stall and plunge the tip into the fire. In a few seconds, he'd set the next stall alight, then the next and the next. The last of the stalls flared up and a great cloud of black smoke boiled up over the arena.

The security guards were in full retreat. One of them, bulky in full riot gear, was fighting desperately just where the HealthCorp stall had been. The athletic lad with the muddy jacket wrenched the baton out of his hand, smashed it into his shin and pushed him out of the way

The runners were now carrying flaming torches. The great banner to the left of the podium went up in a forty metre column of fire. She felt the heat, beating on her face. She halted.

Grisha lay just in front of her, her face covered in blood, her hand still gripping the banner. Lars lay across her, his head wrenched backwards, and next to him the guard with Lar's hands still fastened round his throat. People were streaming by them on both sides.

Ed knelt down and laid her hand against Grisha's neck. There was no pulse.

Matt fell to his knees beside her.

'There's nothing we can do,' he said. 'There were too many people.'

'Too many people.'

She looked up. The Entrepreneurs were crowding onto the podium staircase, shoving each other out of the way in their desperation to escape. Some of them threw themselves over the side-barrier and ran towards Exchange Avenue. She saw a young woman slip off her high-heeled shoes and jump, landing awkwardly and clutching at her ankle. She fell forward and was lost in the turmoil. Franklin, Ed realised, was nowhere to be seen.

An older man appeared at the front of the podium, ignoring the flames below him. He took something out of his mouth and shouted:

'Peace! Let's negotiate, we can do a deal.'

Ed saw he was holding a cigar.

Something hit him hard in the face, drawing blood. People were pelting him with small change, handfuls of it, a hailstorm of money. He stared round bewildered, his hand on the red smudge on his cheek. Then the giant screen exploded and crashed forward onto the blazing stalls. Great gouts of flame burst upwards. When next she could see the podium it was a mass of fire. Dense black smoke rolled out across the city.

# 53

Dain and Anna reached Exchange Avenue ahead of the mob.

'I know where he'll go,' she shouted. 'There's a private car-park. Only the Entrepreneurs have access.'

She raced towards a grey metal door in the side-wall of the Avenue, just next to the Premium Stand. He caught up with her as she wrenched it open.

They were in a downward-sloping corridor with cream breeze-block walls lit only by emergency lights at floor-level. It was so much quieter away from the riot in the stadium. He caught the faint echo of a door shutting somewhere ahead of him.

'Keep behind me,' he said. 'He's dangerous.'

'Shh! I know.'

She was still ahead of him, half-running. They moved as fast they could down a metal staircase. He caught her at a T-junction.

'You go that way,' she said, turning left.

He hesitated but she was already some way away from him, running fast. He followed the other corridor round a corner, down more steps, through double doors and into the underground car-park. It was empty apart from a sleek black limousine at the far end. Franklin stood with his back to him a few paces away, his arm raised to summon the car. There was a tiny rent in the sleeve of his immaculate suit.

Dain felt an absolute confidence in himself. *I have him, and Anna's not here, she's safe!*

'Franklin, you are under arrest. You are charged with the crime against exchange.'

Franklin whirled round and stared at him.

Dain continued. 'You have full commercial rights …'

Franklin slipped his hand into his pocket and pulled out the handkerchief. He spoke in his rough residence-block voice:

'Captain Lucas! I'm sorry, I forgot. It's Mr Lucas now, isn't it? This is private property. Get out before I send for the Enforcers.'

He took a pace forward.

Dain folded his arms.

'Don't move. Seems I was right about your colleagues queuing up to talk to me. We have all the evidence about what goes on in the Colonies. We know how you fix prices. We've got witness-statements on how you rigged the wage-rates today. You saw what happened in the stadium. People have seen through you. You're finished.'

Behind Franklin the massive car was sliding silently towards them.

Franklin took another pace forward, frowning, and slipped the handkerchief back in his pocket.

'You tried to arrest me. That was an insult. Then you raided my colony. That is the second insult. Now you smash Jobs Mart Day. Today we will settle accounts.'

He whipped his hand out of his pocket. Dain saw the light glinting on a small thick-bladed knife. Franklin jabbed the knife towards him.

'Where are your Enforcers now? I told you: I like to win.'

His blue eyes glinted. He jabbed the knife forward again:

'Get back!'

The only thing Dain could think about was the blade of the knife, faintly discoloured, serrated along one edge. He'd have one chance to grab Franklin's wrist next time he jabbed with it.

Someone was moving behind him. Dain felt hands grab at his arms. He twisted from side to side. The grip tightened.

Franklin grinned, showing his teeth:

'I think you forgot about my driver.'

He took another pace forward. Dain braced himself to kick out.

He heard a door creak open and caught sight of movement by one of the pillars. Anna was sliding along the wall as quietly as she could, her face calm as if she knew exactly what she planned to do. Franklin gave no sign of knowing she was there.

'Get back!' Dain shouted. 'He's got a knife!'

Franklin raised an eyebrow.

'Don't think you'll catch me out with that one.'

He feinted with the knife then lunged forward. Dain put all his strength into the kick, but he knew he was too slow. Anna threw herself forward, in front of him. He jerked back, smacking the man holding him against the garage wall. The grip on his arms slackened.

'Anna!'

Her back was pressed hard against him. She was slumped forward, curling over the knife.

Franklin stood without moving, his face aghast.

'She shouldn't have done that,' he said almost in a whisper. 'I never wanted to hurt her. When we interviewed her in the Tower why didn't she say "Yes"? We were ready to do business. She was an Entrepreneur. She shouldn't have got in the way. There was nothing in it for her, nothing at all.'

He released the knife and rubbed his hand back across his hair. His shirt sleeve was stained scarlet. There was a red smear across his forehead.

'Nothing in it for her,' he said again, shaking his head slowly. 'Why did she do it?'

He held his hand in front of his face and stared at it. It was covered in blood.

Dain was filled with an immense calm. He had his arms round Anna. He turned her towards him. Her lips were so warm. Why was there no feeling in those eyes gazing up at him, dark as black satin?

'Anna, say something.' He spoke to her gently. He didn't want it to sound like a reproach. 'I told you to stay back. If only you'd stayed back.'

She seemed to weigh nothing at all.

He was aware of movement around him, of someone talking urgently to Franklin and of a car door slamming and a vehicle sweeping past him and away. He sank down slowly onto the floor. The wall made a good support for his back.

He had Anna in his arms, her face cradled against his chest. They needed to rest. There was something they had to do, but he couldn't remember what it was. Market World. Hero of Enterprise. Young Trader of the Year. Youngest Member of the Guild. Now he had her here in his arms.

*Everything,* he thought. *She had everything and she gave it for someone she loved, not for a God in heaven or for One Law or to stand on a podium on Celebration Day.* He brushed a lock of hair tenderly back from her cheek. Once he thought her eye-lid fluttered. He heard the clatter of boots running towards him, people calling out.

# 54

Ed gripped Matt's hand in hers. The crowd swept them along, onwards, down Exchange Avenue and out onto Central Boulevard. A gleaming plate-glass shop front occupied the prime position directly opposite them. She'd only seen it once before. That was on Celebration Day, when she'd had Matt leaning on her shoulder, her arm round his waist, and they thought the Enforcers were after them. It seemed such a long time ago. Now it was evening and half the city was there, a great mass of people, carrying them towards the mannequins in the plate-glass window: three impossible bodies, tastefully draped in furs, gazing impassively back at the mob.

The lights in the shop snapped off. Almost immediately the fore-runners of the crowd, one of them a broad-shouldered black man in a T-shirt with a HealthCorp logo, were through the door. The lights flashed on, faded and were on again. People were hurling the clothes out of the shop, out onto the street.

'Grisha and Lars,' she said. 'They should be here. This isn't what I wanted.'

'I know. But we have to win.'

The crowd was spilling both ways along the street. She saw shop windows stove in on both sides of them. Luxury goods were strewn onto the street. People were carrying off clothes, televisions, toys, anything they could carry. She saw another window crash outwards. A thickset woman in hot pants stepped through from inside, her face vivid with excitement, holding a model trainset in a glossy box. A blond-haired man was trying to push a fridge along the pavement.

Further up the crowd had reached Franklin's flagship food store. A burly man in a suit appeared on the threshold, shouted something about Enforcers, and abruptly stepped back, slamming the door behind him. The door opened again. It was a young woman shop assistant, in a smock, tight skirt and high heels.

'It's all yours,' she yelled to them.

Ed saw her push her way into the mob.

On they went, towards the Halls of Law and the towers at the heart of the city. Suddenly, at the end of Central Boulevard the crowd hesitated, halted and swirled backwards.

'What's happening?' she shouted, but no-one seemed to hear her. Matt forced his way through and they were at the front.

Ed saw a double line of Enforcers blocking the boulevard, their visors down and the whips thrust forward in their hands. The light from the shop windows glistened on their body armour. For a few moments no-one spoke. She heard the crash of another shop window shattering behind them.

One of the Enforcers stepped forward, laid down his whip, pushed up his visor, and removed his helmet. Ed recognised Adam's face, scarred from eye to mouth, unsmiling.

The dark-skinned man in the HealthCorp T-shirt was standing in front of him.

'Let us through,' he shouted. 'Market World's finished, and so's the One Law.'

He raised his voice and shouted:

'We don't believe in it anymore! We don't believe in it!'

He turned to the crowd and raised his right fist. A great roar of sound swept past Ed and Matt, over the Enforcers, out over the city:

WE DON'T BELIEVE IN IT!
MARKET WORLD'S FINISHED!

People were pressing forward. Ed saw the Enforcers tense themselves, readying their whips. She glanced up at Matt.

'I don't like this,' he said.

She gripped his hand tighter.

'We can't give up now.'

Adam fixed his eyes on the man in the HealthCorp T-shirt for a moment. Then he shifted his gaze to the crowd.

'Citizens.' He spoke loudly, not shouting. 'No more! Your Enforcers have impounded all goods in these stores. We will distribute them fairly. Understand that: fairly, not by who can pay and who can't. The One Law is at an end.'

He gestured to the Enforcers, who laid down their whips, raised their visors and removed their helmets.

'All of you listen to me. We are no longer Market World. I say again, the One Law is at an end. But hear this too: we will not be a Broken Land.'

He paused.

'The fire in the stadium is now extinguished. We will burn nothing more. If anyone objects, let him speak.'

The brown eyes ranged across the crowd. Silence. Then a great roar of sound.

NO MORE ONE LAW! NO MORE ONE LAW!

Ed found herself bellowing out the words with everyone else. She heard Matt's voice, deep, like a preacher, beside her. She shouted until her throat hurt.

Adam was holding up a hand for silence.

'President Wells is under arrest. As I speak, my officers are detaining the surviving Entrepreneurs. They will face justice. I repeat: we will not become a Broken Land. There will be no bosses and no warlords.'

He paused again and let his gaze rove across the crowd.

'If anyone objects, let him speak.'

Silence, then Ed heard people murmuring all around her, the sound growing to an excited babble among the crowd.

Adam continued:

'One more thing. Earlier this evening I detained Franklin's limousine at a roadblock. He attempted to escape on foot and made an unprovoked attack on a citizen with a small-bladed knife. He fell on the weapon while being arrested and sustained a serious injury. Efforts to resuscitate him were ineffective.'

Adam folded his arms and surveyed the crowd.

'Franklin was a criminal. He used the One Law to rob and cheat and exploit. He cheated you. He fixed the prices you pay. He rigged rents. He paid you starvation wages. He did not hesitate to use lethal force against those who stood in his way. There will be a full enquiry into his conduct and the conduct of those who worked for him. It will include the circumstances of his death.'

Everywhere people were turning to their neighbours, talking, calling out. Ed drew Matt close to her.

'It's worth it,' she said. 'We hated Franklin, we hated Market World. Now we're free. And I'm here with you.'

Someone was singing at the back of the crowd, a deep bass voice that carried over all of them. Others took up the song. Ed couldn't make out the words. It didn't matter, others joined in. It was all about justice and making the world free and building common wealth. A red-cheeked black-haired man with a great belly next to her was belting out the words, his whole body swaying with the effort.

'Look!'

The woman next to Ed was pointing upwards, over the heads of the Enforcers.

Ed stared, and turned to Matt:

'The lights in the towers! They're going out.'

Her face glowed, lit up by the shop-windows around them.

'They've given up. They've abandoned the towers.'

No-one spoke. Ahead of them she saw the lights were winking out in the towers, first individual lights, then whole floors, whole sections in darkness. The toadstool, the exclamation mark, the dagger, the swan, the gantry, the space-rocket, the fir tree, all of them were fading, merging into the night sky. The last to disappear was Franklin's tower, the tallest of them all. The lights in the myriad tiny windows still blazed out as the others diminished. Suddenly these lights too were extinguished, all of them at once, leaving a faint after-image in her eyes. Then that too faded away.

'Don't you see?' she shouted. 'We've won! There's no more One Law, no more Franklin, no more Entrepreneurs, no more Colonies.'

She had her arm round him. She felt he'd always be there with her.

'Yes,' he said. 'We've won.'

# 55

Matt pulled Ed to the side as the crowd flowed past them, following Adam and the Enforcers towards the Halls of Law.

'Ed, this isn't my scene. I always wanted to be in the country, in a village, away from all this. Let's leave them to it.'

She remembered the ploughing at the colony, how he'd gentled the heavy horse, how he'd fitted the bridle to it, how he'd leaned back against the traces, forcing the ploughshare downwards into the soil, mastering the horse. She reached up and touched his face:

'Yes, I think maybe I've had enough of the city too. But this is something I've got to see.'

She knew she'd never have got through the crowd without Matt there, forcing open a path in front of them. The plaza in front of the Halls was brightly lit and packed with people. People were standing on the steps. Most of them she didn't recognise, but she saw Adam to one side, his eyes ranging over the crowd, silent.

The muscular man in the HealthCorp T-shirt, who introduced himself to the crowd as Winston, did a lot of the talking. Eve was there in her tattered fur coat, wisps of grey hair escaping from her hat, with a huge glittering broach on her collar. Many of those in the crowd seemed to recognise her. They shouted out her name:

'Eve! Eve!'

She remembered how Grisha had taken them through the tunnels. She squeezed Matt's hand. Other people came up the steps to talk to the crowd and then stepped down.

Ed found it hard to follow the discussion. Winston had started things off:

'Citizens! This is a great day for all of us! Together you have defeated Market World. Tomorrow will dawn on a kinder, gentler City. No more greed!'

Someone took up the slogan:

'No more greed! No more greed!' echoed from the façade of the Halls of Law, and back from Franklin's Tower, distorted to a blur of sound.

More people came out on the steps talking, arguing, demanding. Ed recognised the young woman with braided hair she'd seen racing across the arena in the first close-up of Jobs Mart. She wanted to know how they'd get jobs. Someone else was talking about schools and who'd teach in them. The tall woman said they should set up a committee to help people sort out the day nurseries. Someone else said they should send an expedition north to release the colonists.

The discussion went on for a long time. Ed felt herself grow sleepy, leaning against Matt there in the plaza. She felt herself distant from it all. The night was growing chillier but she didn't feel cold.

People were discussing jobs, what they'd do about the residence blocks, the buses, the hospitals, how they'd organise everything.

She heard a familiar voice. Adam was on the steps, staring calmly out at the crowd. She noticed how everyone fell silent when he spoke:

'Citizens! The world has changed and the Enforcers will change with it. The One Law is at an end. There has been enough violence. Our first priority is to protect all citizens. After that we will help in distributing the supplies you need.'

He paused. Ed realised that he spoke with the same calm certainty that Dain had.

'No more bosses, no more Franklin. The time of the One Law is at an end. The city is now yours. Do with it as you wish.'

Cheering broke out at the front of the crowd and spread backwards. A great wave of jubilation broke over her and Matt. She heard people shouting:

'Adam Steele! Adam Steele!'

He raised his hand. The crowd fell silent. A great smile spread slowly across his face. Then Ed saw him shake his head.

'The city is yours,' he said. 'You must build the world you wish to live in. Good luck!'

He turned and started moving towards the pillars. A tall woman just in front of Ed shouted:

'But why are you doing all this?'

Adam thought for moment and said:

'I joined the Enforcers to serve the people. Franklin betrayed me, he betrayed all of us. We must help one another. That's all there is.'

He moved away from the steps, out of the floodlight area into the shadows at the side of the building and was gone.

# 56

Ed rested her head against Matt's shoulder.

'Heard enough?' he said.

She could hear someone on the steps behind him arguing about an interim government. A woman's voice was talking about how they'd hold elections. Other people were saying it was too early. *Will it make a difference?* Ed thought. She wanted something she could do, something there in front of her, something she could succeed at.

She nodded.

They made their way slowly through the crowd and down the Main Boulevard. She saw glass on the pavement where Exchange Avenue joined the boulevard, but it only lasted for a couple of blocks. A couple of young people were sweeping it to one side. She realised that most of the shops had a group of Enforcers standing in the doorway, keeping watch.

*Adam's work,* she thought, *order in the city.*

There weren't many people about. Those she saw were moving fast, making for the plaza.

She stopped.

'Did you see what happened to Anna and Dain? Last I saw them they were in the arena, quite a way ahead of us. I looked in the crowd, but I couldn't see them anywhere.'

He looked down at her, his blue eyes glistening in the light from the shop windows.

'I don't know. They're not really like us. They were always at the centre of things. They'll be busy sorting things out, organising. They'll be OK.'

'I'd like to see them, just to say good-bye.'

'We'll be back sometime, when we've got settled. I just want to make a go of it in the village. We could head back to Fernhill. I know my way around there and there's a black-smith's shop, they always need help.'

Away from the city centre, the streets were in darkness. They walked on, into the narrower streets among the residence blocks, carefully picking their way. As they walked the street lighting suddenly came on, so that they found themselves passing between pools of light, always another pool ahead of them, and another, vaguer, beyond that.

They passed a café that was still open.

'Let's eat,' said Matt, 'I'm hungry and we've got a long way to go.'

He pushed open the door.

Ed looked round. They were the only customers. The proprietor sat on a high stool at the bar, a fat, round-shouldered man in a grubby mess-jacket, his face pallid.

'Two coffees and what you've got: bacon and eggs?' asked Matt.

'You can have whatever I've got,' said the proprietor. 'No, you don't have to pay.'

He moved listlessly to the coffee urn.

'Haven't you heard?' he continued, over his shoulder. 'All this stuff in the city about the Commonwealth? They want to give everything to the workers.'

He turned and fixed his gaze on Matt.

'Bloody good thing. I've been trying to make a profit out of this place for twenty years. Good luck to them, I say. They can have it. I'll be a worker too.'

'It's not about profit,' said Ed, but he'd already turned back to the stove. 'It's about sharing things out. Being fair.'

She realised she was addressing his back.

'That's as maybe,' he grunted. 'But the oven's got to be cleaned, who's going to do that? No-one likes cleaning ovens.'

Matt glanced at her and she sat down at one of the tables. Chipped Formica. Everything about the place told of a hard struggle for survival, she thought, from the grubby menu cards, obviously weeks old, to the dog-eared magazines in the rack, to the missing 'N' in 'SUNSHI E CAFÉ' on the window.

She touched Matt's hand and smiled.

'No more bosses. It's not going to be easy.'

'Nothing ever is. You just have to look after each other. That's what Adam said. You showed me that, back in Re-education, out at the Colony.'

She tried to smile at him, but suddenly she found her eyes full of tears. Her body shook with sobs. Matt started up. He had his arms round her.

'Ed, what is it?' he said gently.

'It's nothing.' She held him to her. 'It's just that I'm so happy.'

The proprietor glanced round at them, then back at the frying pan on the stove. He ran a hand through his thinning hair. *Young love,* he thought, *whichever way you looked at it, bidding or no bidding, it's kind of nice.*

He cracked the eggs carefully on the side of the pan.

# 57

Dain entered the residence block where he'd always lived on a warm May evening some six months later. The Commonwealth was now established and Market World was history, but there was still much to do. He crossed the landing, turned the handle as quietly as he could and edged open the door to his flat. He paused to listen, and then moved stealthily across the hallway. He took the big cut-glass vase and filled it one-third full. He unwrapped the flowers, carefully crushed the stalks and placed them in it.

Peonies, he thought, crimson, golden, purple, cream, yellow, pink. She always loved peonies. She'd once said they made her think that spring was truly here. The flat was very quiet. He remembered how she'd been the first time he saw her, Celebration Day, pushing her way to the front, standing there, her eyes on him, and saluting. He stood there for a full minute. There was still much to do.

He sorted everything out in the kitchen, picked up the vase, and carried it back across the hall. He placed it on the side-table in the room at the back of the flat, where the afternoon sun fell full on it.

He bent down and spoke softly:

'Wake up. Wake up, darling.'

He loved this moment in the day, when he got back to the flat, when Anna would be asleep and he could sit there and feel he was protecting her. He sat on the chair next to her, watching for the faint interruption to her breathing as she stirred, catching the exact instant when her eyelids first parted, then opened wide, and she looked up at him.

'Dain!'

She stretched, then reached up with both arms and pulled her face close to his and kissed him. His heart filled with tenderness for her. He lowered her back gently onto the head-rest. Then he leaned sideways, so she could see past him.

'Dain!' she exclaimed, 'they're lovely! Thank you so much, you know I love them.'

Her eyes lingered on the blossoms.

'I've still got some friends in the Old Market,' he said. He wasn't going to tell her how much they'd cost.

She looked back at him. He saw a new pallor in her face.

'How did it go today?'

'Successful, I would say. We make progress. I spent most of the morning on the apprentice scheme, visiting the academy. Some of those young people are really very good. They're so keen, they'll try anything once you give them the opportunity. And they're sharp.'

He smiled, thinking of how they'd welcomed him: a giant arch of bolts welded together in an intricate design, and a caricature sculpture of his head in different metals with the grey streak in chromium. 'Not easy welding chromium,' the instructor had said.

'They've got sixteen workshops now, everything from welding to brick-laying. They're very excited about the new electronics wing. They've got machines to make printed circuits, video microscopes, remote controlled finishers, you name it. It's full to bursting, we've got the expansion programme underway.'

'And the afternoon? What happened?'

'It wasn't easy. The last case has now gone through, everything fair, everything seen to be fair. All those businesses the Entrepreneurs ran, the supermarkets, the workshops, the buses, the house-building, everything, they've all been confiscated. The city's sorting them out. A lot will become co-operatives. That's what we're training everyone for. It's been six months from the end of Market World and now it's over.'

He rested a hand on hers.

'I was there as a witness of course. I should be used to that by now, but I'm not. I never will be.'

He shook his head.

'Every time, I think of that day in the courtroom, that judge.'

'You did your very best,' Anna said.

'My best. As I was then. If only I'd made them understand, perhaps everything would be different. You wouldn't …'

'But what was the verdict?'

'Guilty. That makes a conviction in every case. Including that judge, the one who hated you.'

Anna nodded.

'That was necessary. You and the others prepared everything very carefully. What happens about sentencing?'

Dain looked up at her.

'Exile. They must never come back, the Entrepreneurs and all their associates. Ex-President Wells too. There's an island for them out in the ocean. Quite fertile, nice climate. Out of the way. We'll give them just enough to get started, and then they'll have to work everything out for themselves. Like we do, here in the city. It'll be a good exercise for them, they'll learn to get on with each other, to do everything you need to do to eat and drink and clothe and shelter yourself. Or maybe they won't.'

Anna grinned, her dark eyes dancing.

'That's a brilliant idea. Whose was it?'

'Adam's, of course. Said he'd been thinking about it for a long time. It's hard to believe it's all over. They're calling it the Gentle Revolution.'

'For some.'

Dain and Anna sat there together in silence, watching the sun set over the velvety blossom of the peonies. After a few minutes Dain said:

'Something else. That's the last of the trials. All my work gathering evidence and standing as a witness is finished. We can take a break, if you'd like that. Do you remember, a long time ago we talked about going up to the mountains, where the snow is? Where the air's so clear you can see an eagle a thousand metres above the peak? Where your nearest neighbour's a mile away? We could take a cabin up there.'

Anna squeezed his hand.

'That would be great. But if you want to go skiing, you mustn't let me stop you. I don't ever want to stop you doing what you want to do.'

'We'll see. Maybe I'll just sit on the porch with you and watch the view and think. It would be good to have time to think. Maybe we could do some writing together. There ought to be a proper history of Market World and the One Law and everything that happened, before it's all lost. Both of us could work on it. It'll take time to do it properly. They'll be lots of research to do in the archives, interviews, checking all the records, the media. All those apprentices I saw today, they need to know the truth. And their children.'

Anna stroked his hand.

'Yes, that's what we'll do,' she said. 'I'd like that. The truth is so easy to hide if the lie's big enough, that's something we've learnt. Shall we eat now?'

Dain smiled. He took the handles and pushed the wheelchair into the dining room, where he'd already laid the table. He poured out the soup and set Anna's bowl in front of her.

'Glass of wine?' he asked.

'Yes, that'd be fine,' said Anna, smiling back up at him. After a moment she added: 'Everything is absolutely fine.'

THE END

## ANNEX: THE ONE LAW

Implemented: Year Zero, Celebration Day

All citizens are equal.
No citizen is a dependant.
No citizen is a slave.
All goods and services are held as private property by individual citizens.
All transfers of goods or services between citizens must be through free exchange between willing buyer and willing seller.
No goods or services may be seized or given or stolen or shared except through free exchange.
Both thief and gifter insult the citizen by treating him or her as less than equal.
The Enforcement Agency calls all to account.
The Enforcement Agency guards all rights.
The Enforcement Agency exacts all penalties.
Only the Enforcer stands outside the market.
Only the Enforcer will never accept payment for service.

This law protects property.
This law protects freedom.
This law protects dignity.
The law stands between the citizen and slavery.
The law stands between the citizen and theft.
The law stands between the citizen and rape.
The law stands between the citizen and charity.
The law stands between the citizen and the Broken Lands.
This is the law that ended the Great Hunger.
This is the law.